I0750544

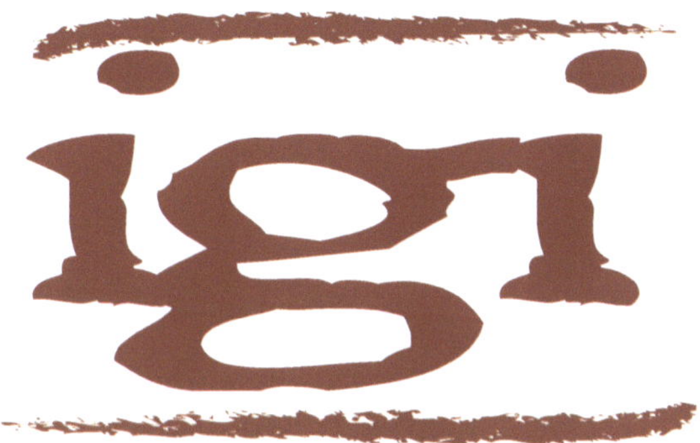
igi

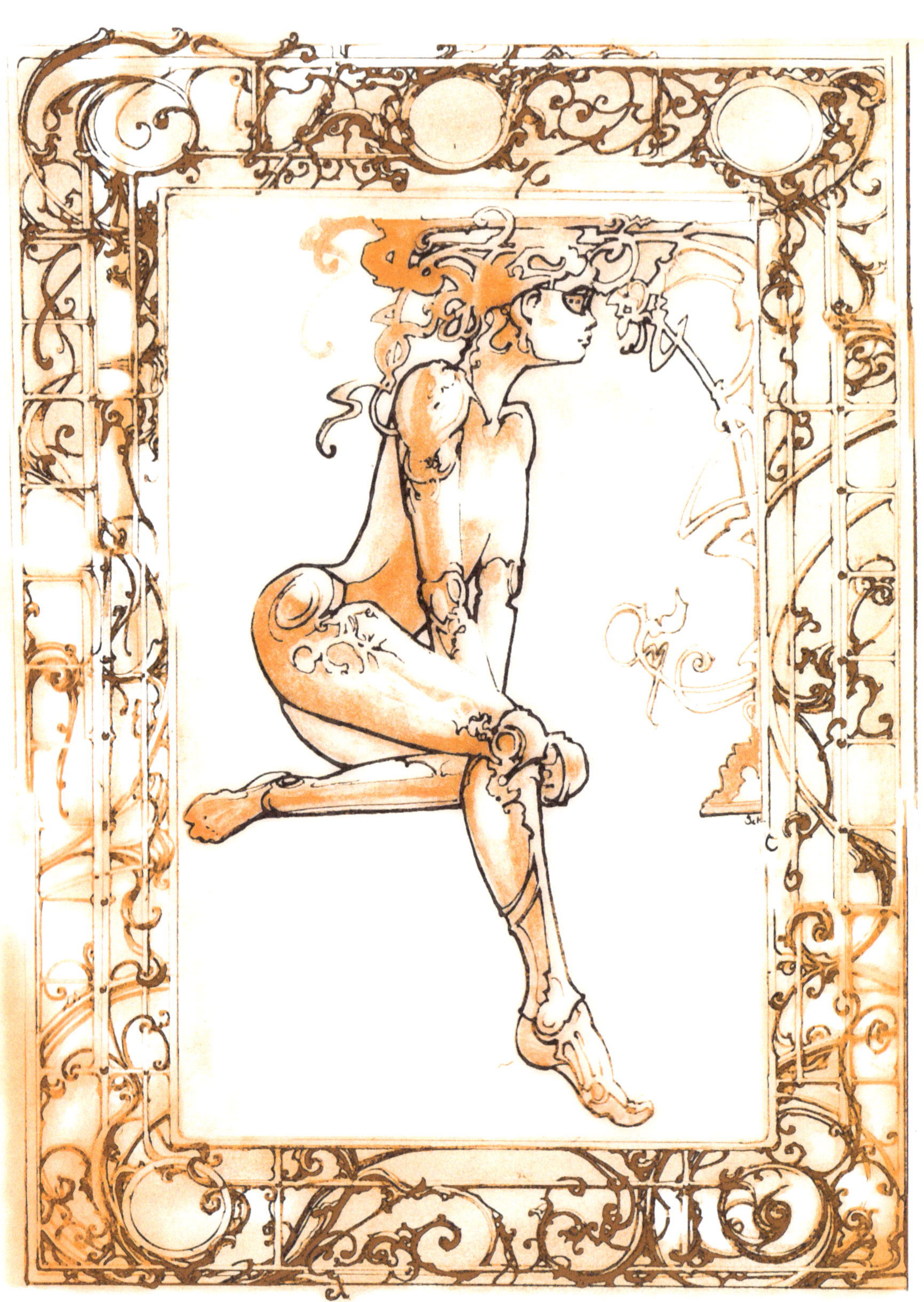

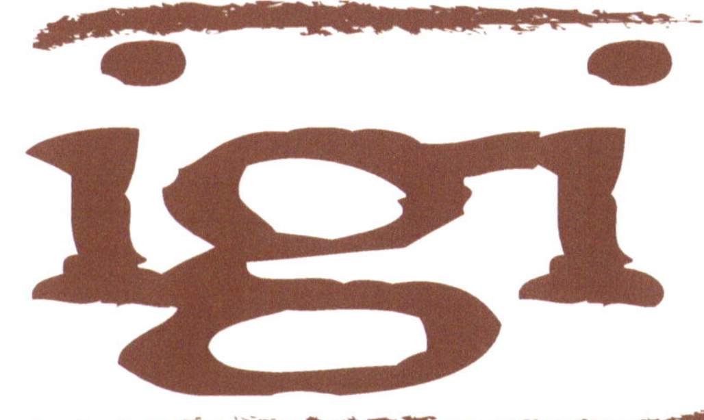

Selected works from

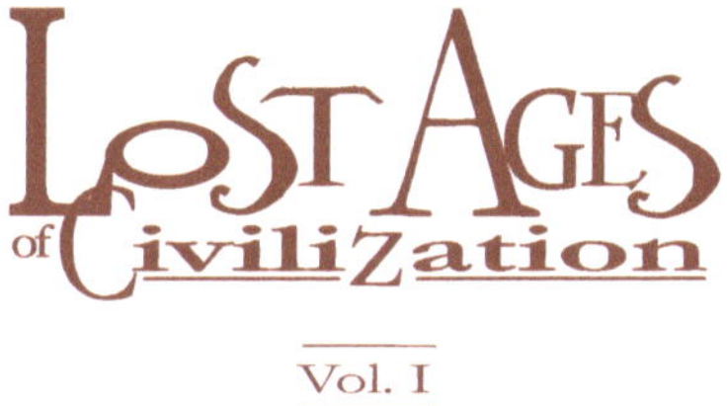

Vol. I

Schel Harris

iRthMoNkeY Press Portland, Oregon

I give thanks to:
The **Kickstarter.com** funding site and the Awesome folks who contributed. Your support and patience has been invaluable to this project and my confidence! **Heather Barrs.** and **Ed Anderson, Marilee Muzatko,**
Andrea and **Jason Nicholas, Ali Sorber! Mr. Martin "Bird" Bickford Brianne Williams!**
Qauuntum Glen is EveryWhere! **Lisa Church, Krissy Bussman, Kelly Gnerre Taylor,**
Tamara Ashton, to whom I must also Thank for your encouragment and "Getting it too"
Laura Burke, John Foxwell and **Erica Hoecten, Jodi! Chapman, Charis Gallaty**
Mindy Boyle, Spyder Monkee! and, **Lisa.**
Of course, Thanks to the in laws **Royal** and **Crystal Bruce** for all your support through the years.
My big brother **Craig** for all the support and understanding through the years.
Joel and Aaron! for supporting everything I do through your friendship and collection of this work. I'm fortunate to have such good hearted, cool people in my Life. Thanks!
Shawna Clymer who, out of no where swoops up this collection of pieces and, inspires me to do more! An amazing Artist who truly shares her own success and wishes it for others.
Barb Frank, for Everything you do! Your generosity and, friendship gives us sanity! I could not have created these books without it. Thanks **Otto**! for bringing us together. The joy and laughter will never be forgotten.
Dee Frank! A most impressively traveled and, talented woman to whom I owe the fact: I may never have to buy paper, mats nor drawing supplies ever again! Mr. **Ed Guy**, Your selfless rescue is nay forgotten!
Andea Oncken for your wonderful house and, your patience with us living in it. **Tyler Armstrong** for always being their for me, even when you're globetrotting
Pop, all the life lessons and skills..You have given a foundation that frees me from fear to pusue my dreams.
Mom, for passing to me this curse that all artist must carry. Too, the encouragement and tools at that early age has begun to pay off! Thanks Mum!

My Wife and Bestest Pal, **Tracie**. Without your encouragement, believing in me and, putting up with the madness that haunts we creative types, I would not be who I am today. Love.

I must include: Mr. Sam Adams and All those who support and, participate in Portlands' own Last Thursdays. You have kept me going year after year with ideas, encouragement and, of course, purchases. Much Thanks!

Portland, Oregon, We Love You!

Cover Image : Caitlyn awake 2010 Schel Harris

Harris, Schel
IGI Selected works from Lost Ages of Civilization by Schel Harris
p.

ISBN- 978-0-692-23646-8 06922364 65

Art

Special editions or book excerpts may be created to specification. Request for permission to make copies of any part of this work are valued and can be directed to the Author via postal or email.

Book and Cover Design by Schel Harris

iRthMoNkeY Press Portland, OR 97211

Contents

Introduction

The inspiration behind this multi volume work I must say is rooted in the fact that the planet is losing ancient cultures and knowledge in our present age. The most intriguing to me is the last remaining ancestors of the ancient Sumerians today called Marsh-Arabs. These descendants of the . "Black-headed people" as the Sumerians called themselves continue to live as their ancient families did. Creating floating houses and cattle pens among the ancient reed beds in southern Iraq. The coastal areas of Iran and, Iraq make up the southern boundary of what was referred to as Mesopotamia. Eastern Syria and Southern Turkey make up the northern edges of what was once vast forests and fertile plains. Now, Very few Marsh-Arabs survive in their ancestral homes due to modern dams and endless wars across these regions. Many efforts have been made to extinguish these people of the reeds by draining the marsh lands and damming the Euphrates river. So, too are the efforts to save these marshes and it's inhabitants, some with little interest in preserving this fading culture. Relocation, modern buildings and open communication with the world around them has all but deteriorated the last remaining remnants of the language and culture that has survived over 5000 years. The ancient myths and stories in the native tongue are soon to be lost forever. The legends of heroes and gods that created modern civilization are soon to be only translated artifacts of lost civilizations found in museum basements.

These Marsh-Arabs are the direct descendants of the people who gave us Astronomy, Farming and irrigation, geometry, written language, bricks, the useful shape- the square, the axled wheel, the hoe, many, many word roots still used today, the DC battery, copper wire, coins, Time - sixty second minute, sixty minute hour. or as in his work, ***History Begins at Sumer***, **Samuel Noah Kramer** lists some firsts' that originated in Sumer. including The First Schools, The First Bicameral Congress, The First Historian, The First Case of Tax Reduction, The First `Moses', The First Legal Precedent, The First Pharmacopoeia, The First `Farmer's Almanac', The First Experiment in Shade-Tree Gardening, Man's First Cosmogony and Cosmology, The First Moral Ideals, The First `Job', The First Proverbs and Sayings, The First Animal Fables, The First Literary Debates, The First Biblical Parallels, The First `Noah', The First Tale of Resurrection, Man's First Heroic Age, The First Love Song, The First Library Catalog, The First Liturgic Laments, The First Messiahs, The First Literary Imagery, The First Sex Symbolism, The First Lullaby, The First Literary Portrait, The First Aquarium.

The ancient literature from whence all notions of religion and culture sprung has opened my eyes to the truth behind books once held in high regard such as the Christian Holy Bible. This truth gives me hope and an inspiration to share what I've found the way I know best, Art!

Through the past five years, I've been fortunate enough to have participated in the local monthly "street fair' held during the longer Spring / Summer months here. Last Thursday as it's known across the country has been vital to my chosen arts path. Never have I had as much positive feedback and support as I have received here in the NW. Often, I've heard the suggestion to make a book of my artwork. Since my art was inspired from my great city and, my on-going personal study of ancient cultures, particularly Sumerian cultures, I felt there was plenty to work from.

The original intent was a simple book. A "coffee table" book as it's sometimes called. Just a book of images from the past years work. Then, maybe I just put a few of these cool prehistorical Sumerian quotes in the even pages. Well, I should give some background to who is "saying" this quote. I should squeeze in my sci-fi story somewhere since thats where this piece or, that piece came from. Into, I better research that...and this.

Research led to more head-scratching information which led to more research that just had to be used in the book! And so it went. Four Years, Three computers, 214 illustrations, One solo gallery show, three group shows, Three rewrites, Six flash drives and, finally, not one, nor two but, THREE books later...We come around again to the original plan.

There are few words in this book but, a sprinkling of excerpts from volume 1 have been included. Many of these excerpts are direct translations of ancient stories given us by our ancestors. The paintings and ink works that best represent the storys' chapters were chosen for this book from the large Volume 1. A collection of stories, quotes and, art works depicting the arrival and final demise of prehistoric civilizations. Formed from fact, historical knowns and mythology, this epic is told in the first person and spans more than 12,000 years!

An attempt to publish a single book that includes all three of the final books would place it financially out of reach to print and, for anyone to purchase.

Believe it when I say I am not a fan of the current trend as in films. Where a story that could have been told in fifteen minutes is stretched out over two or three, 3 hour movies and, years apart! Bah!

This book in your hand is simply an Art book. No need to wait nor buy a ticket to see the "other" parts later. This volume is to share a few pieces of art inspired by and, created for the book-
Lost Ages of Civilization Volume 1.

Much Thanks and Enjoy!

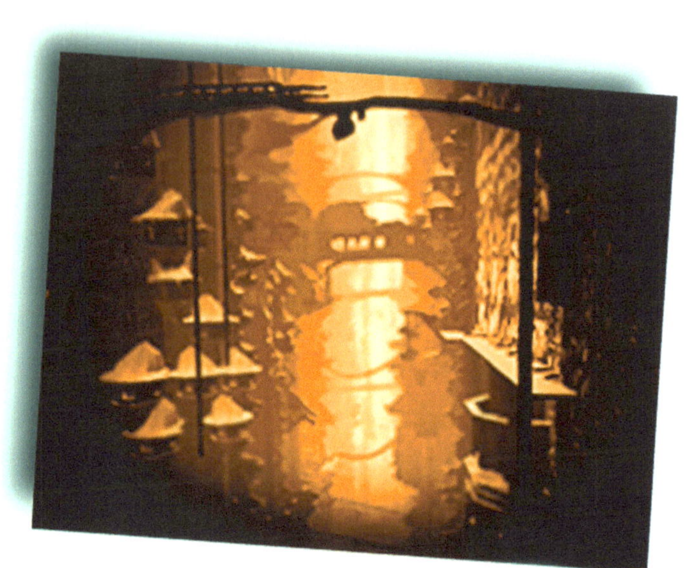

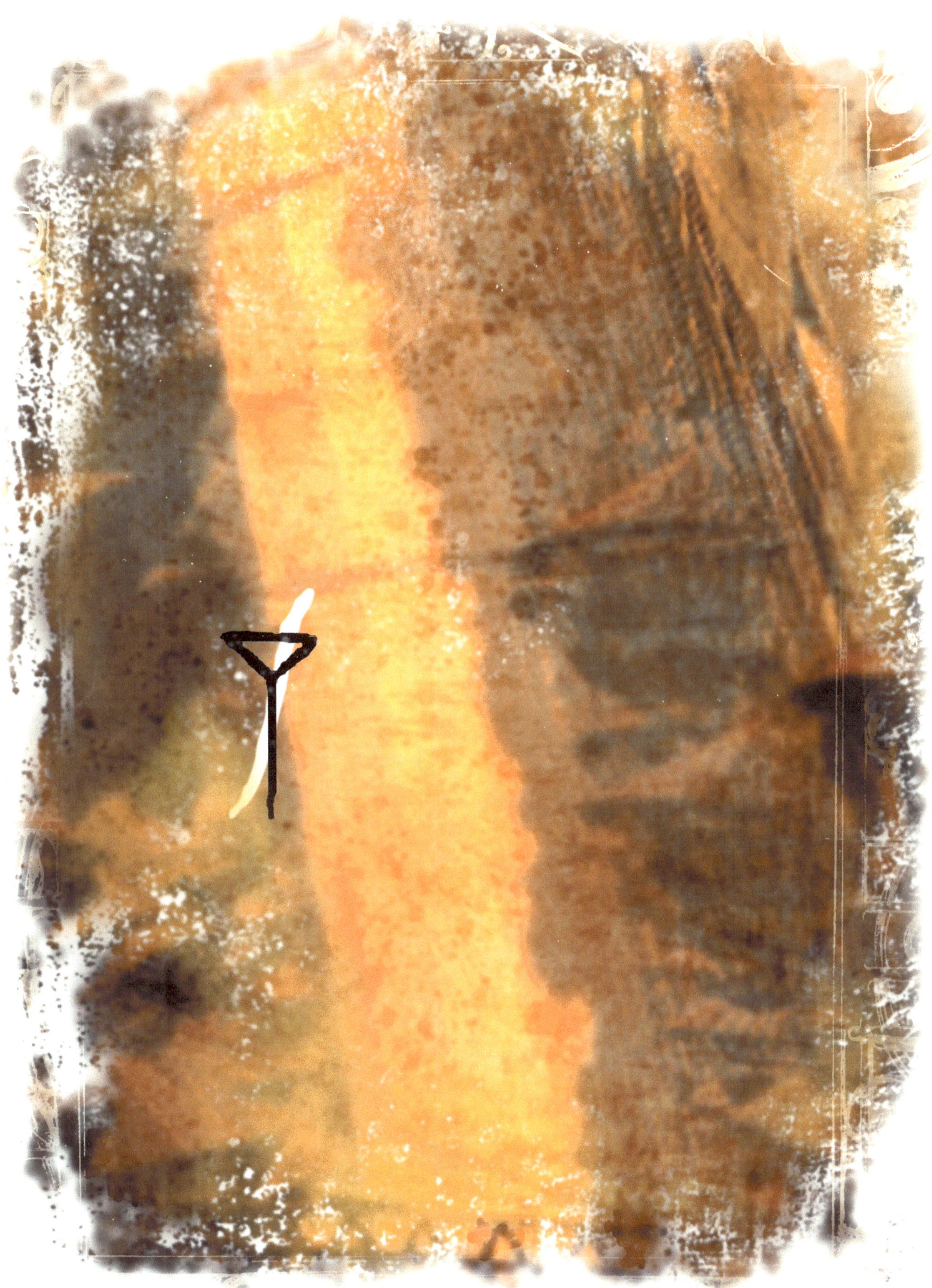

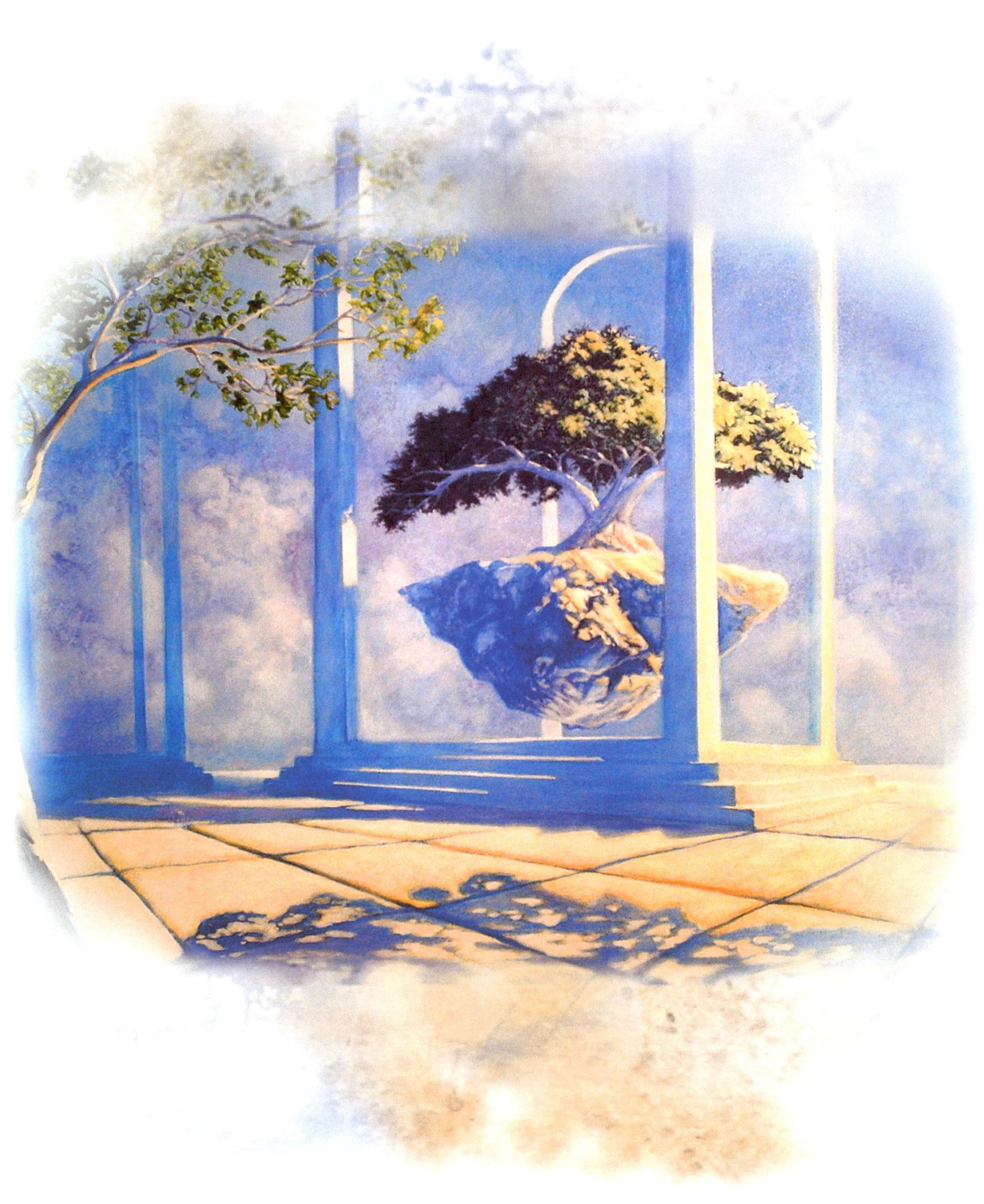

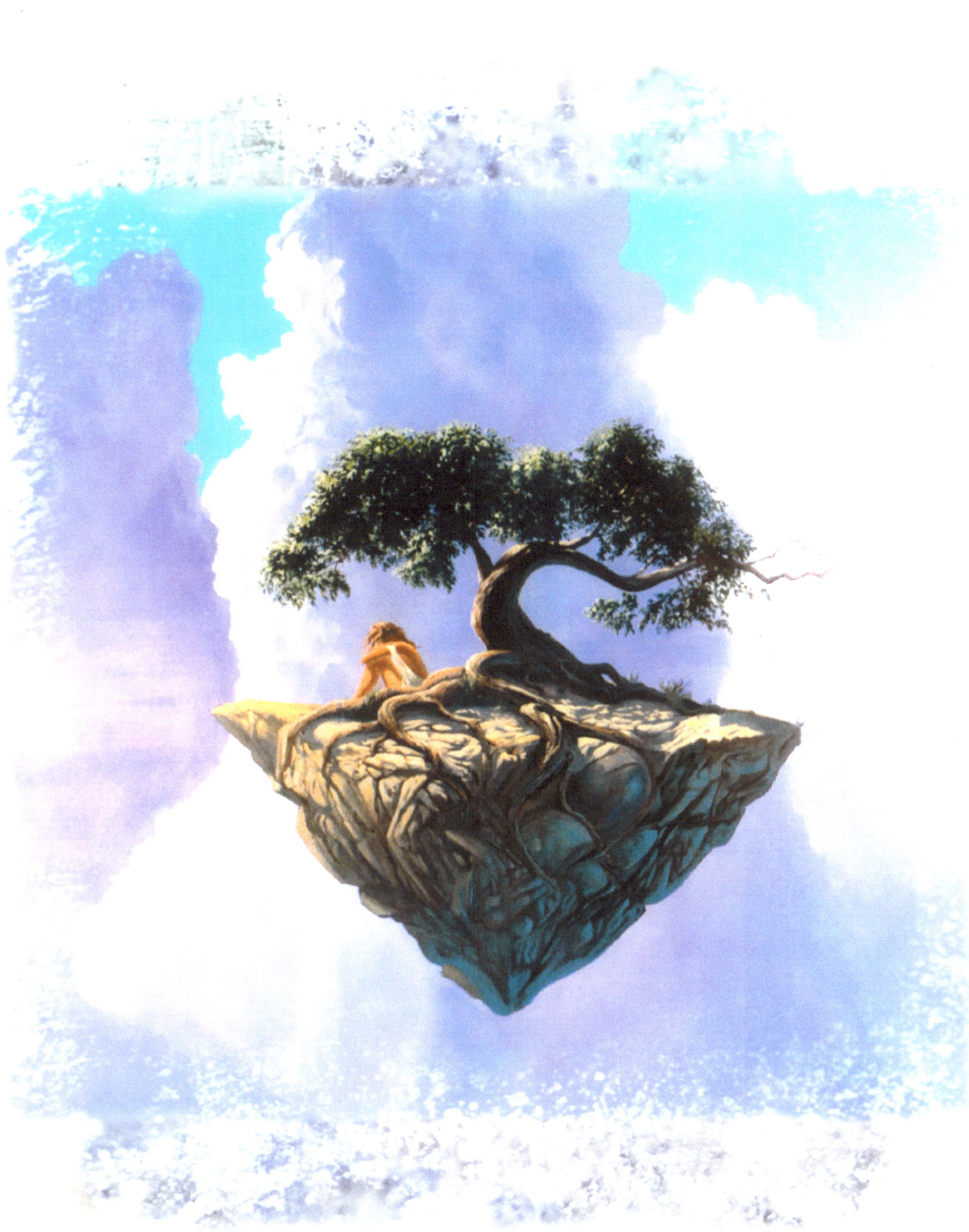

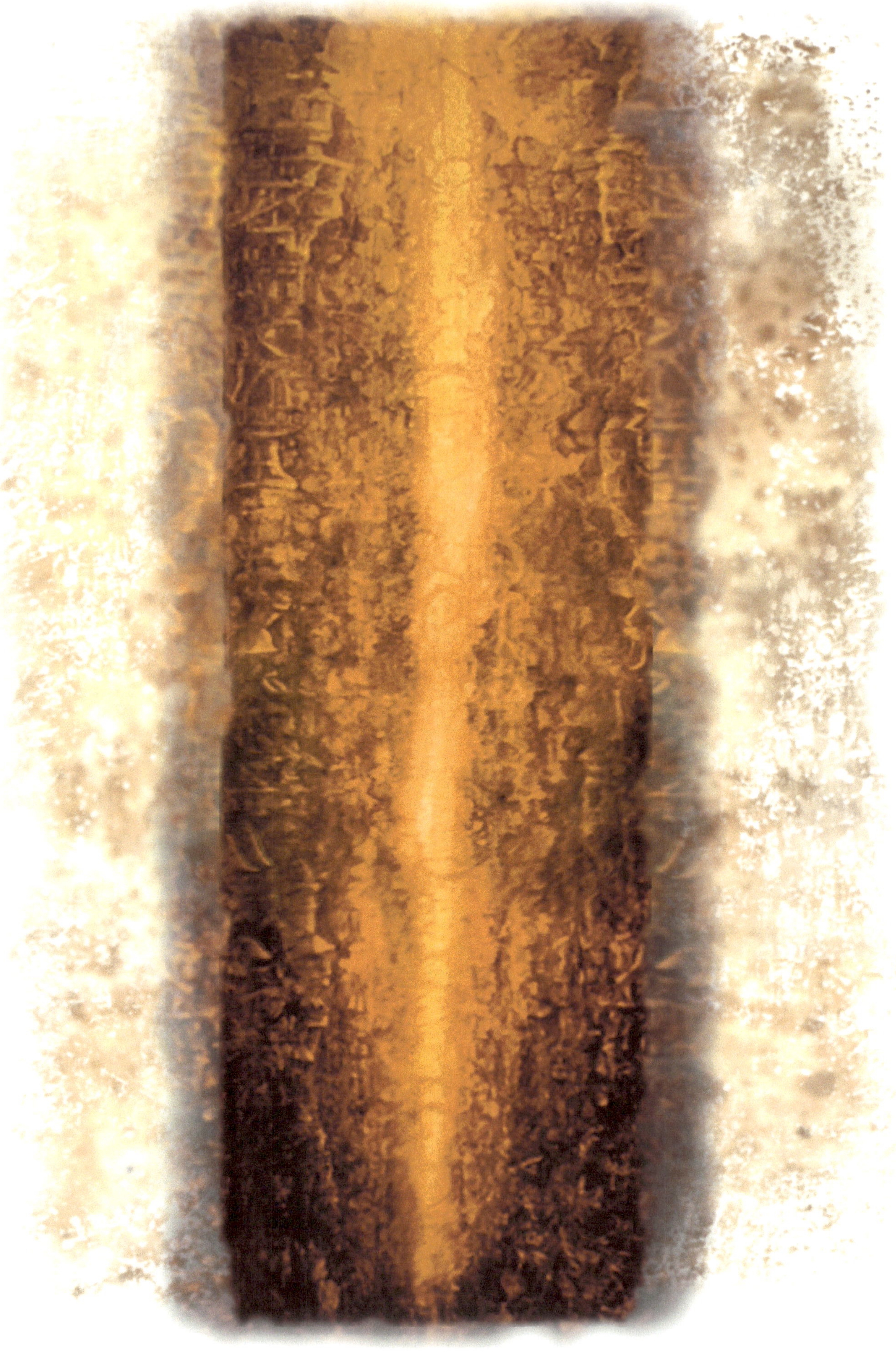

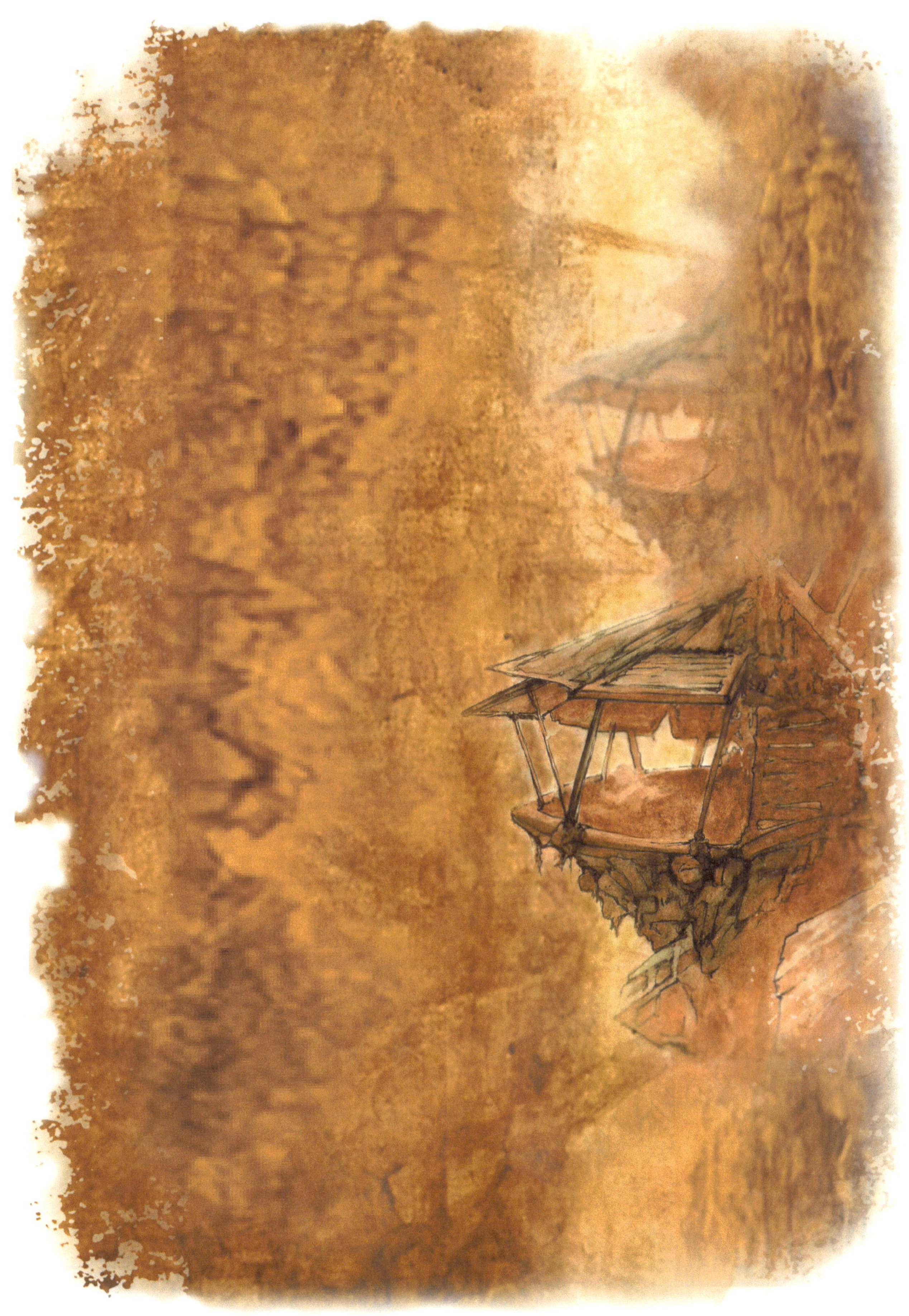

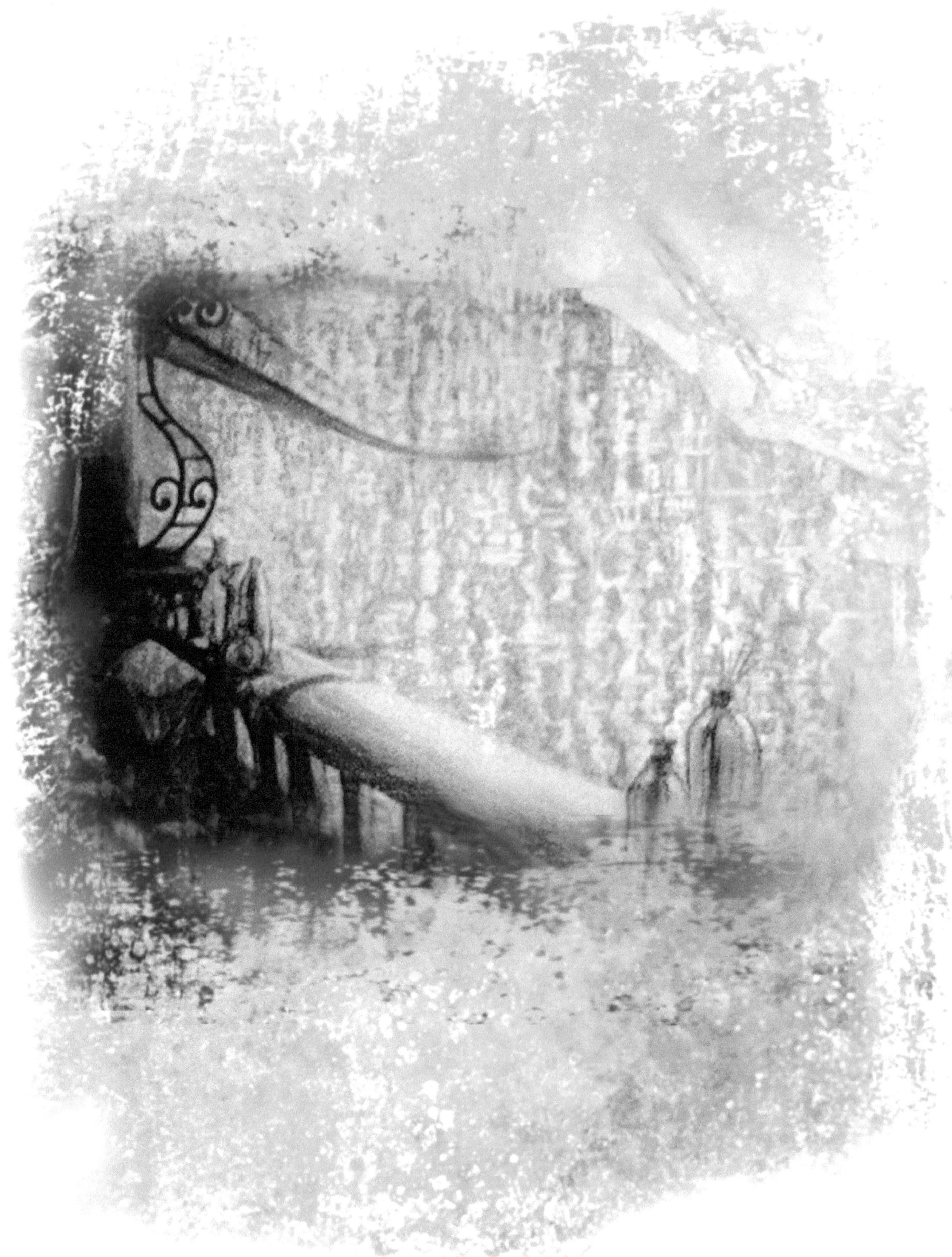

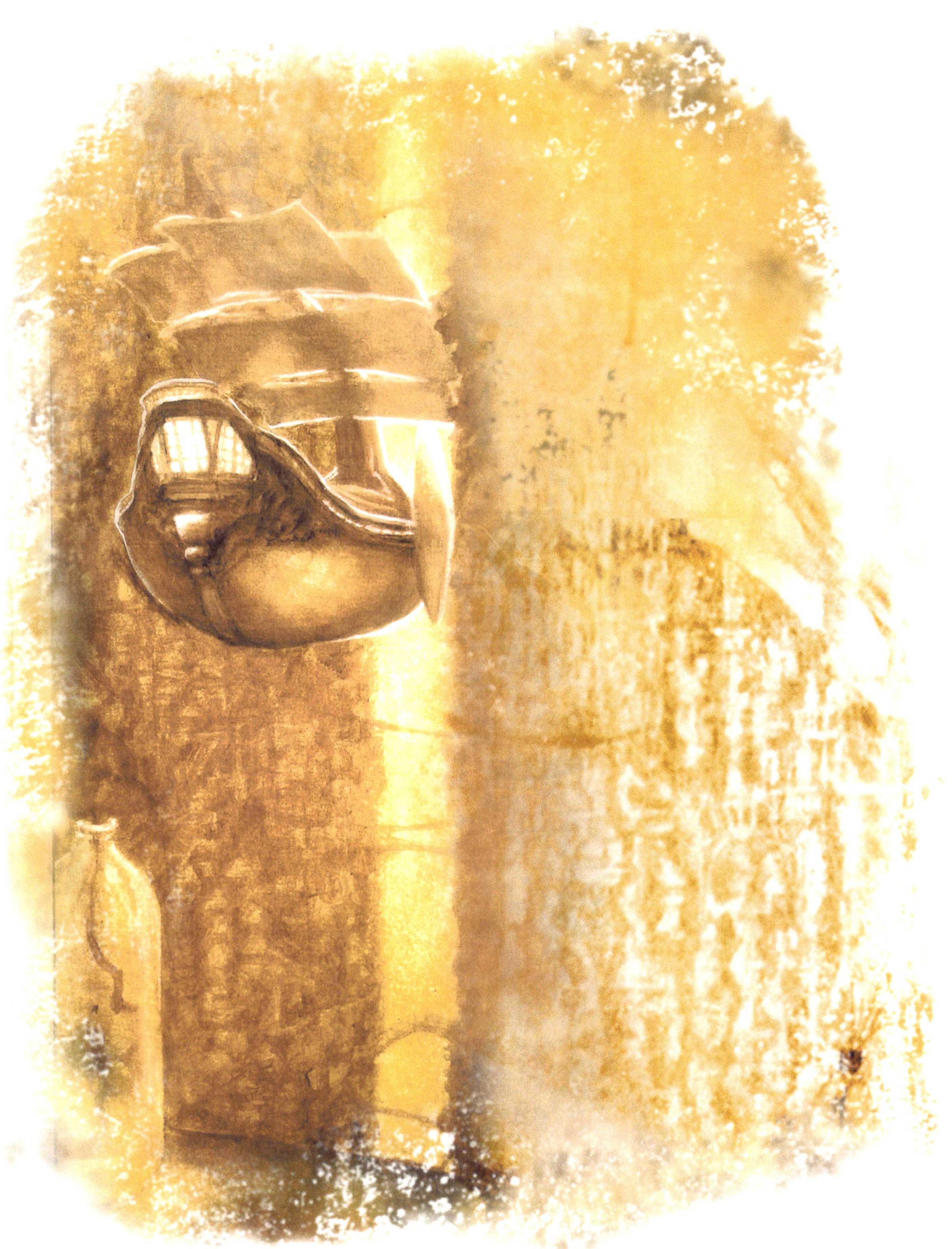

Upon I wake this morning, the gi had abandoned I on rooftop! The dim amber light of day came. I saw others on the roof as well. Huddled in small dark clumps they remained silent. Only occasional whines of a child were heard. As I beheld the surroundings, one from the roof edge moved with haste through the crowd in whisper. As he passed, the groups would stumble about to stand grabbing cases and boxes into their arms.. Soon everyone was on foot stepping to the roof edge. I sat watching as they without sound passed. Offspring beheld I in bewilderment. I too stood and collected I satchel when a low rumble could be heard that turned to hiss as a ship ascended into the sky above. It dropped slowly down again until it was beside the waiting crowd. I stopped in step. Was I to follow this design, to leap aboard this ship for no known purpose? As to why I was here and what to be done was unknown. So too was the design for an ancient ship loading passengers in the city at dawn!

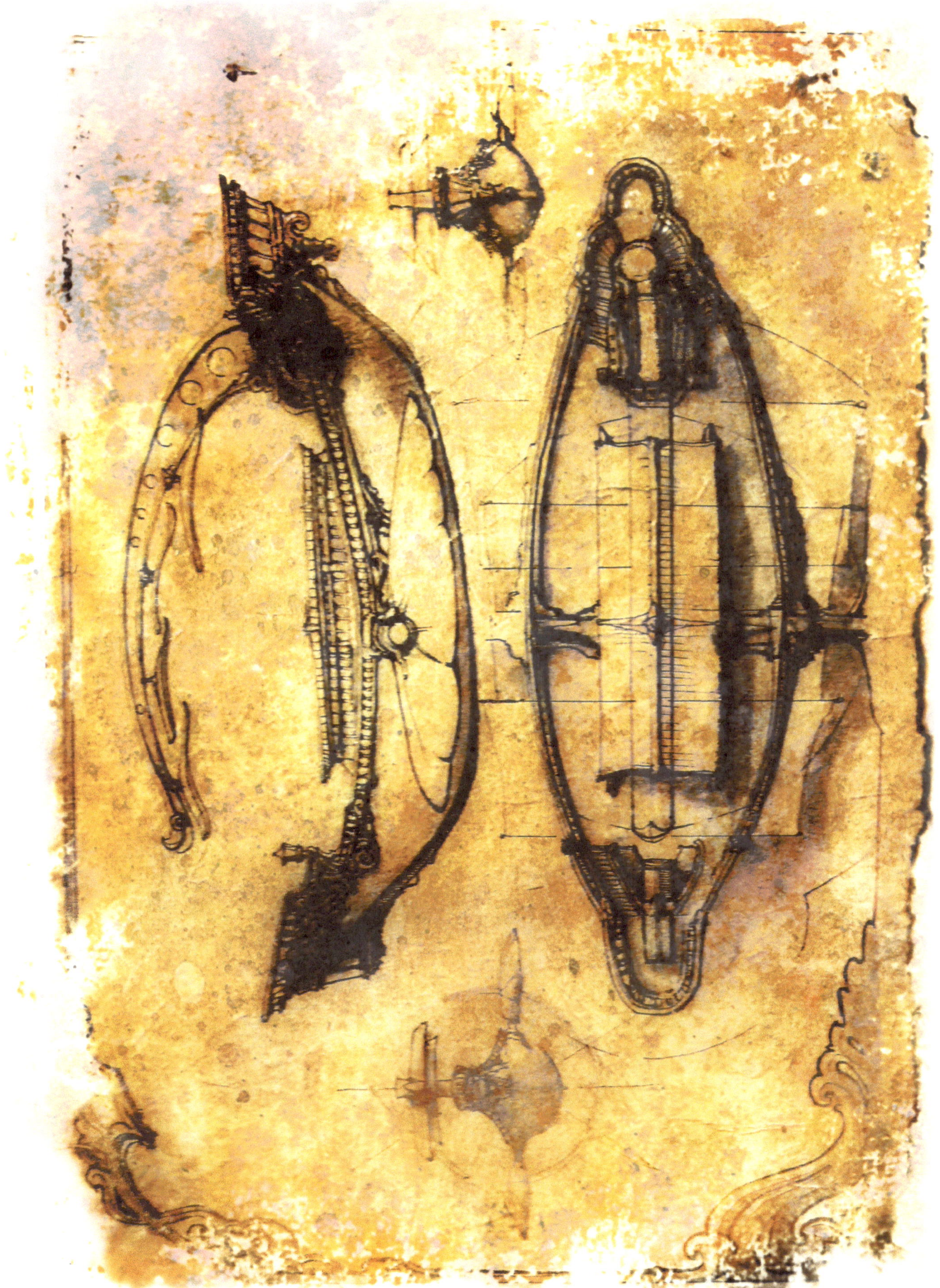

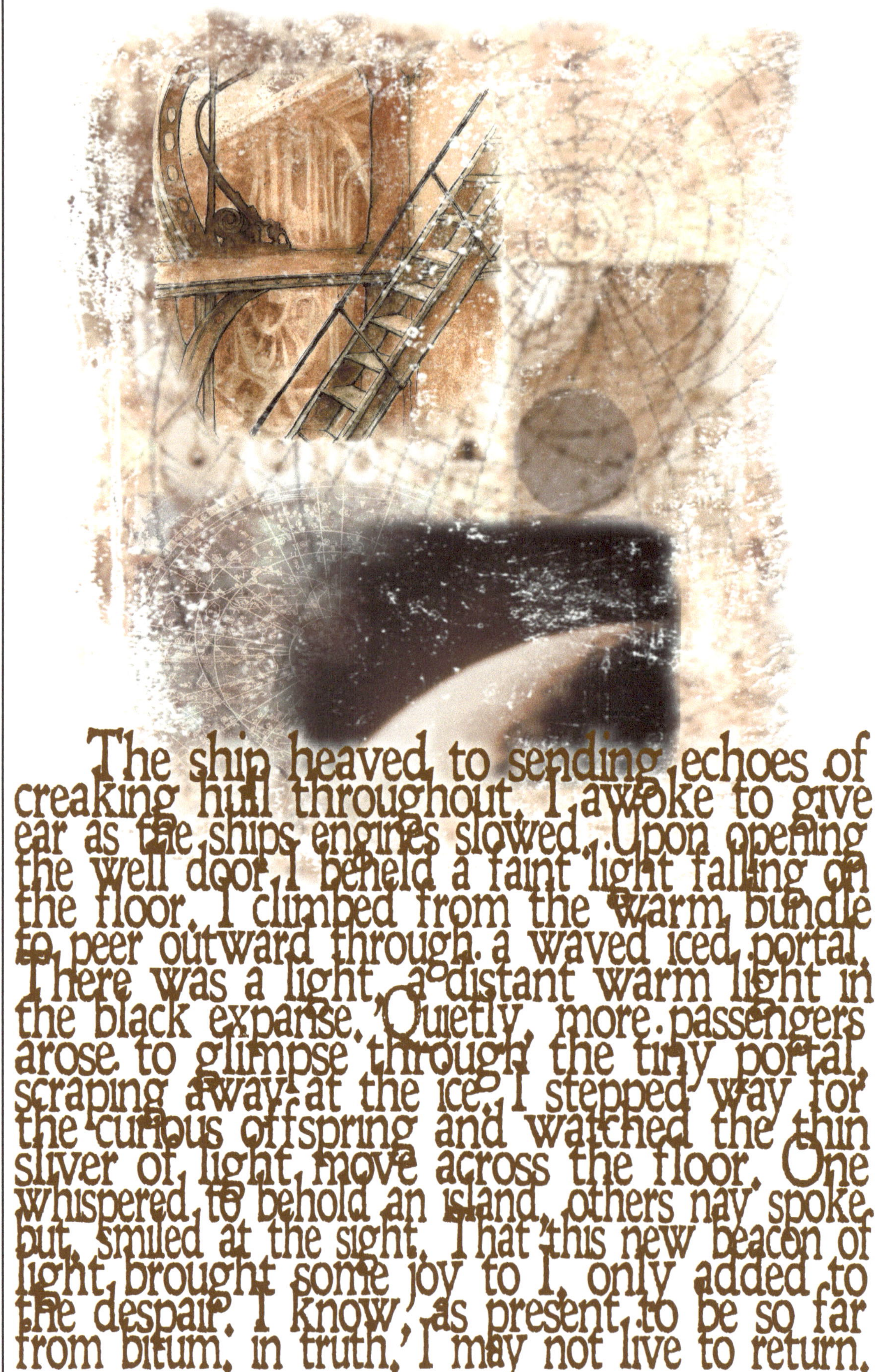

The ship heaved to sending echoes of creaking hull throughout. I awoke to give ear as the ships engines slowed. Upon opening the well door I beheld a faint light falling on the floor. I climbed from the warm bundle to peer outward through a waved iced portal. There was a light, a distant warm light in the black expanse. Quietly, more passengers arose to glimpse through the tiny portal, scraping away at the ice. I stepped way for the curious offspring and watched the thin sliver of light move across the floor. One whispered to behold an island, others nay spoke, but, smiled at the sight. That this new beacon of light brought some joy to I, only added to the despair. I know, as present to be so far from Bitum, in truth, I may not live to return.

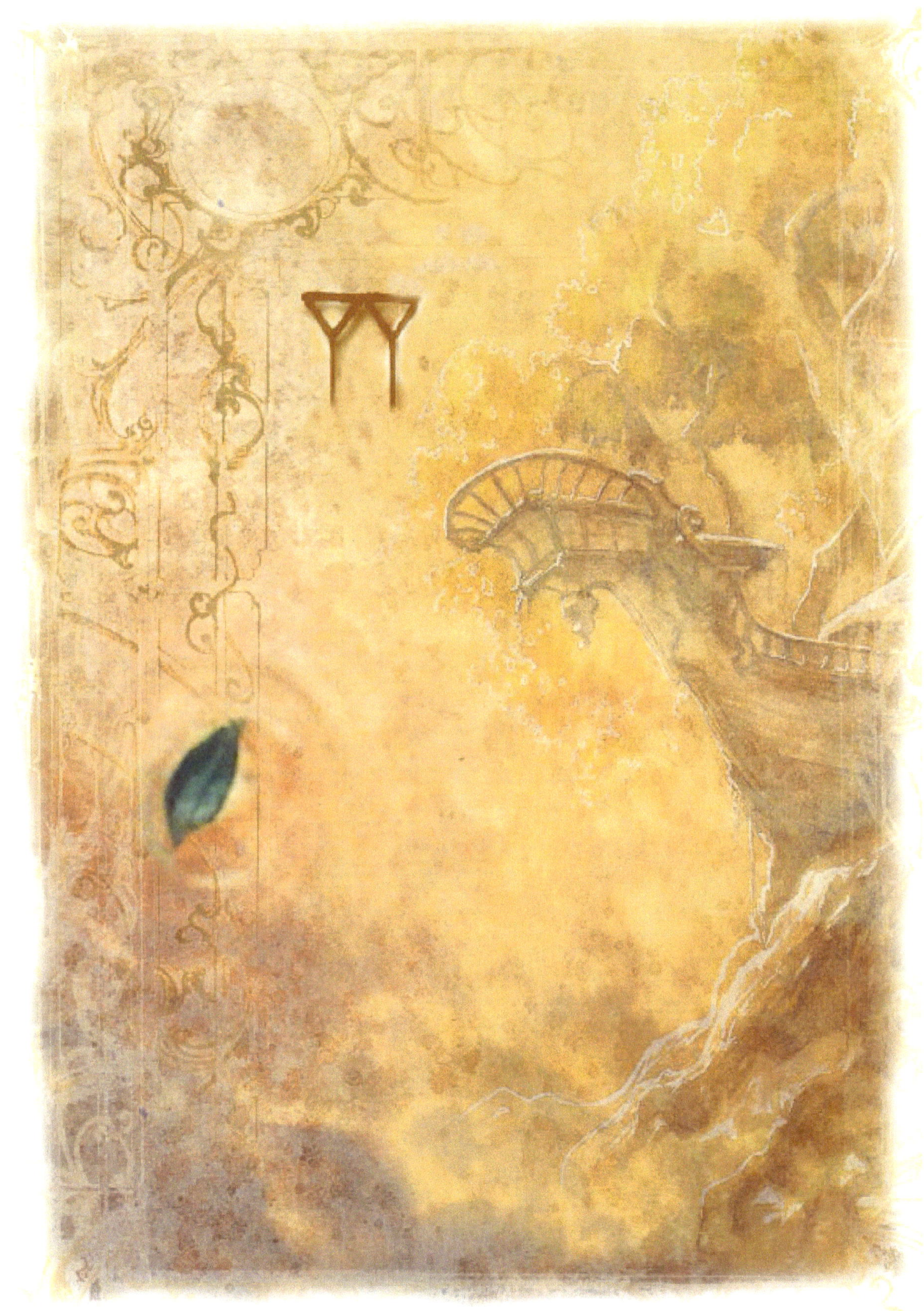

Rains steadily fell in through every seam. The ship groaned long and deep as it slowly rocked back dropping shards of hull with every motion. All was quiet, no engine droning, no voices. Just a storm outside beating on the deck. A few passengers called out for others, joyful shouts arose. The broken ship tilted away from its split and rain dumped in through the upper decks. Lightning flashed giving brief glimpses of the chaos. The gi tried to climb through the wreckage with little success. Soon more gi came with oil lamps and began slowly clearing a path.

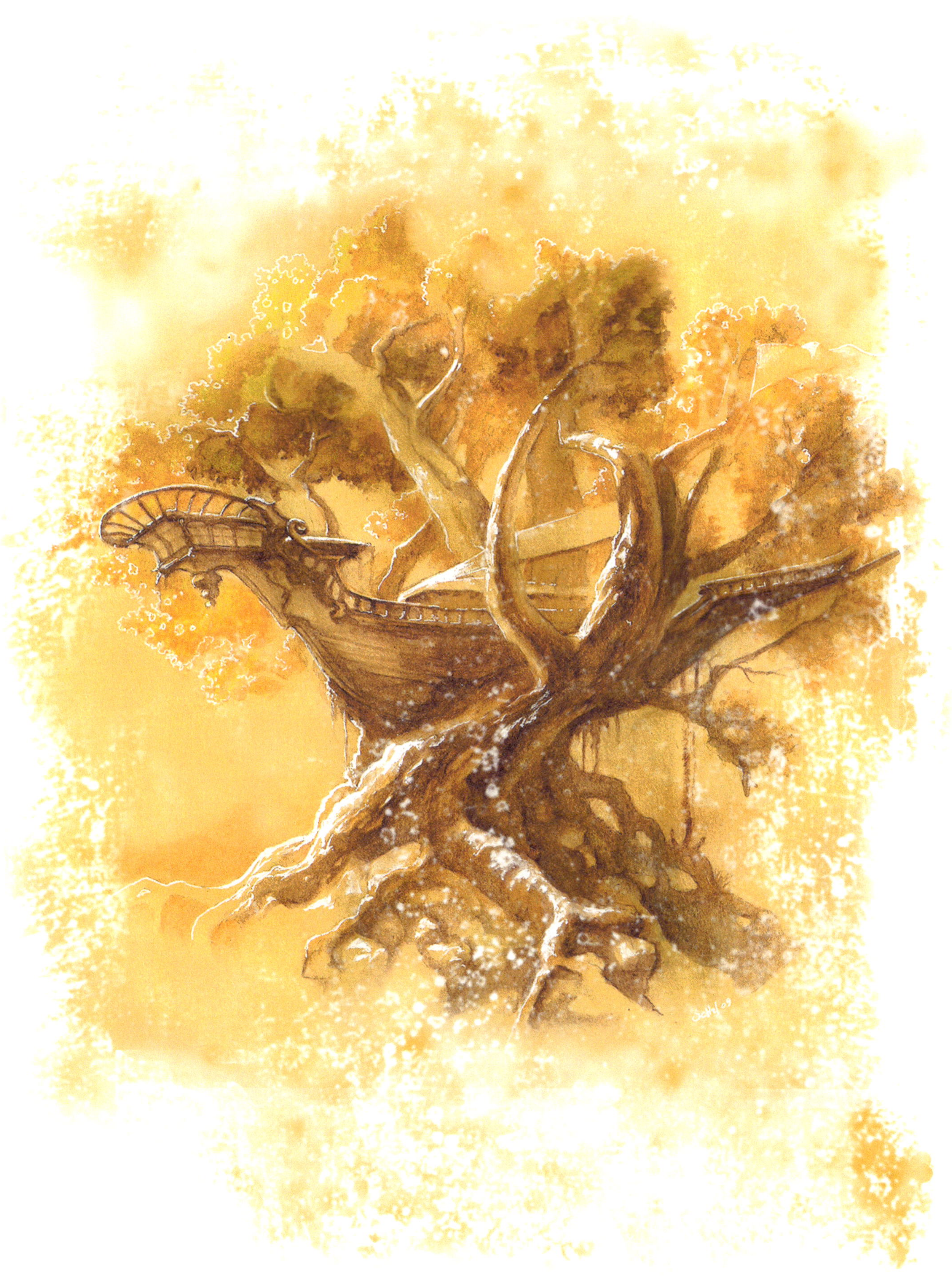

I was drawn to crawl out through the hole shorn open in the hull. A doctor followed closely behind and we made our way down massive stones below the ships resting place. What we came to behold was beyond anything our minds could comprehend. I experienced a transformation, an awakening, as though I had been in slumber until that moment. A truth of a new awareness, a second new life becomes my conciousness.

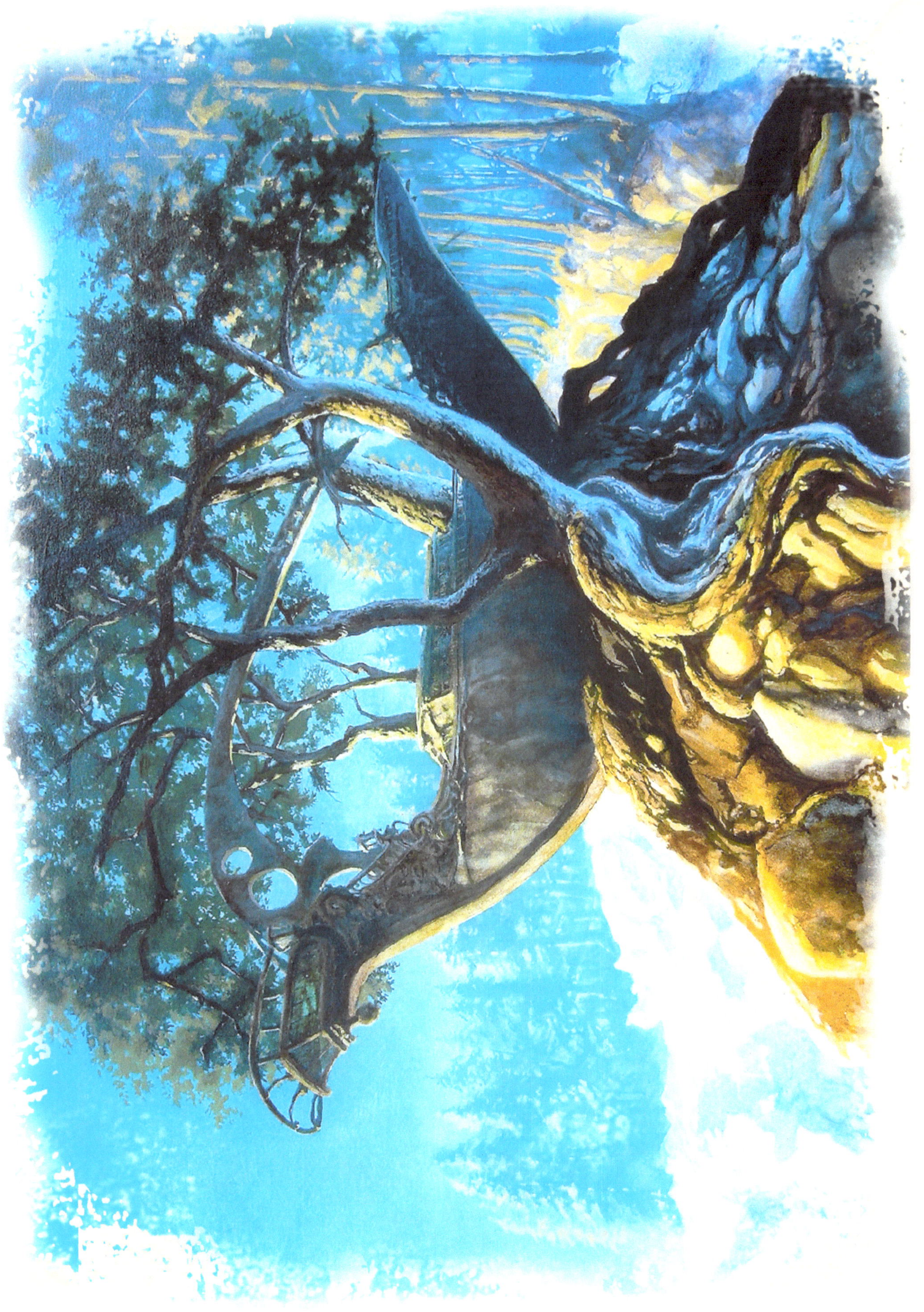

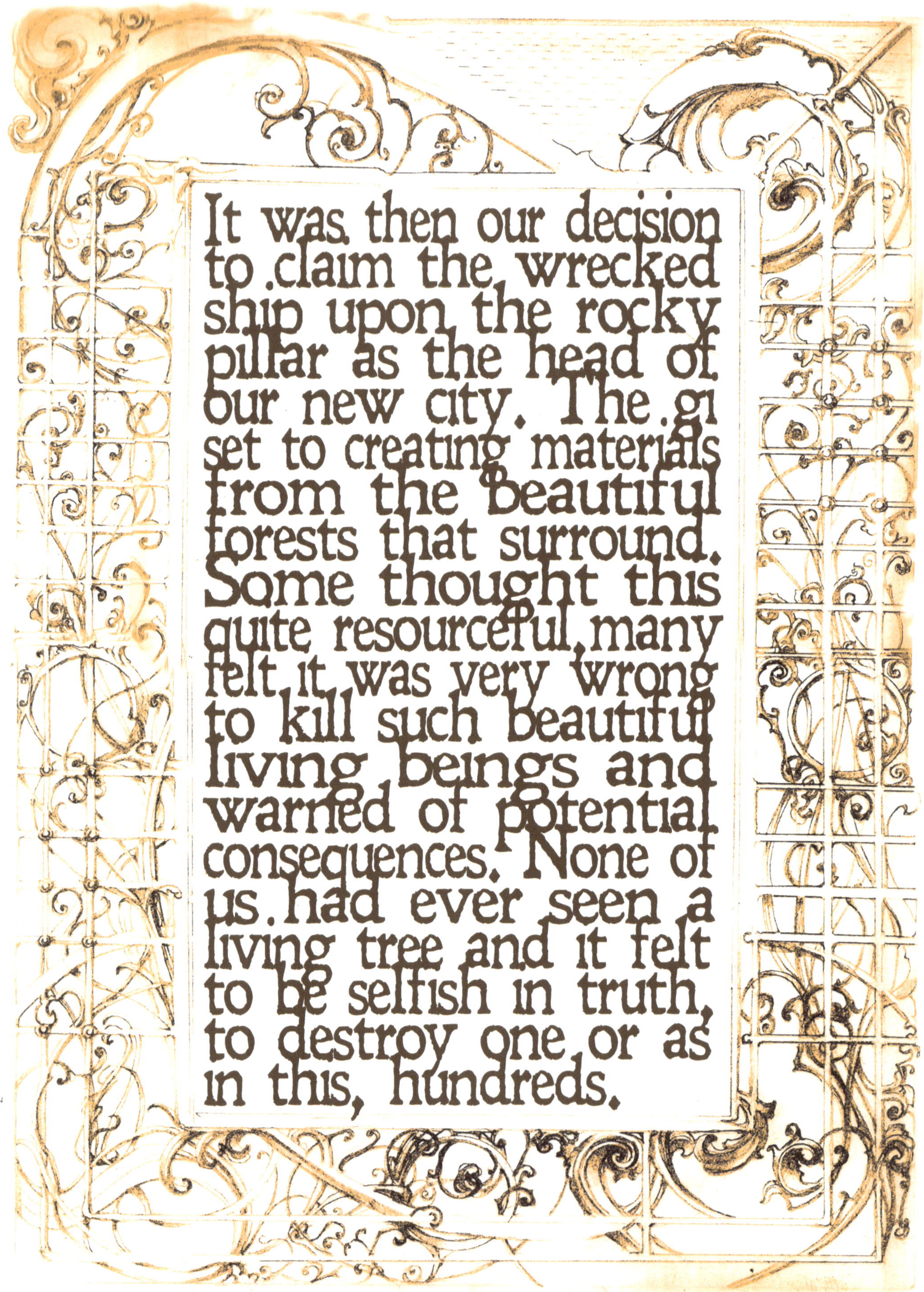

It was then our decision to claim the wrecked ship upon the rocky pillar as the head of our new city. The gi set to creating materials from the beautiful forests that surround. Some thought this quite resourceful, many felt it was very wrong to kill such beautiful living beings and warned of potential consequences. None of us had ever seen a living tree and it felt to be selfish in truth, to destroy one or as in this, hundreds.

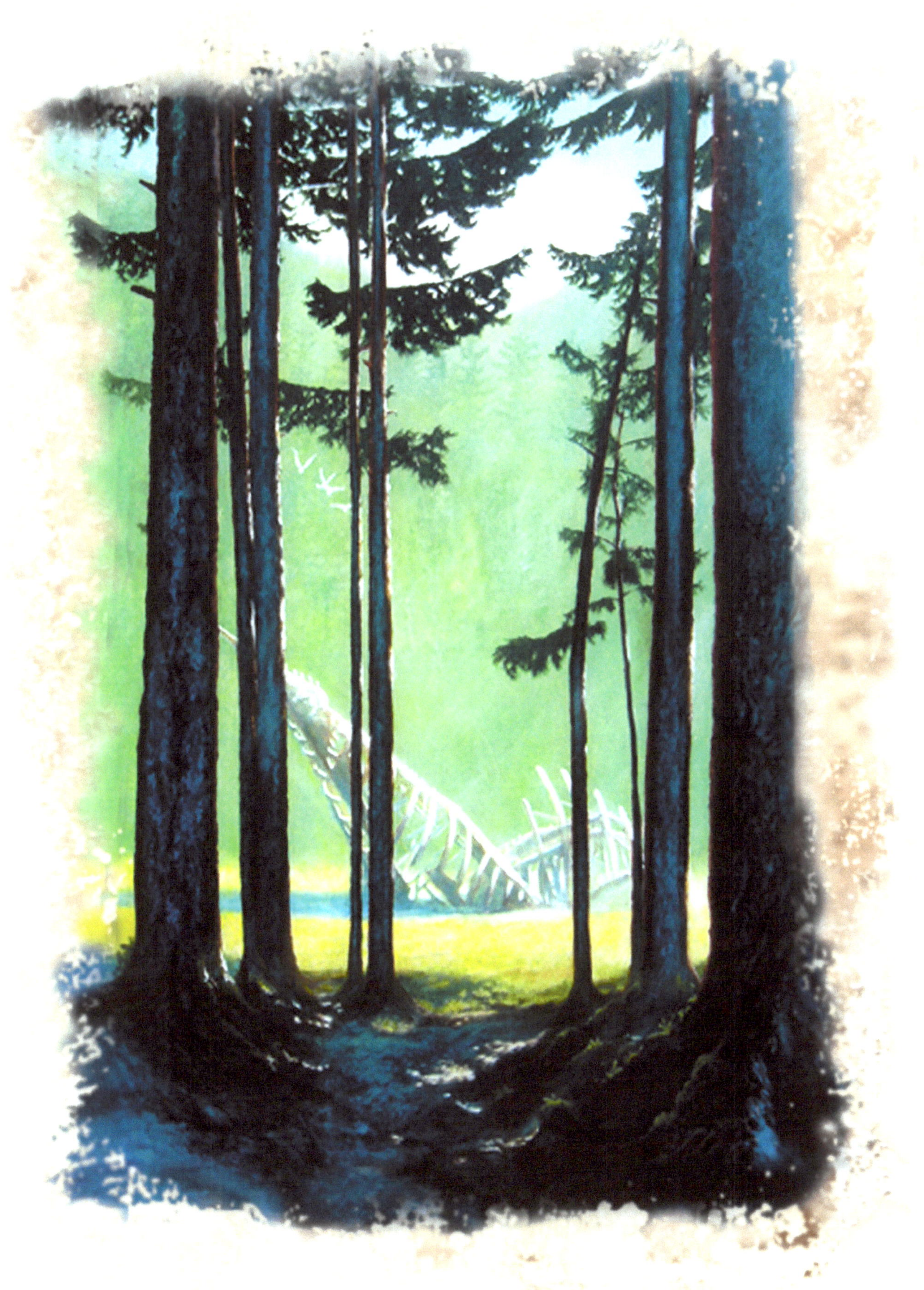

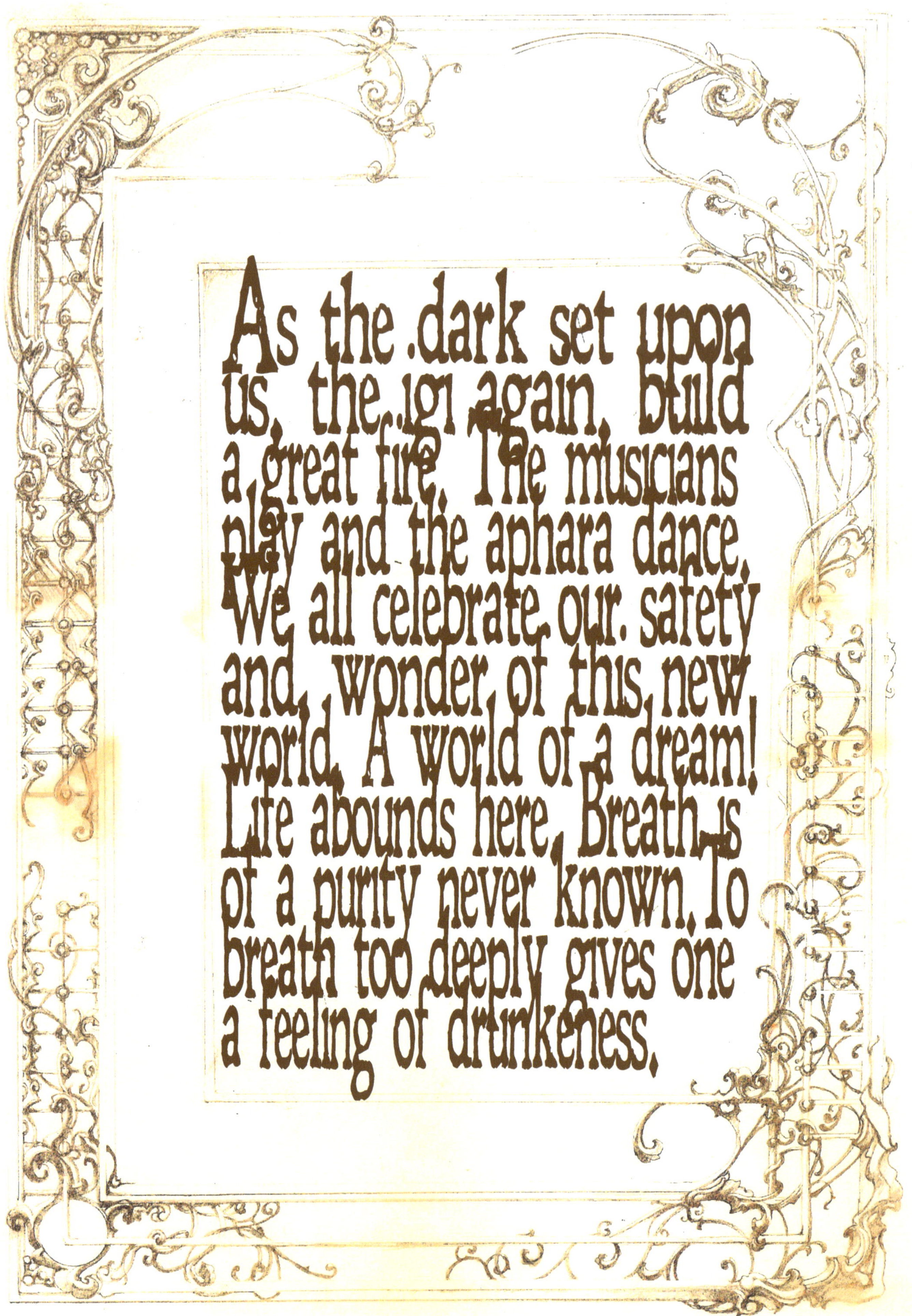

As the dark set upon us, the igi again build a great fire. The musicians play and the aphara dance. We all celebrate our safety and wonder of this new world. A world of a dream! Life abounds here. Breath is of a purity never known. To breath too deeply gives one a feeling of drunkeness.

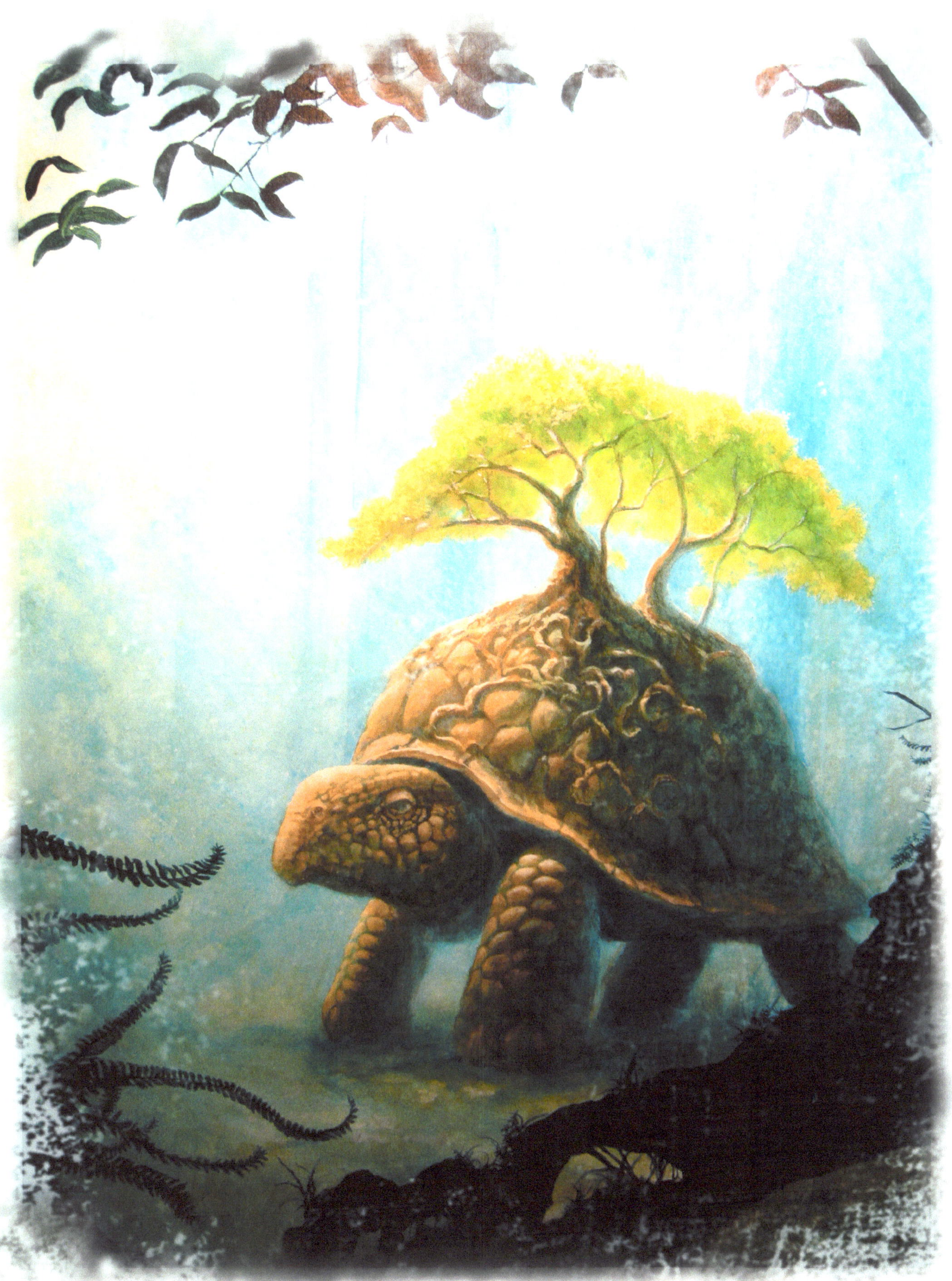

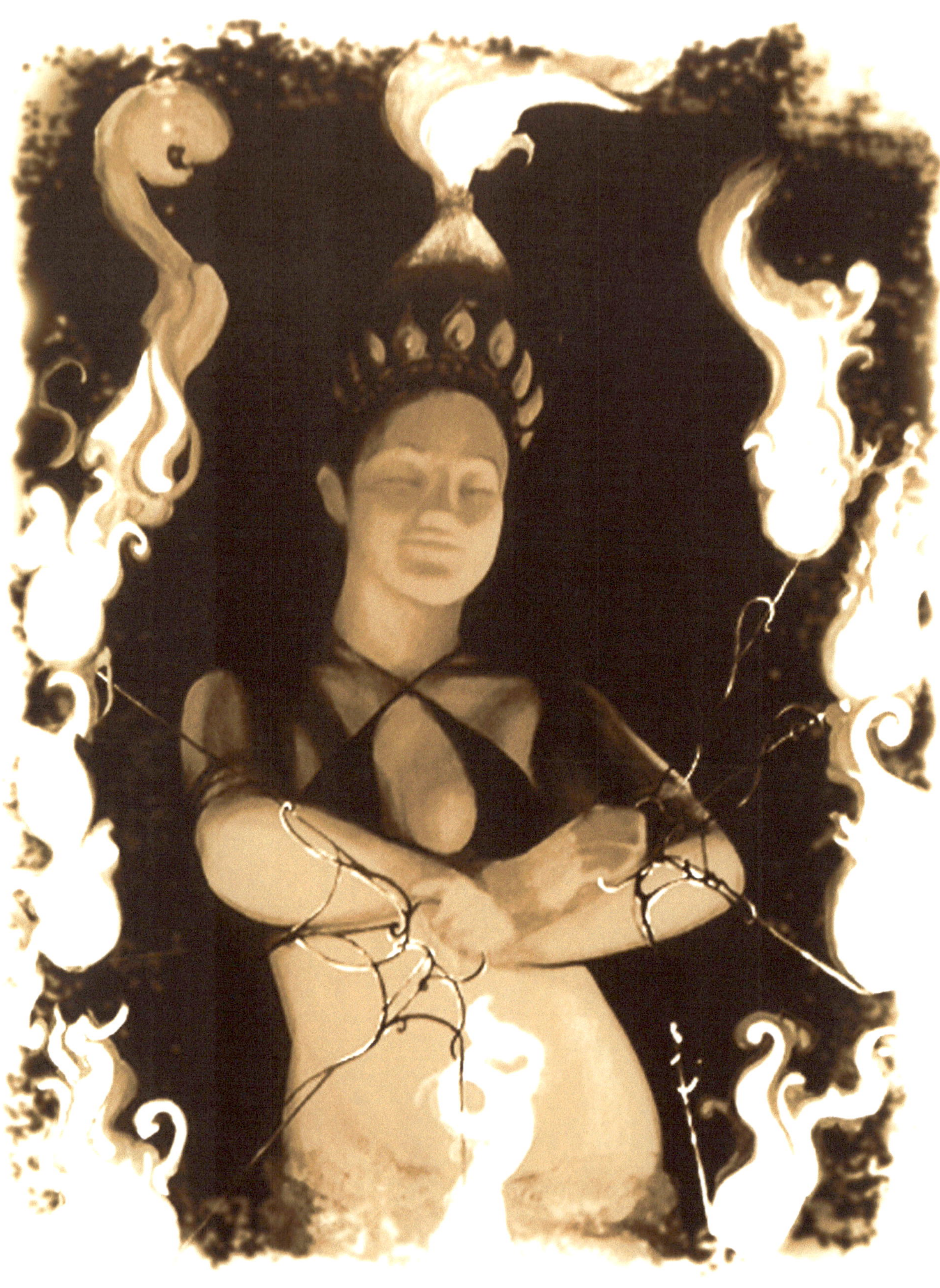

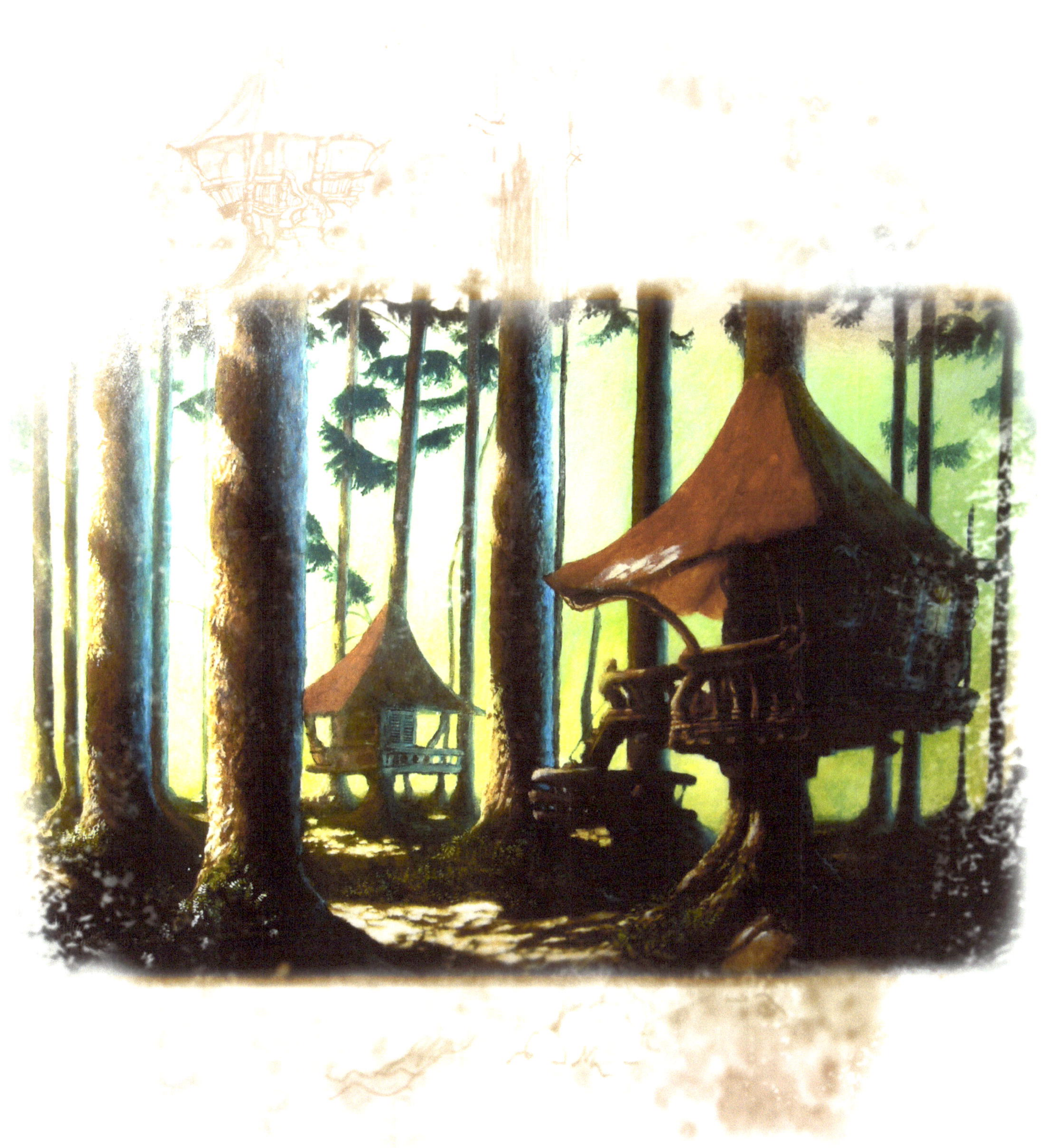

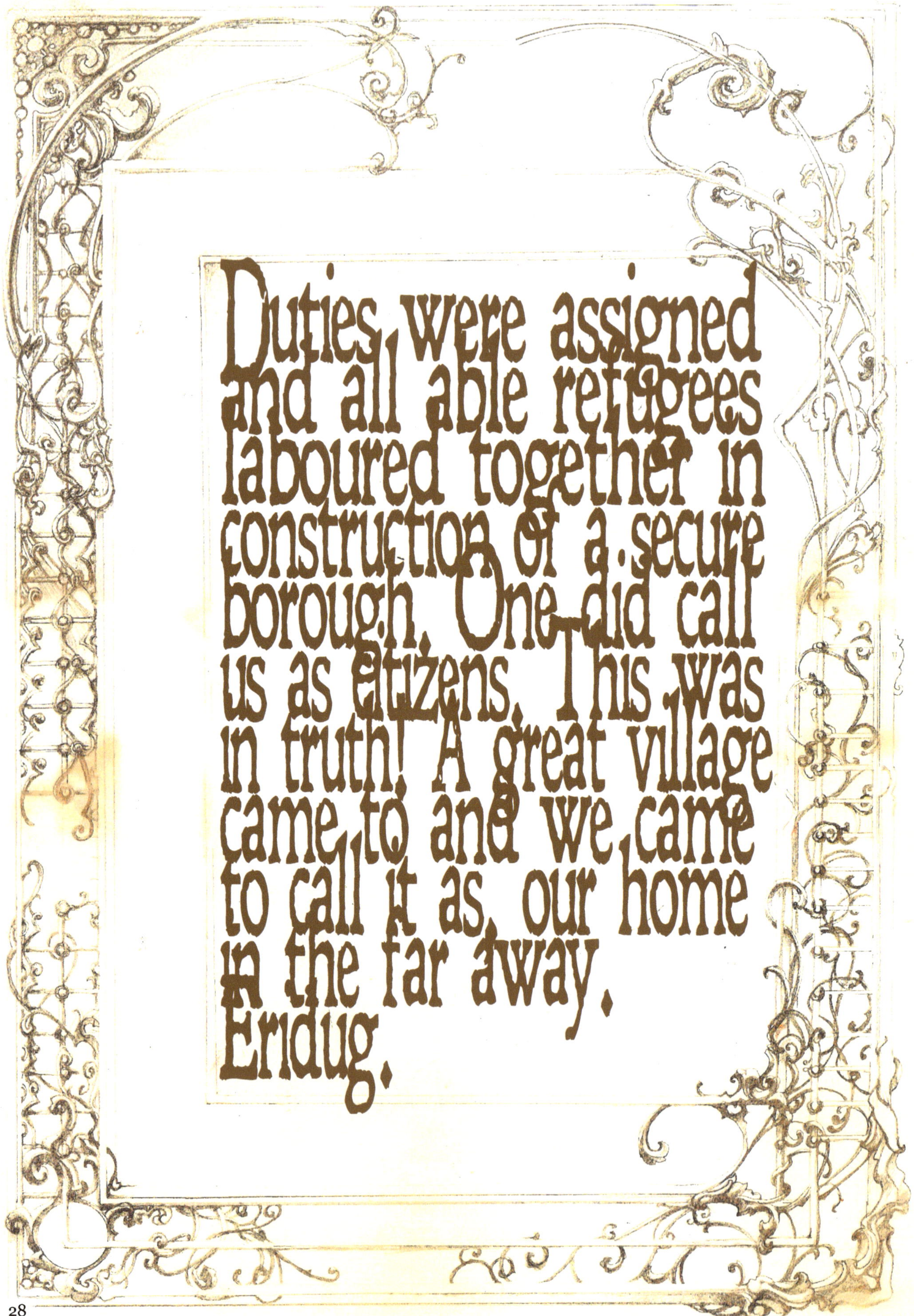
Duties were assigned and all able refugees laboured together in construction of a secure borough. One did call us as citizens. This was in truth! A great village came to and we came to call it as our home in the far away.
Eridug.

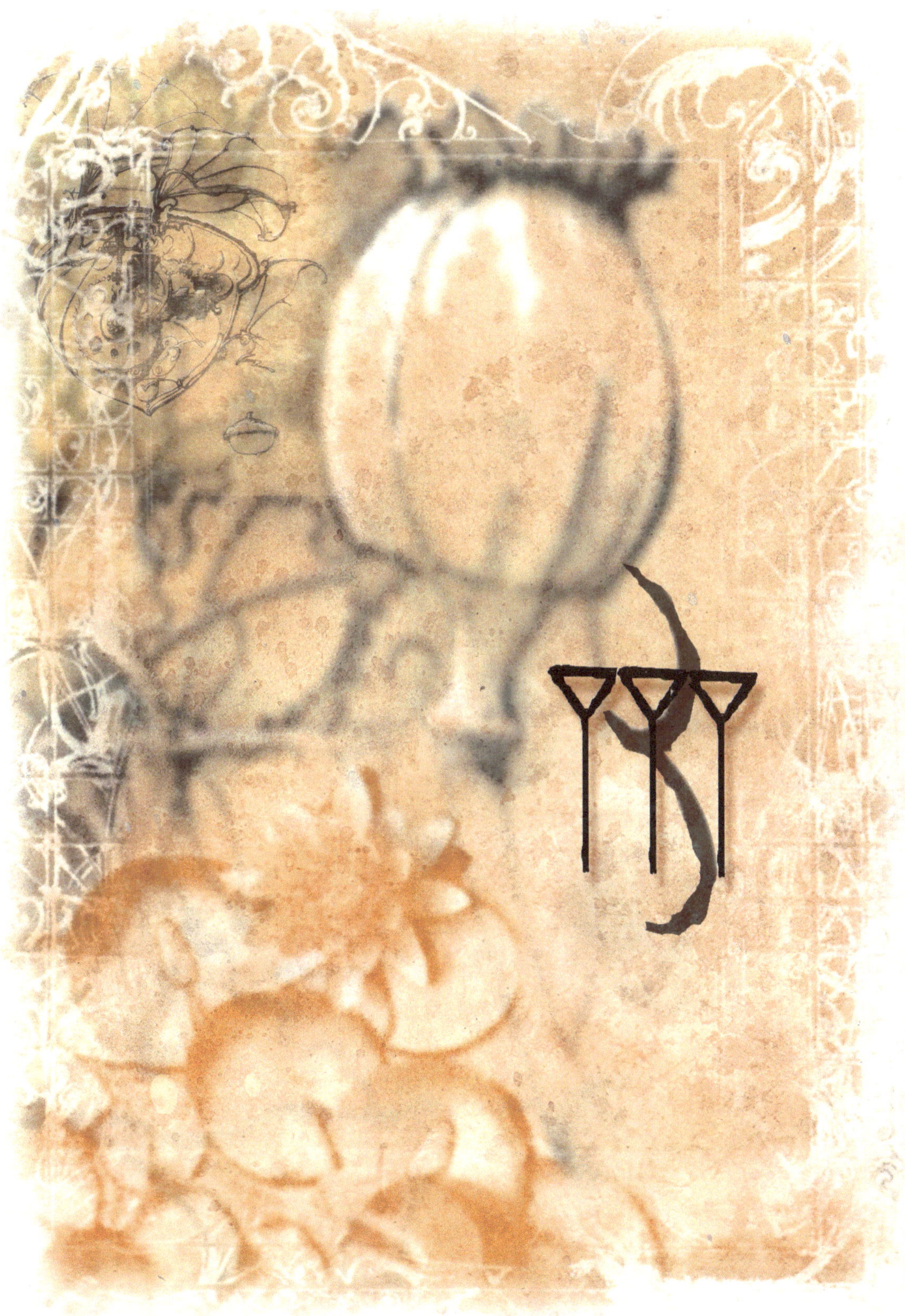

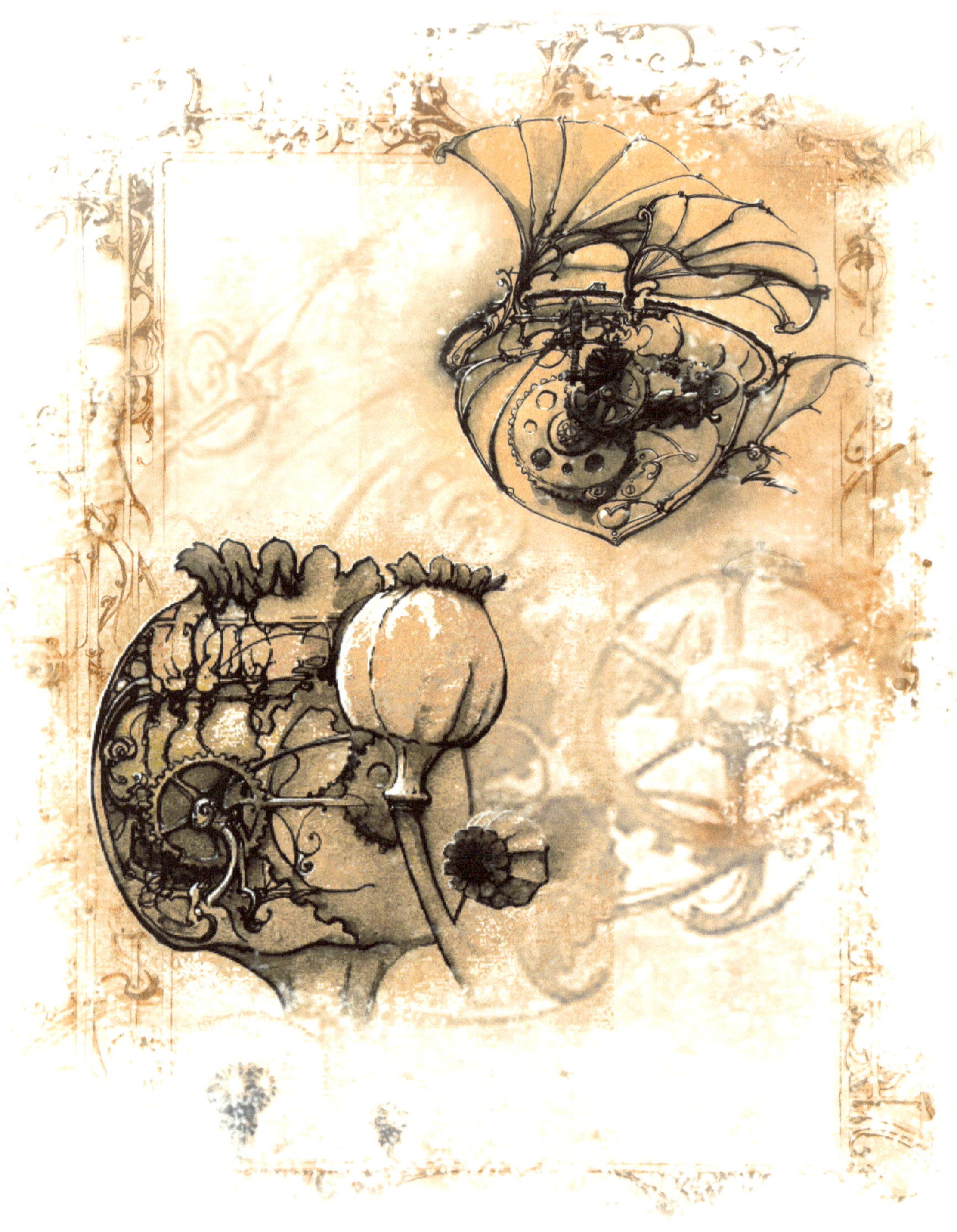

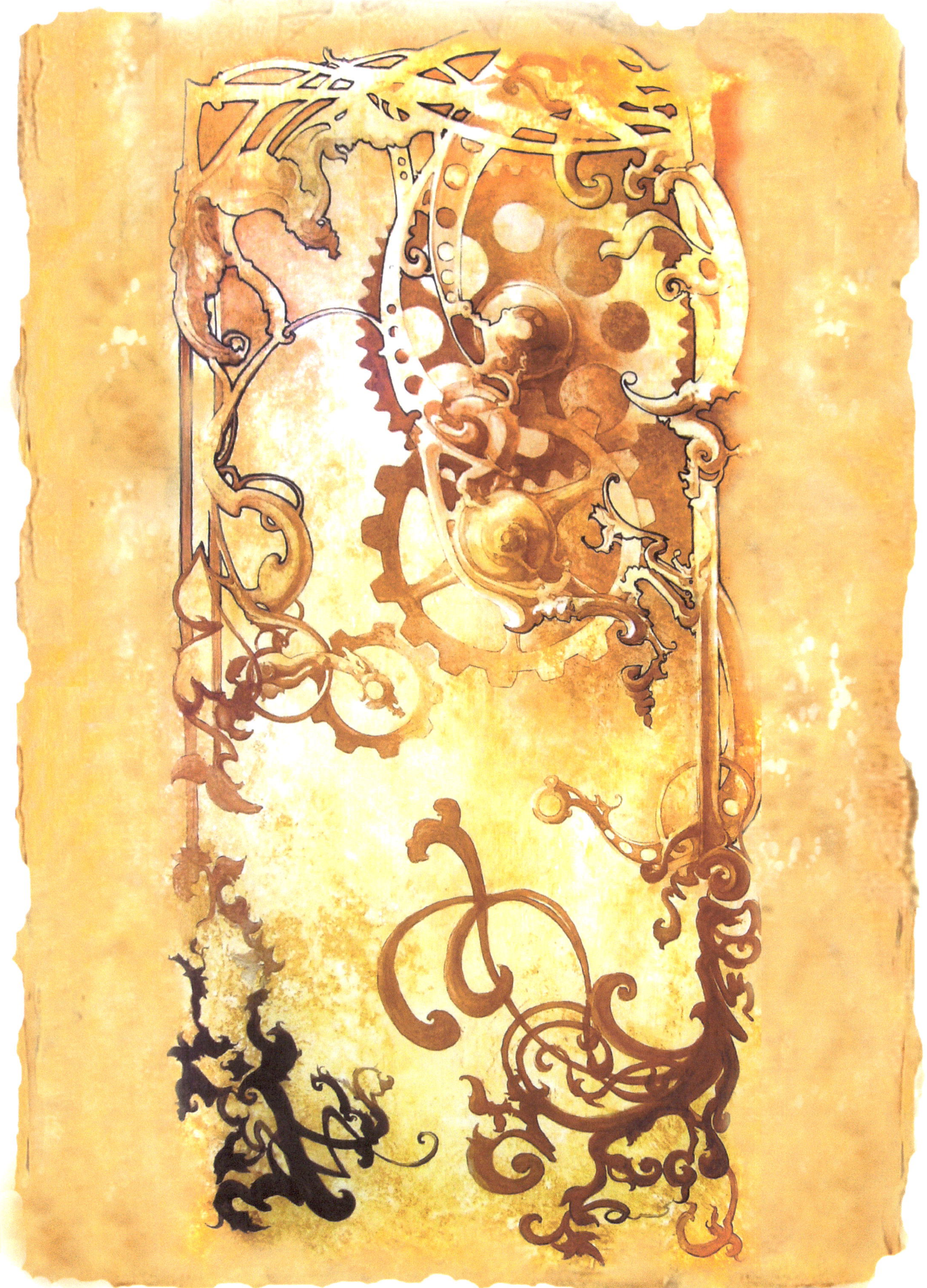

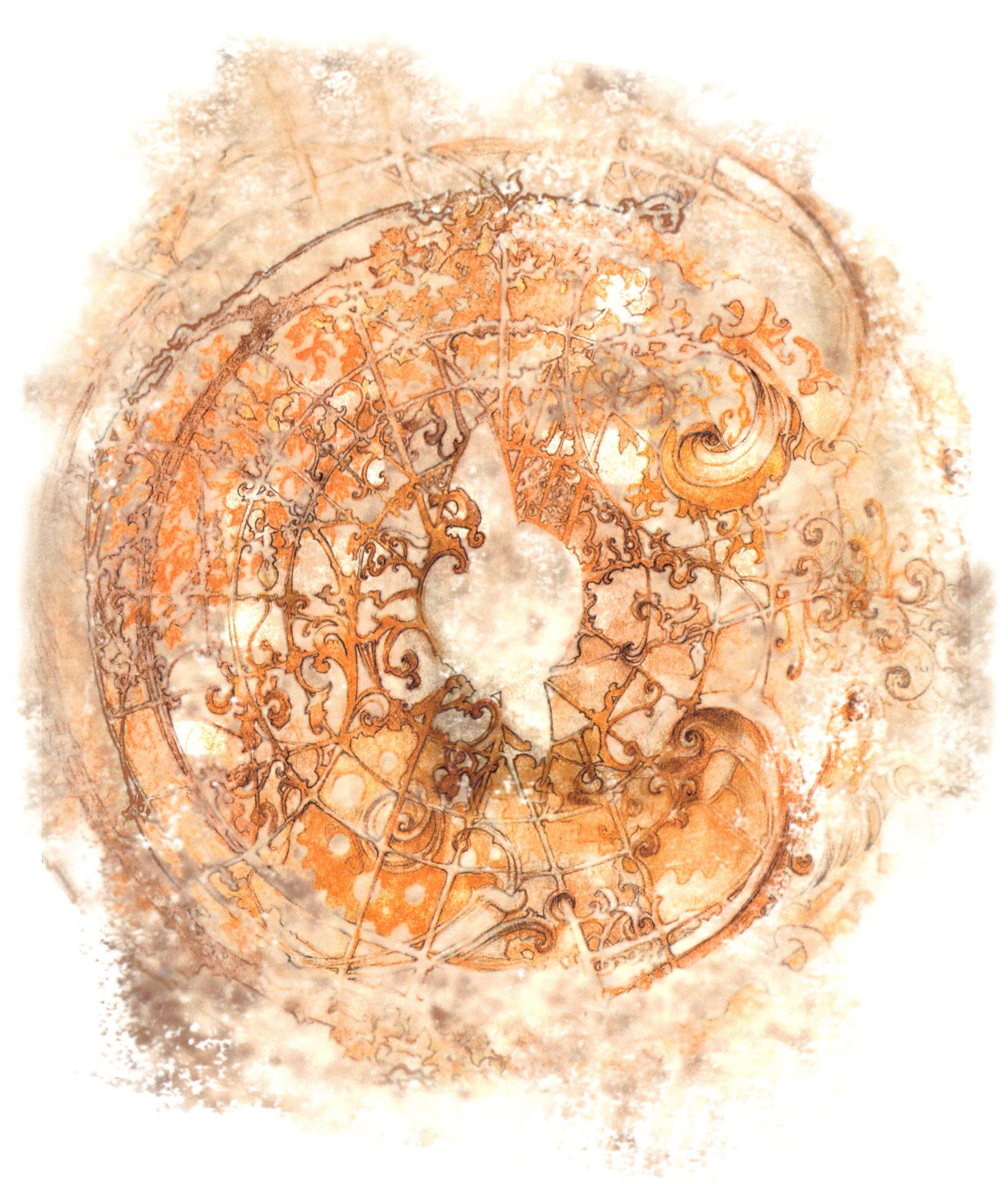

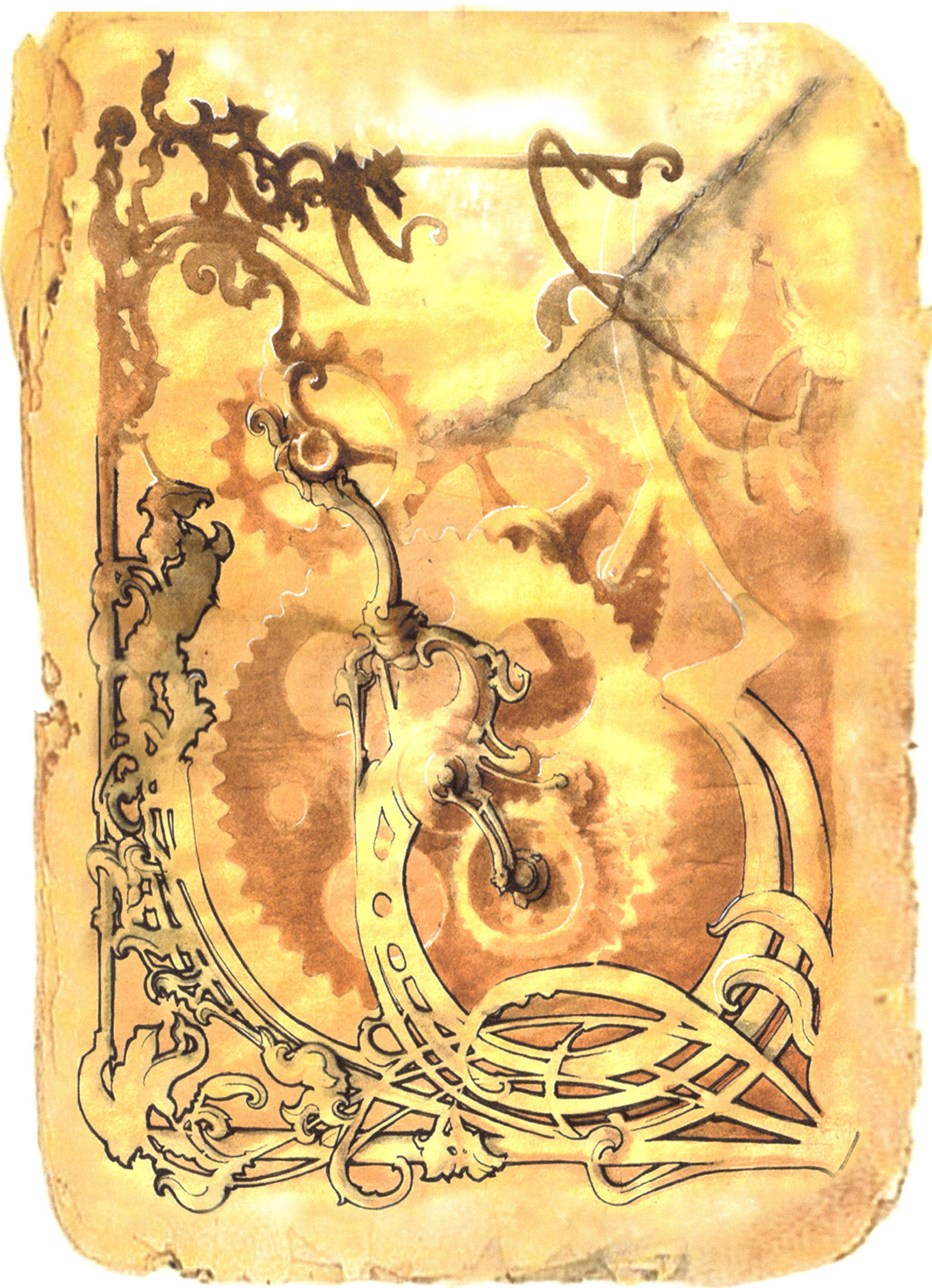

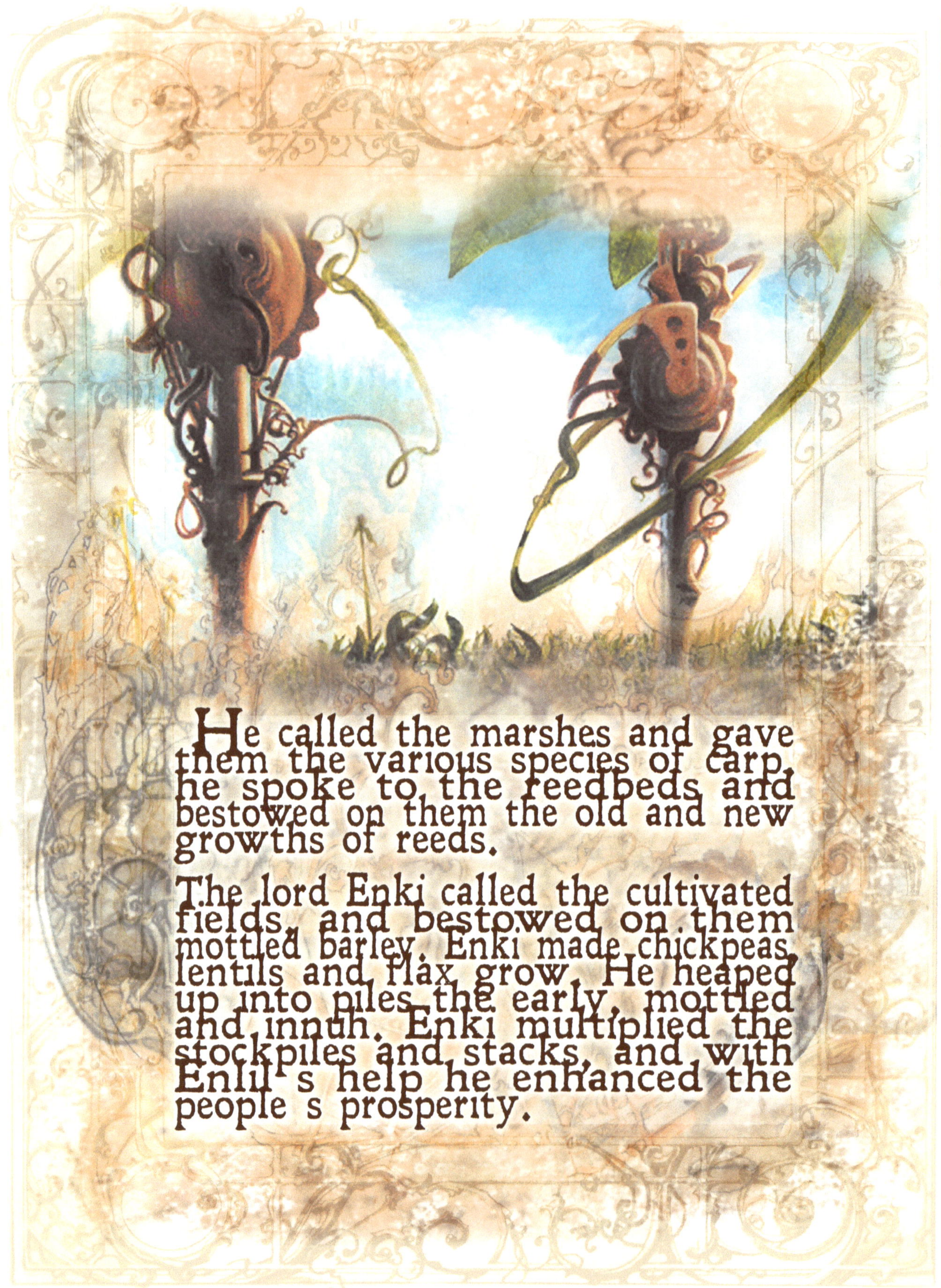

He called the marshes and gave them the various species of carp, he spoke to the reedbeds and bestowed on them the old and new growths of reeds.

The lord Enki called the cultivated fields, and bestowed on them mottled barley. Enki made chickpeas, lentils and flax grow. He heaped up into piles the early, mottled and innuh. Enki multiplied the stockpiles and stacks, and with Enlil s help he enhanced the people s prosperity.

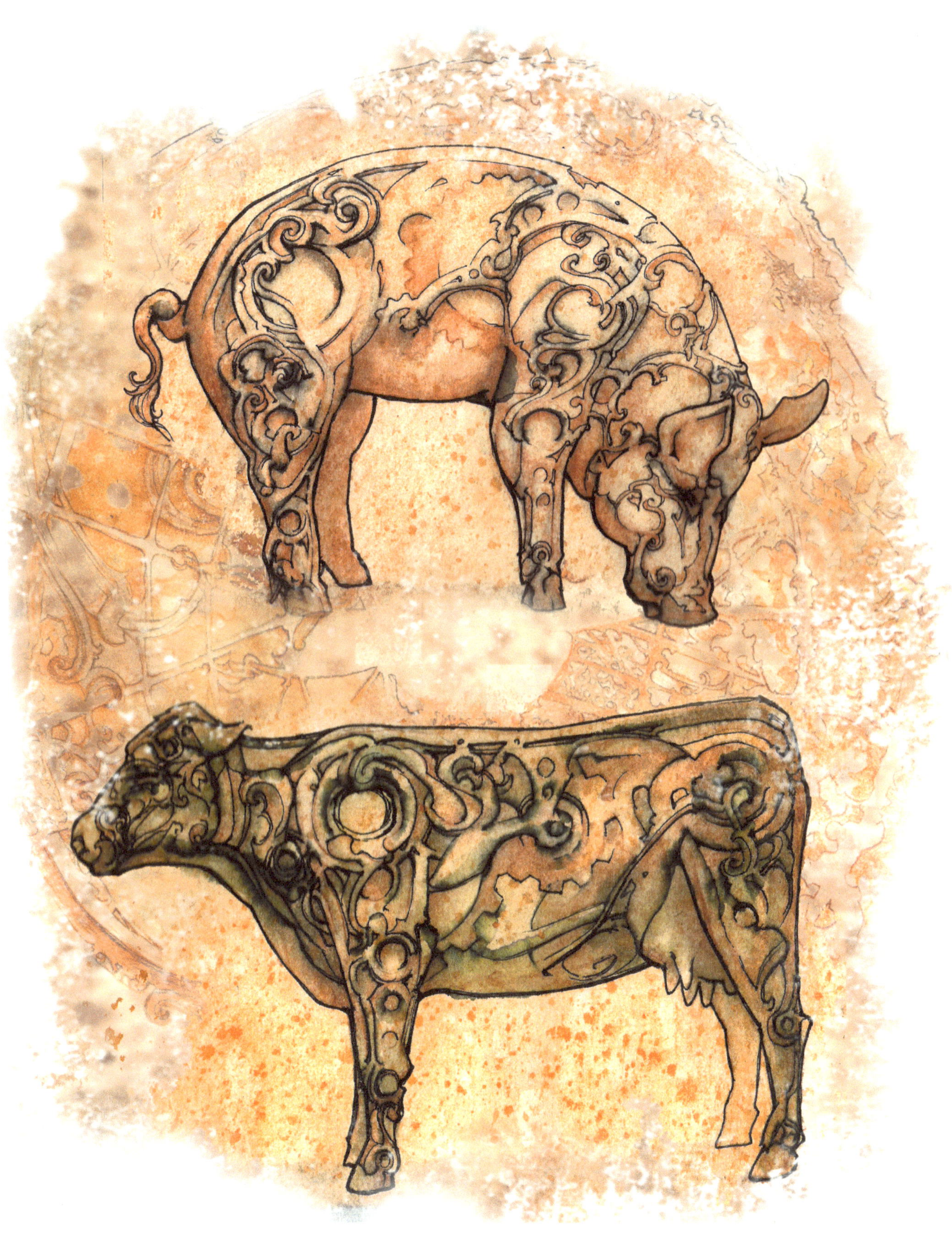

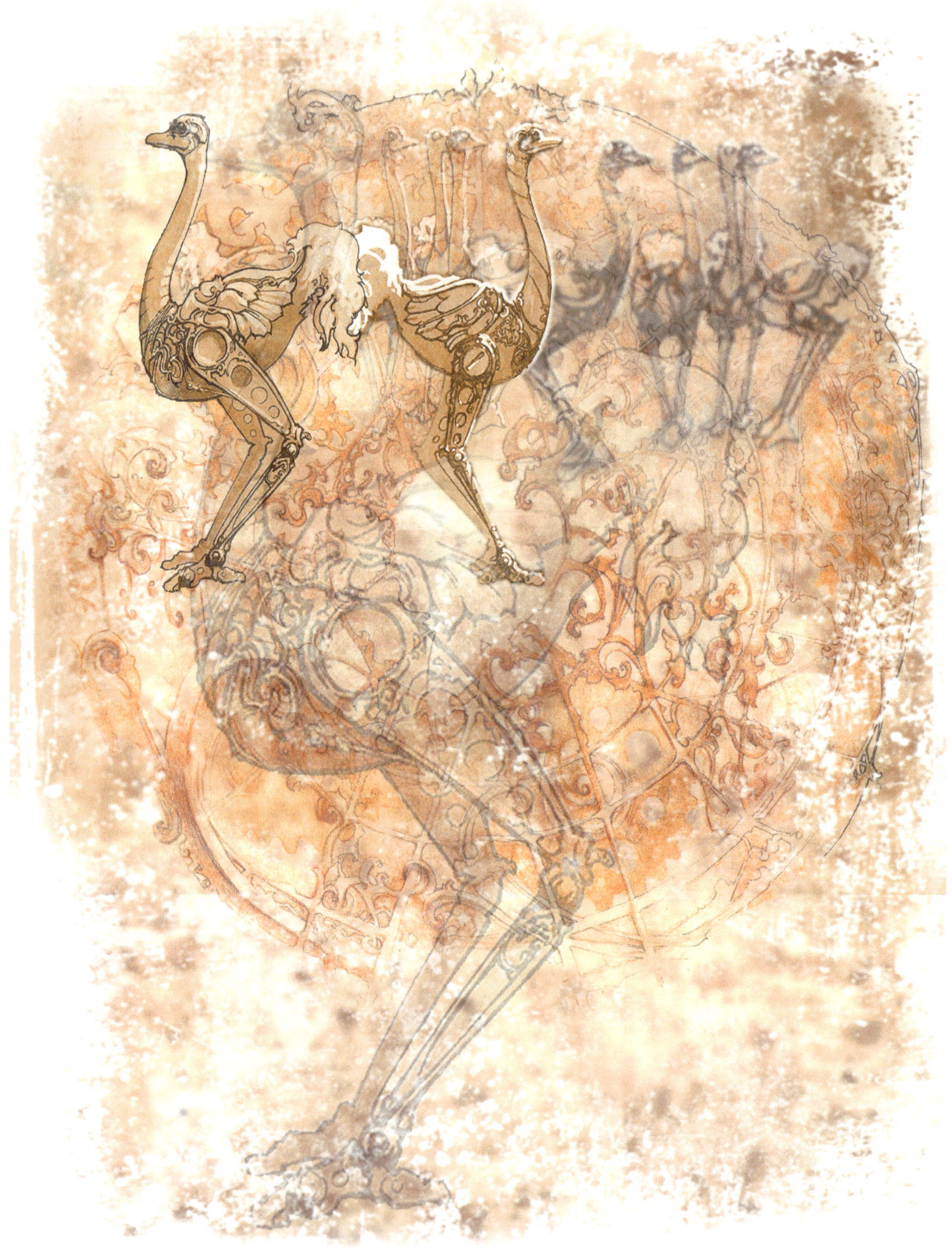

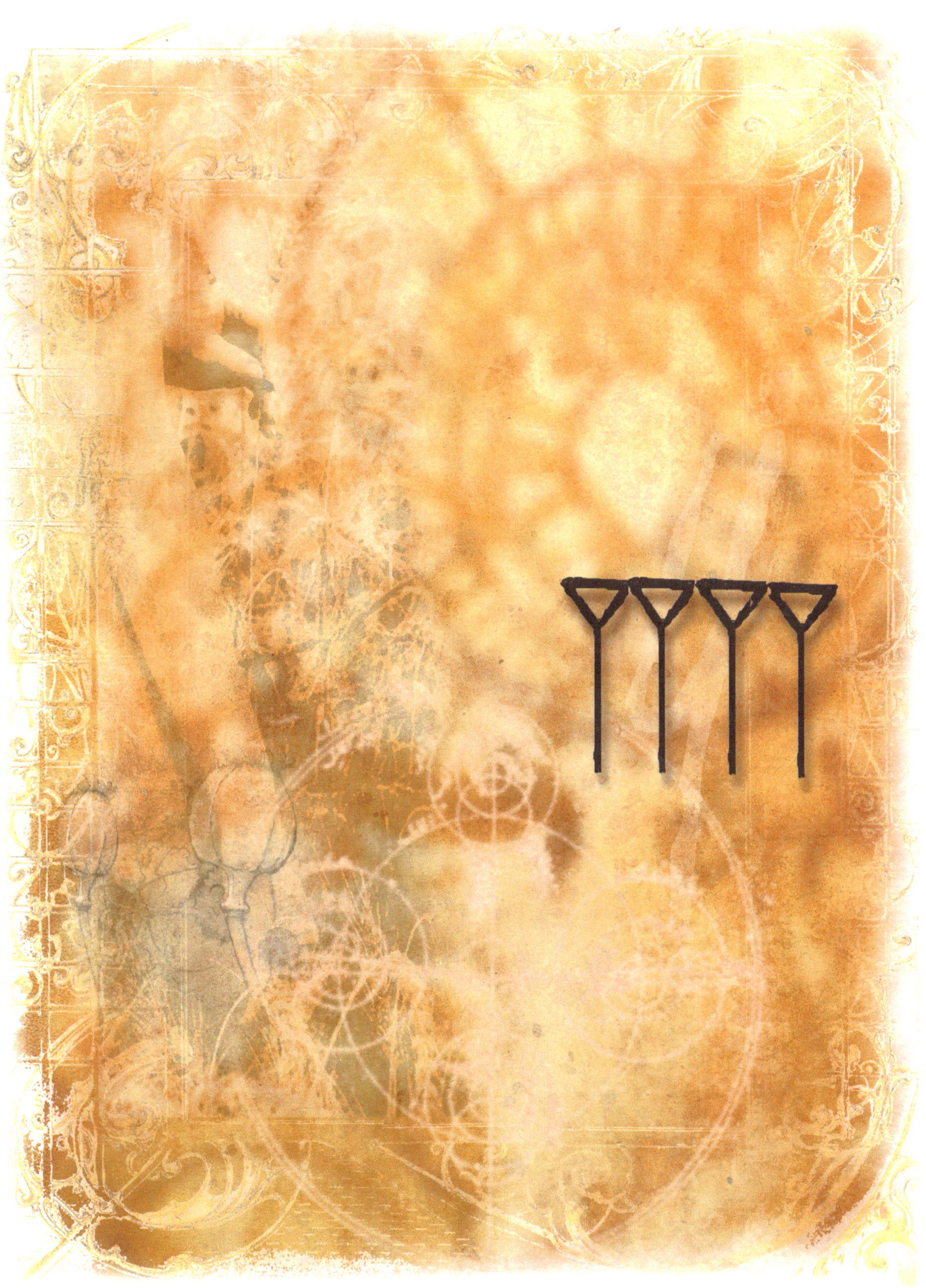

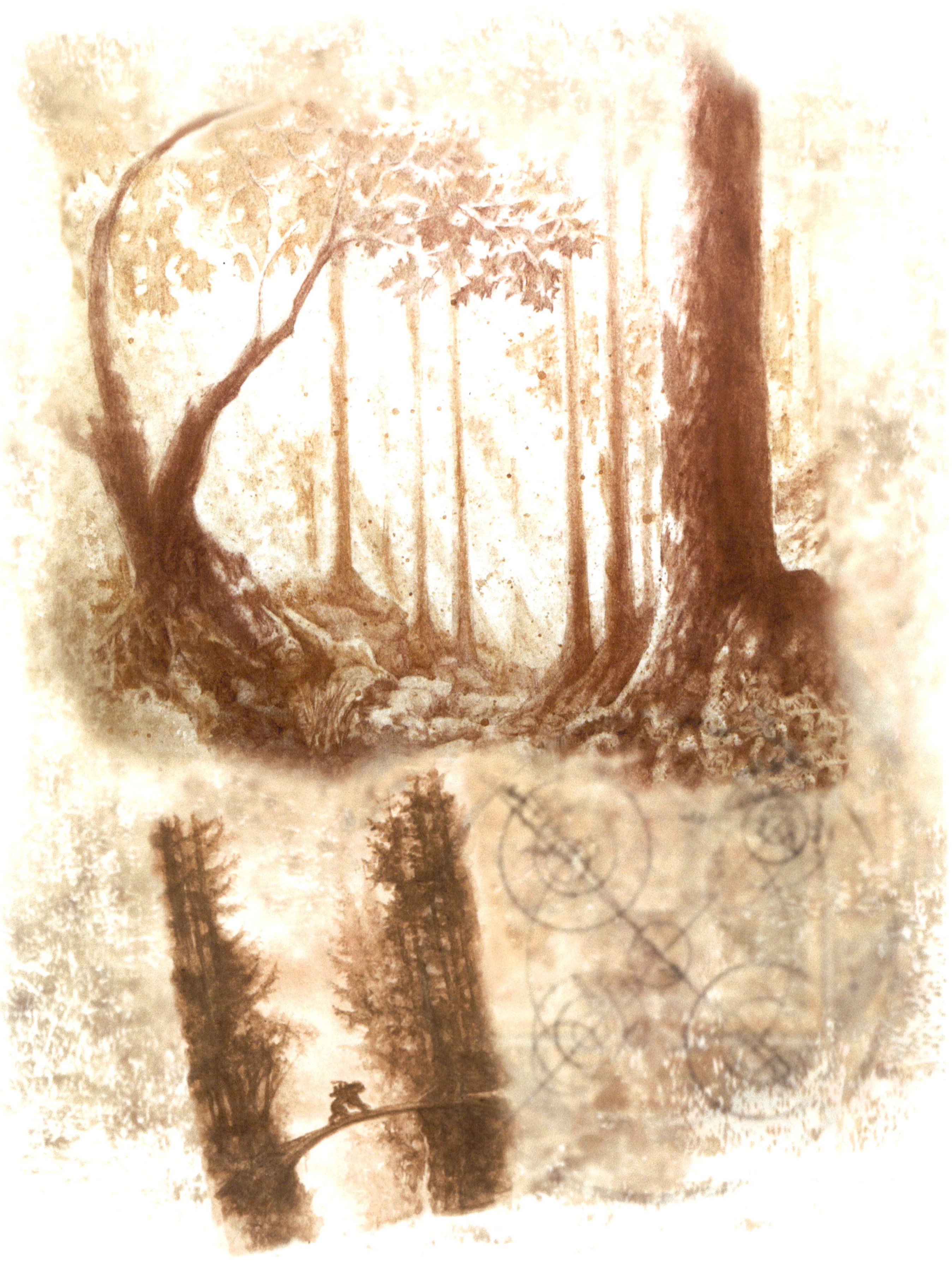

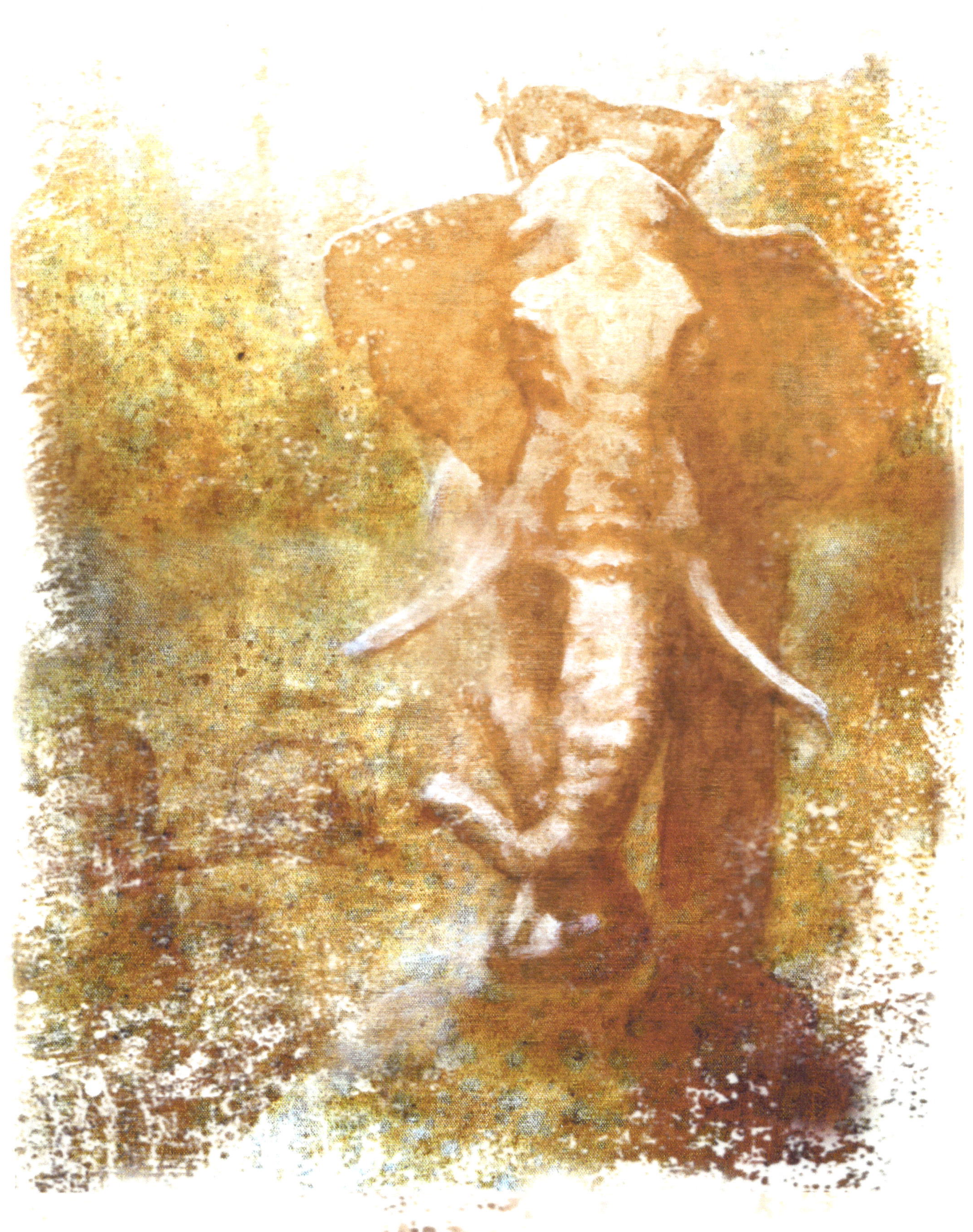

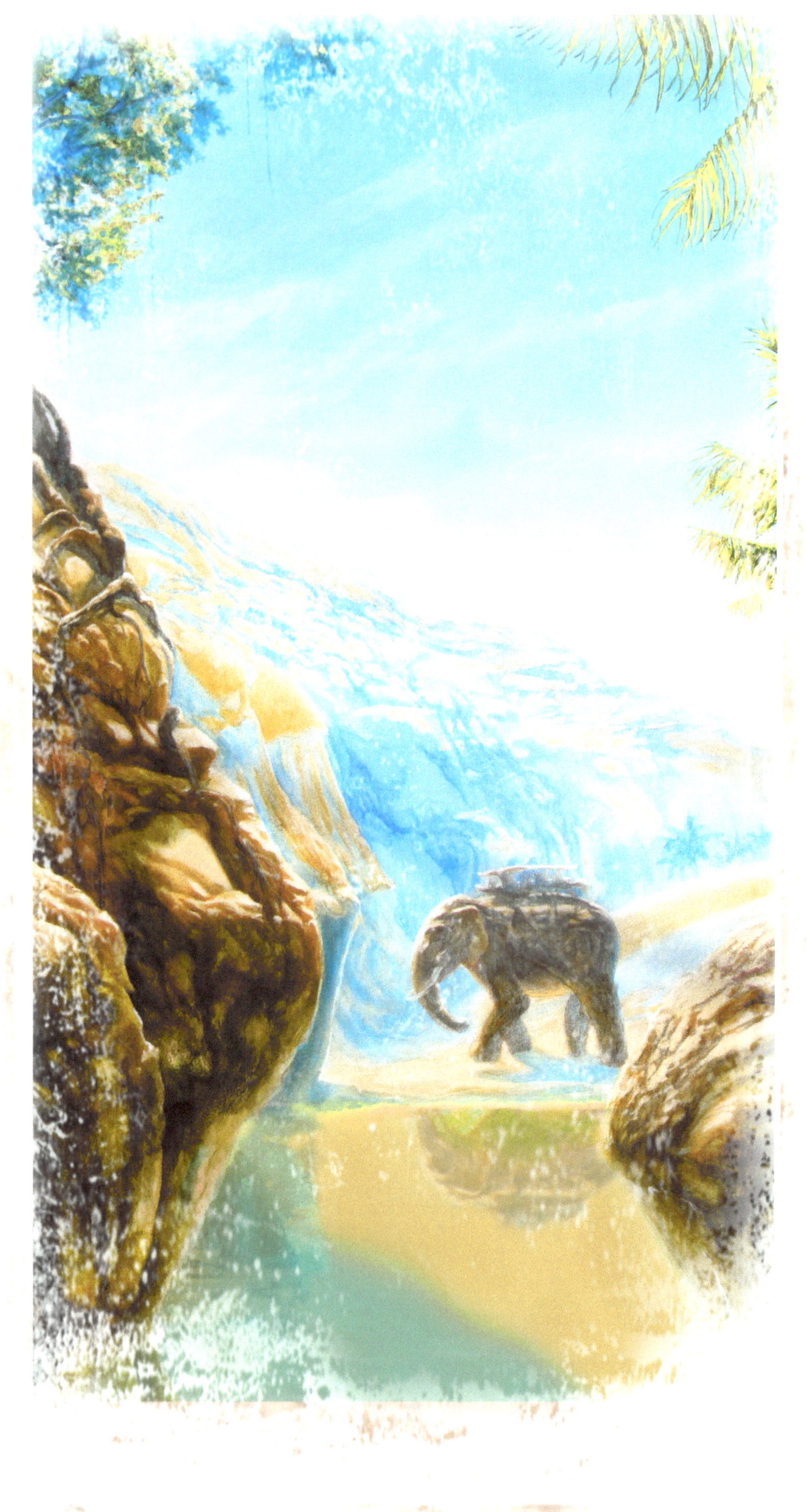

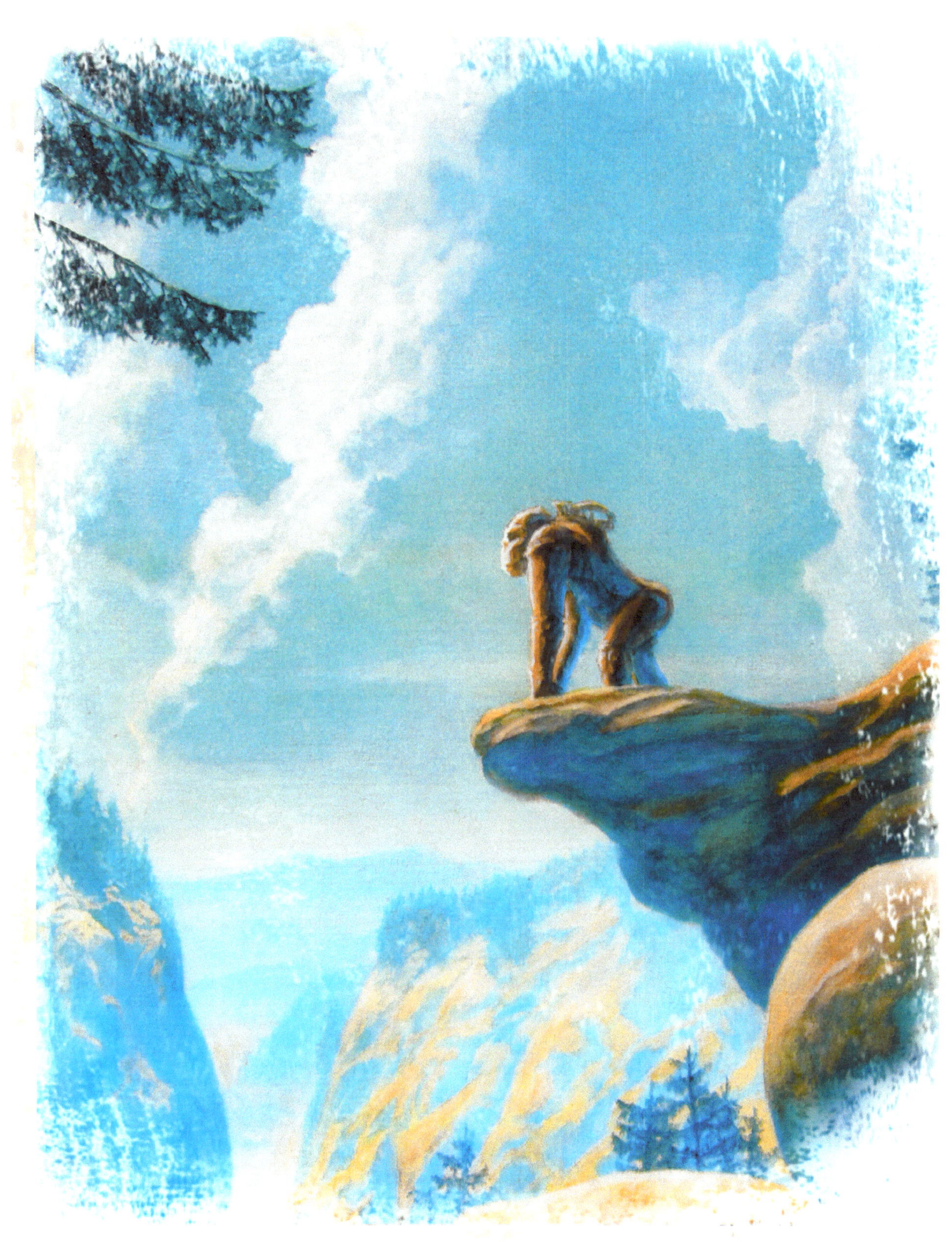

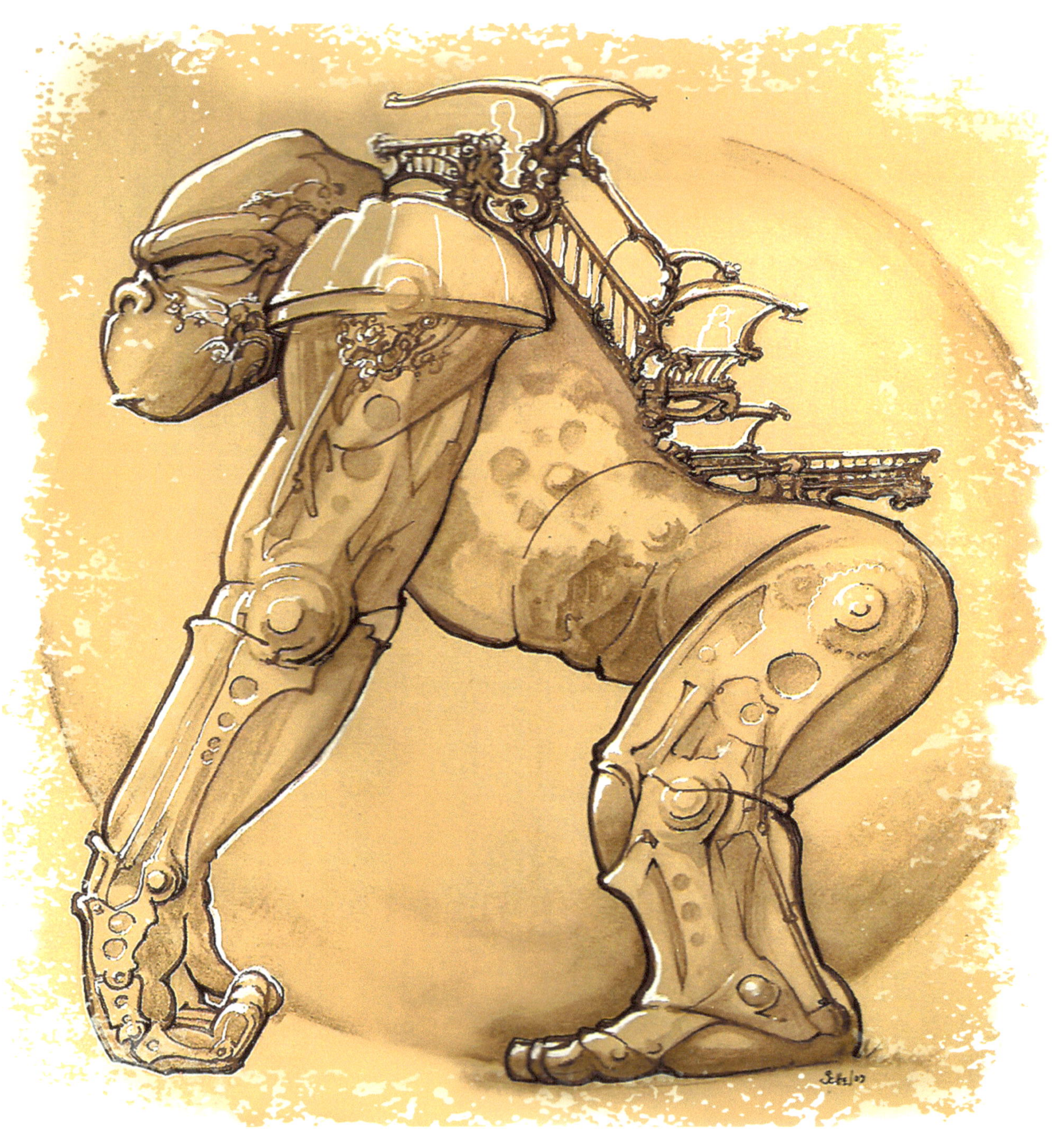

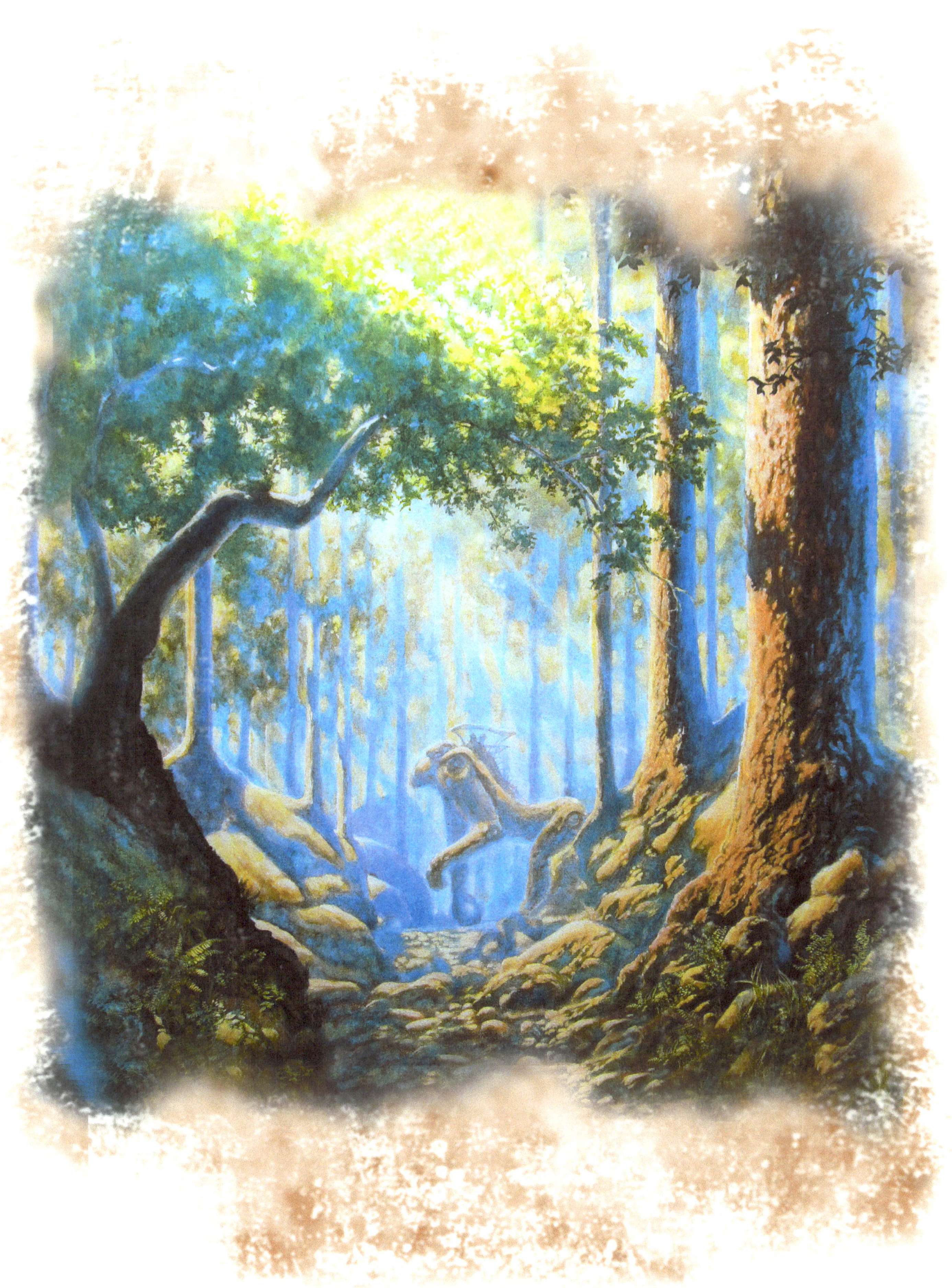

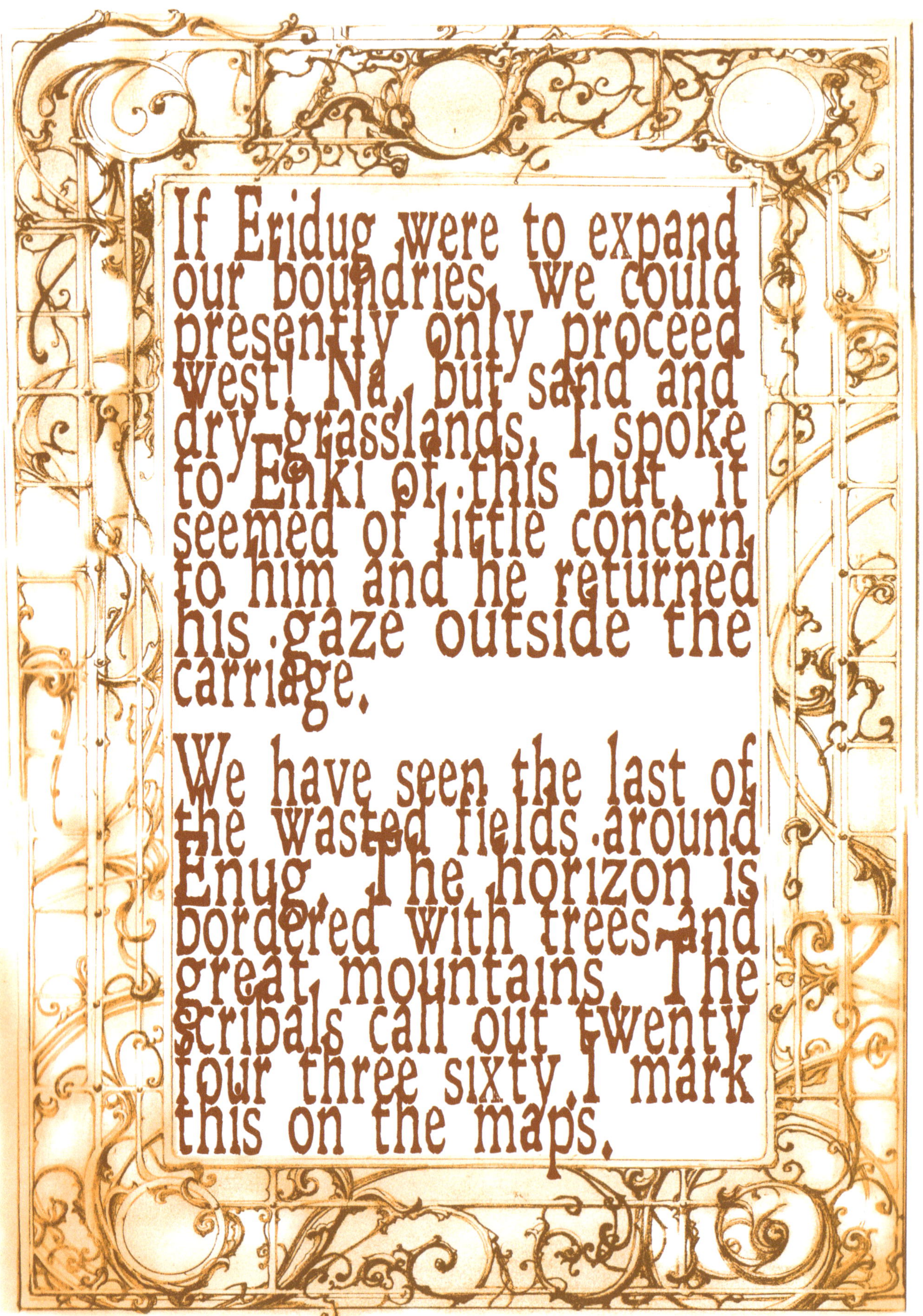

If Eridug were to expand our boundries, we could presently only proceed west! Na, but sand and dry grasslands. I spoke to Enki of this but it seemed of little concern to him and he returned his gaze outside the carriage.

We have seen the last of the wasted fields around Enug. The horizon is bordered with trees and great mountains. The scribals call out twenty four three sixty. I mark this on the maps.

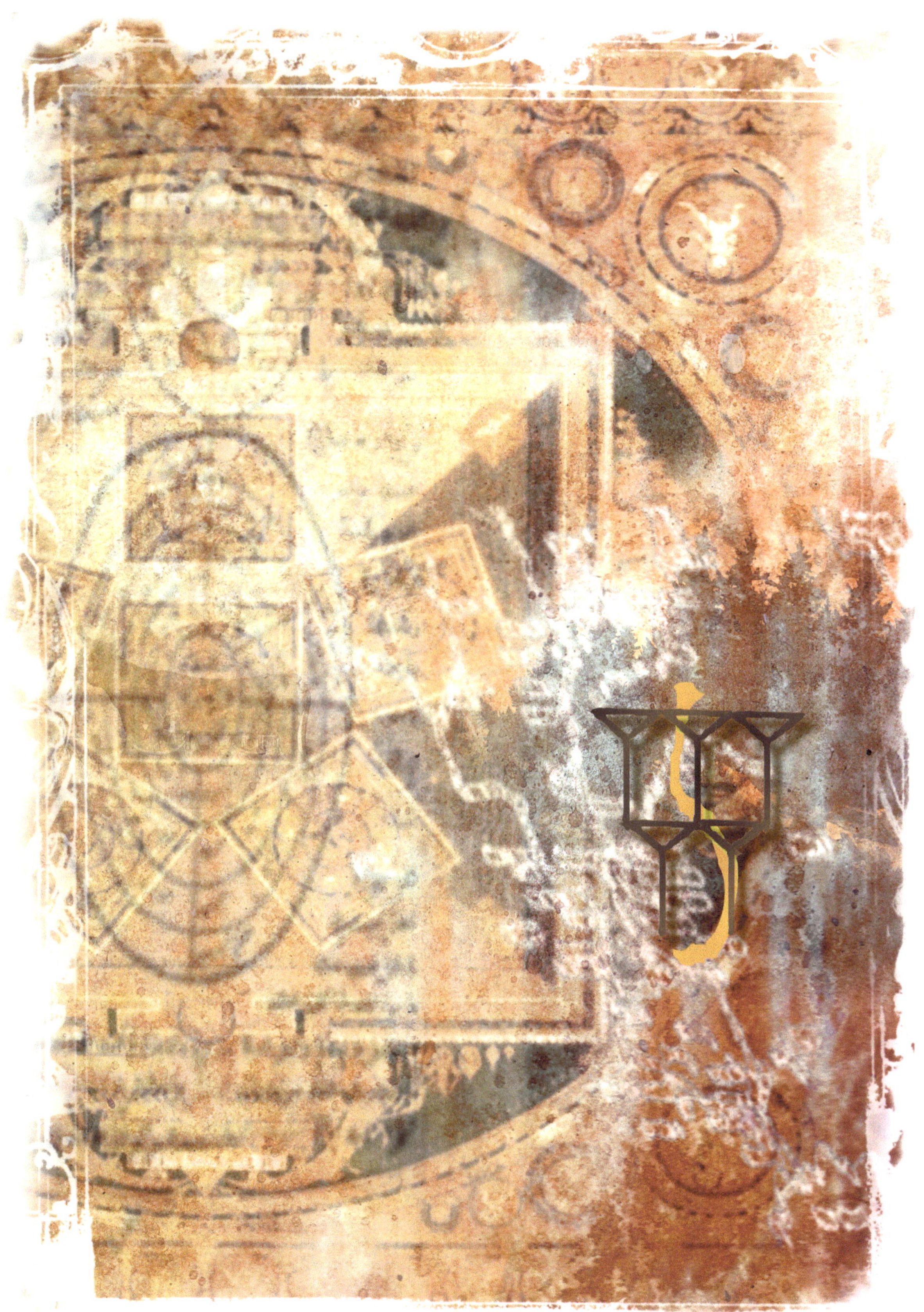

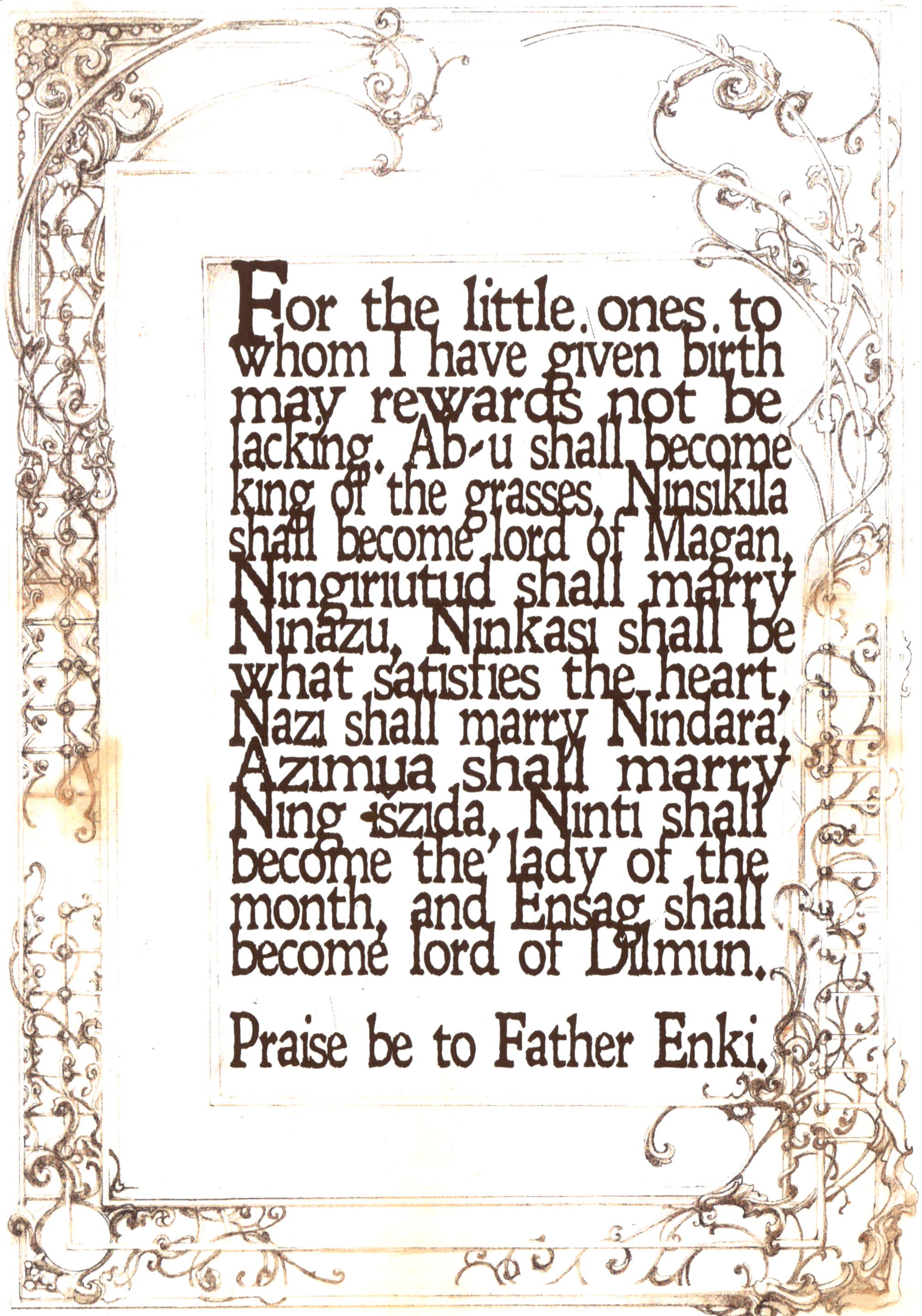

For the little ones to whom I have given birth may rewards not be lacking. Ab-u shall become king of the grasses, Ninsikila shall become lord of Magan, Ningiriutud shall marry Ninazu, Ninkasi shall be what satisfies the heart, Nazi shall marry Nindara, Azimua shall marry Ning-iszida, Ninti shall become the lady of the month, and Ensag shall become lord of Dilmun.

Praise be to Father Enki.

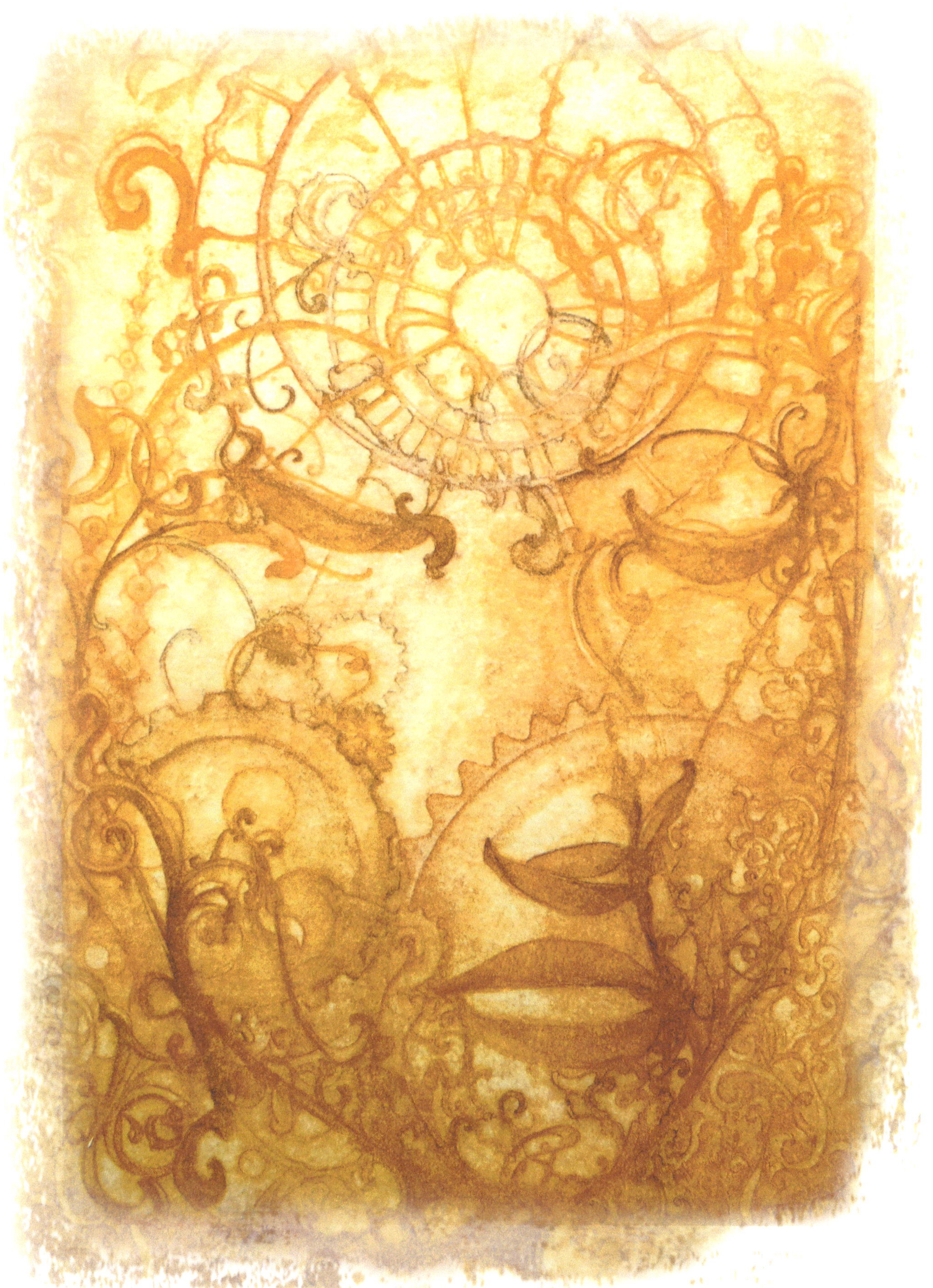

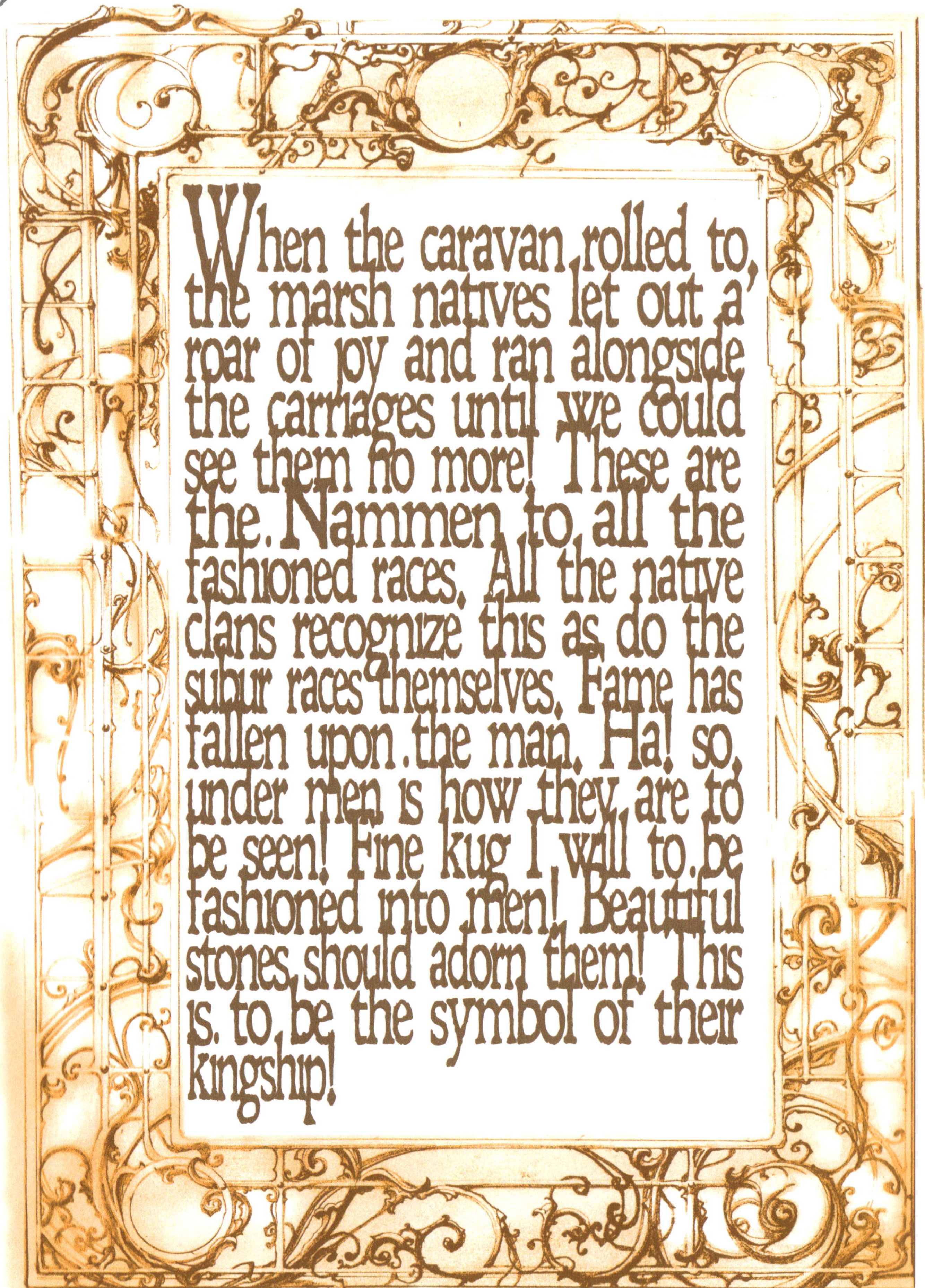

When the caravan rolled to, the marsh natives let out a roar of joy and ran alongside the carriages until we could see them no more! These are the Nammen to all the fashioned races. All the native clans recognize this as do the subur races themselves. Fame has fallen upon the man. Ha! so, under men is how they are to be seen! Fine kug I will to be fashioned into men! Beautiful stones should adorn them! This is to be the symbol of their kingship!

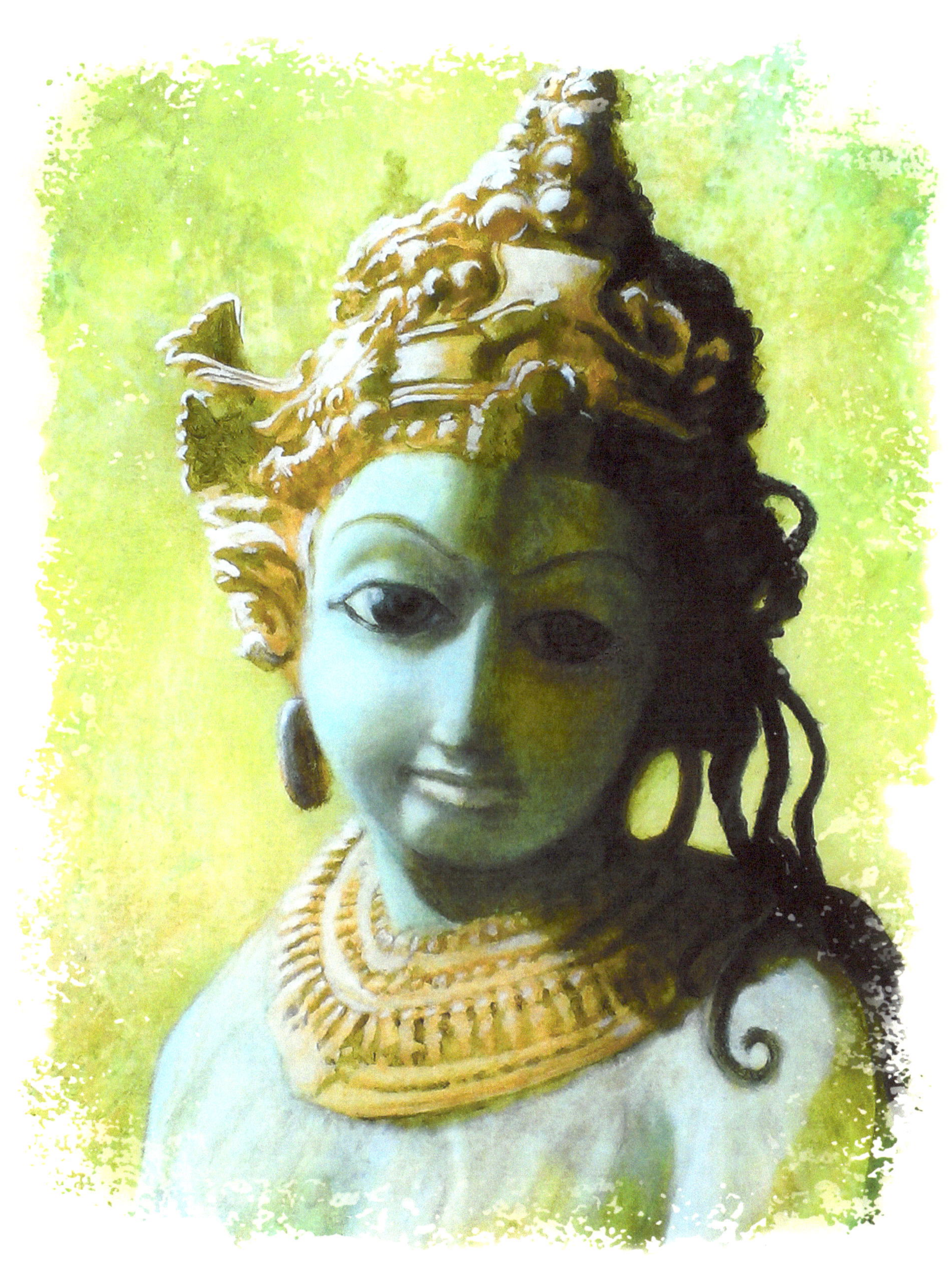

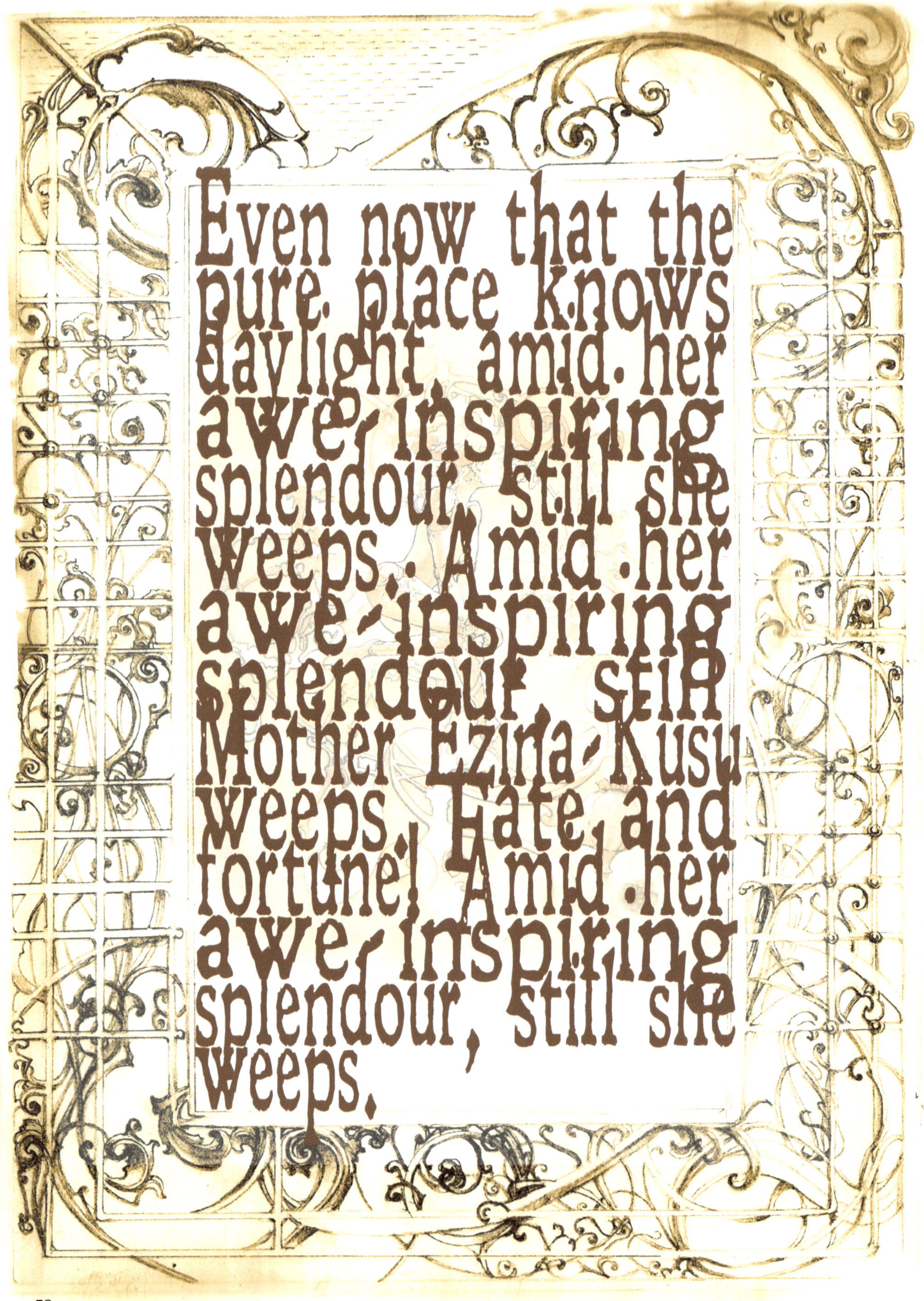
Even now that the
pure place knows
daylight amid her
awe-inspiring
splendour, still she
weeps. Amid her
awe-inspiring
splendour still
Mother Ezina-Kusu
weeps. Fate and
fortune! Amid her
awe-inspiring
splendour, still she
weeps.

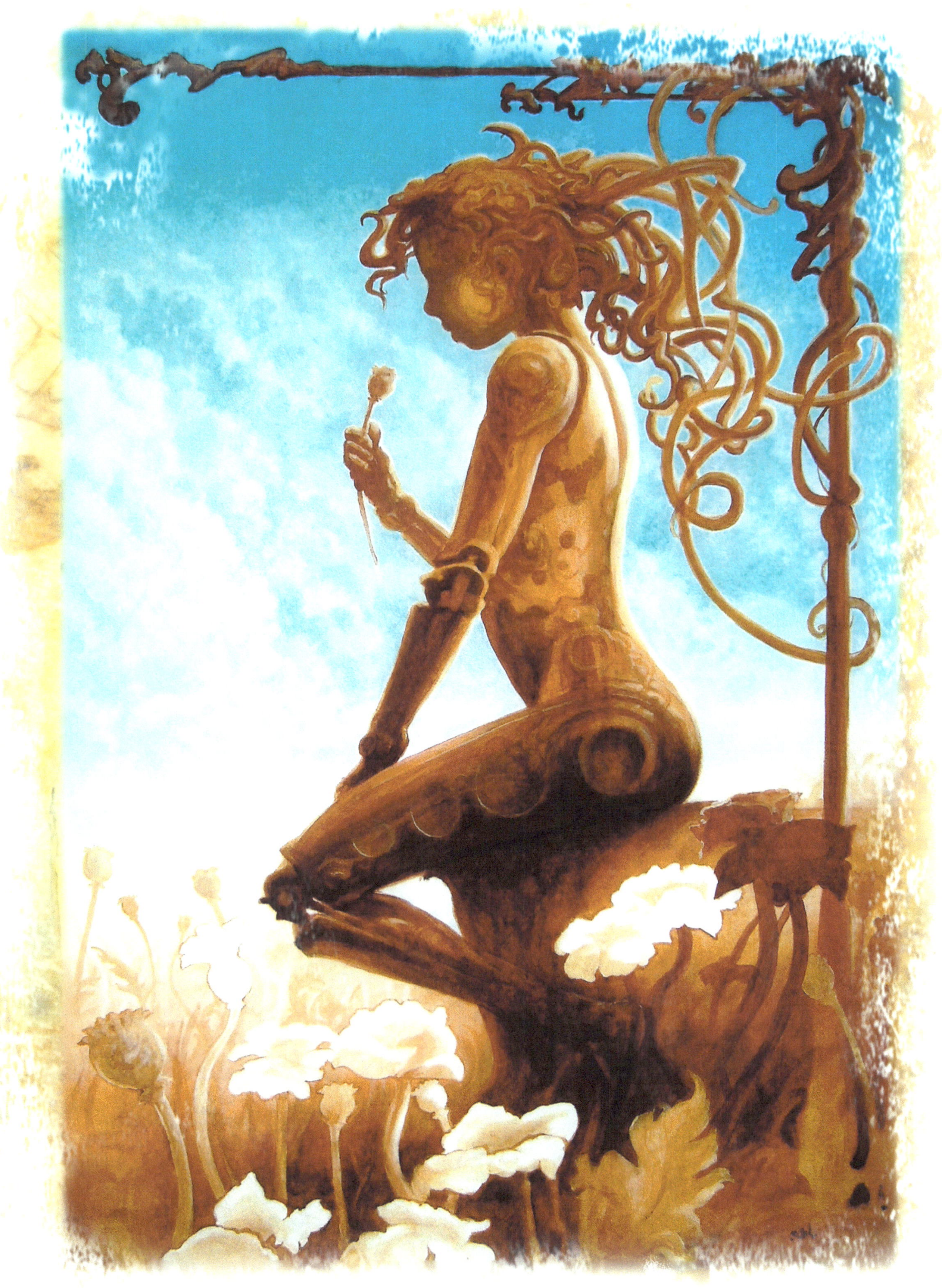

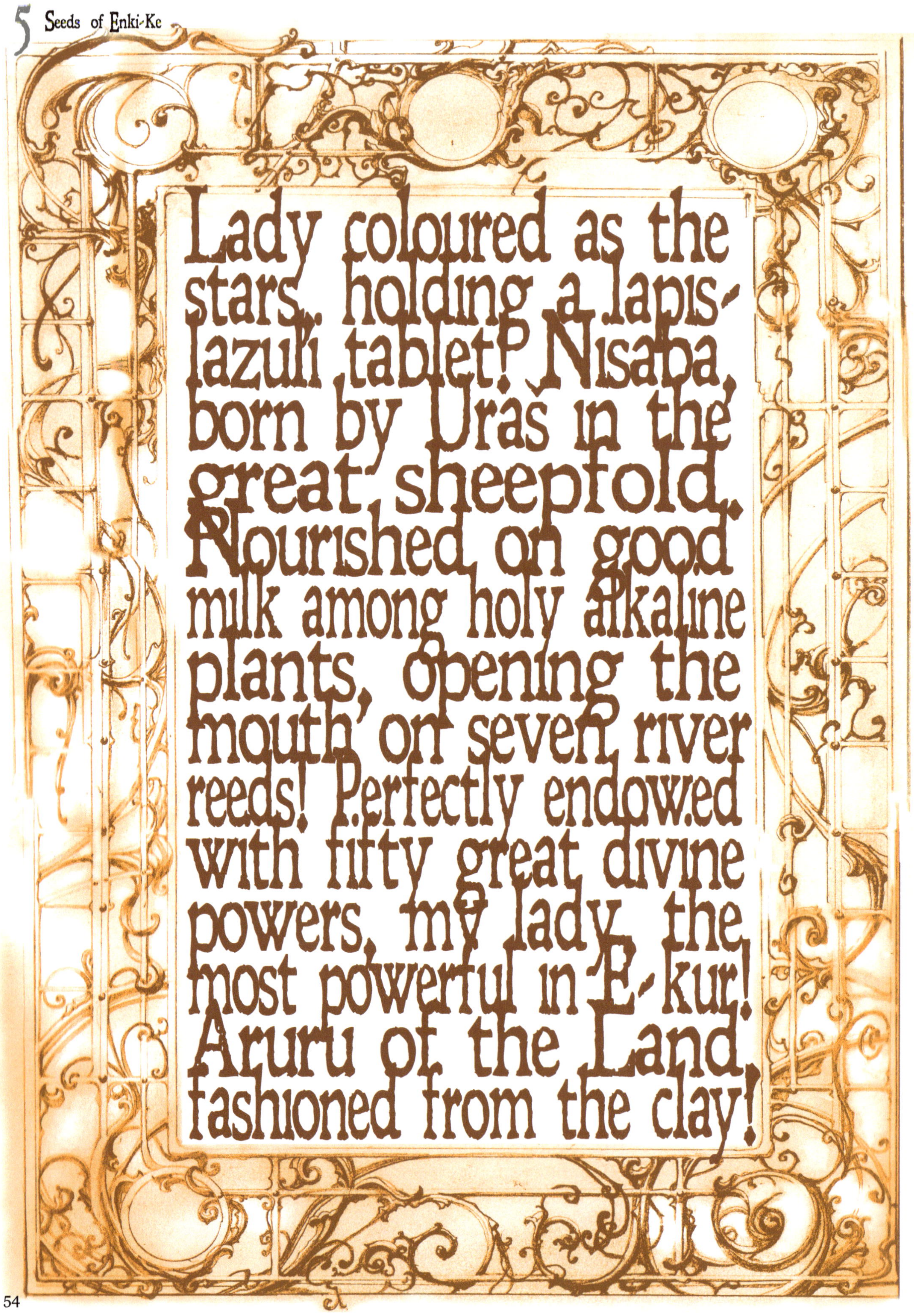
Lady coloured as the stars, holding a lapis-lazuli tablet! Nisaba, born by Uraš in the great sheepfold, Nourished on good milk among holy alkaline plants, opening the mouth on seven river reeds! Perfectly endowed with fifty great divine powers, my lady, the most powerful in E-kur! Aruru of the Land, fashioned from the clay!

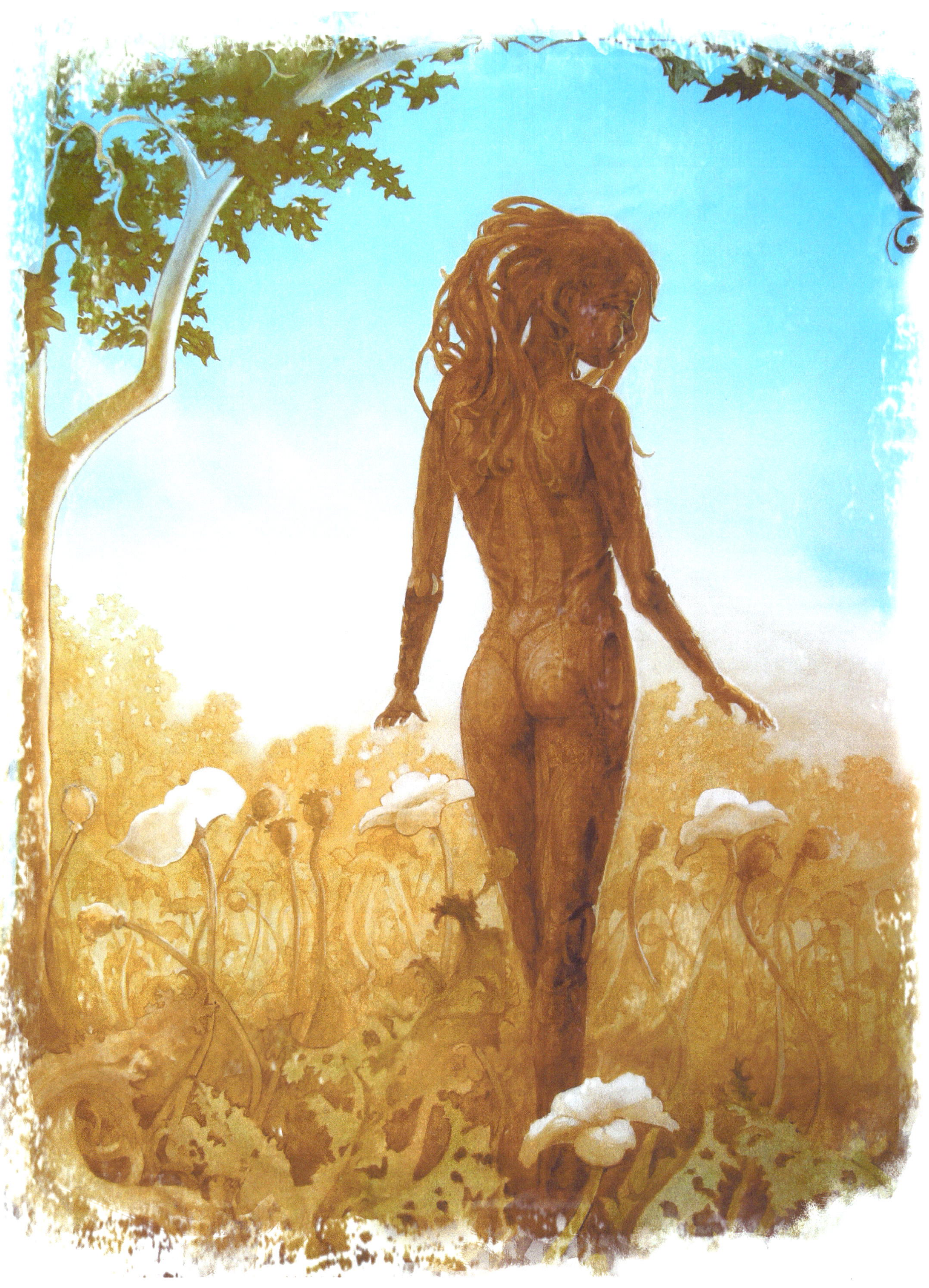

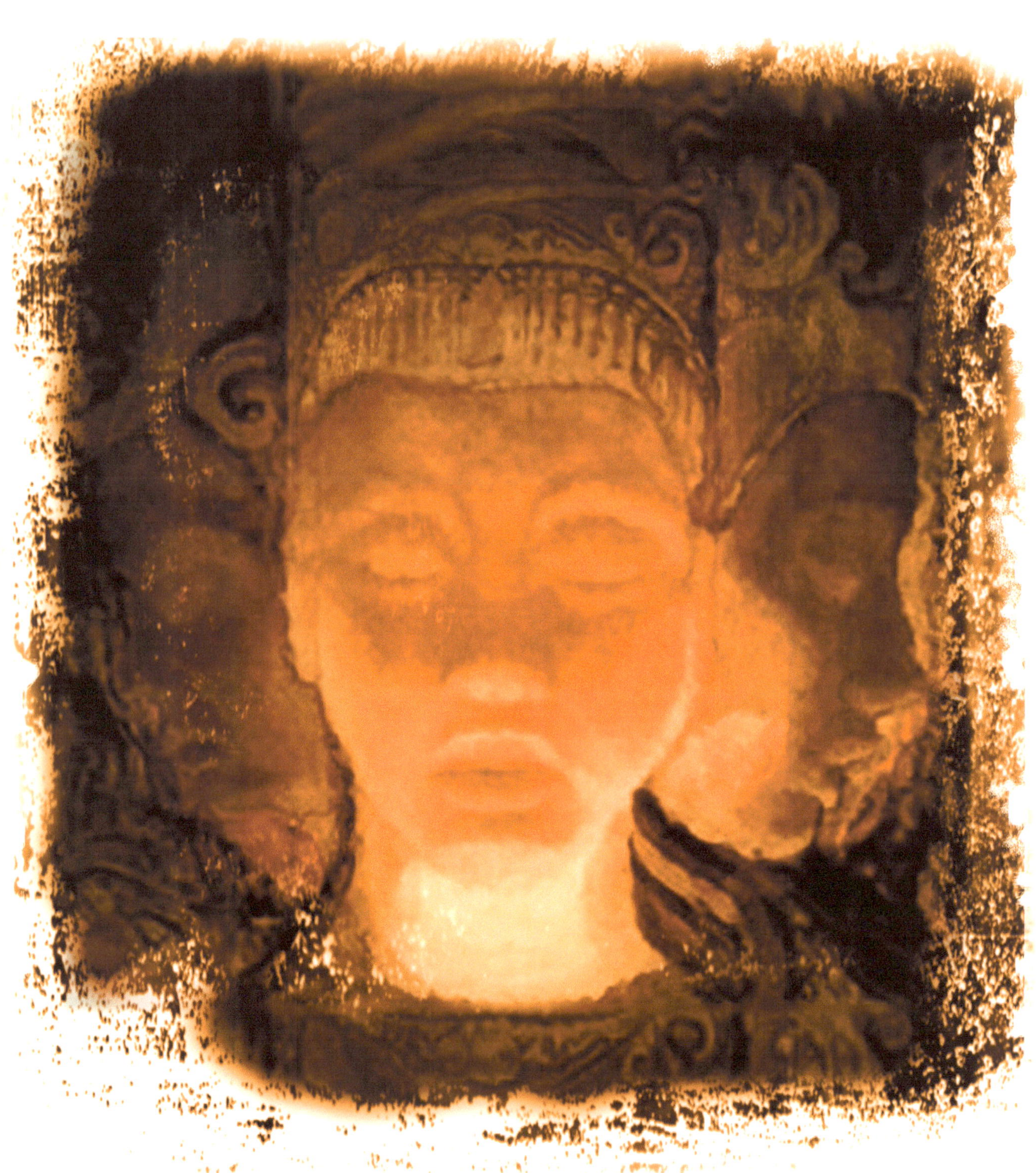

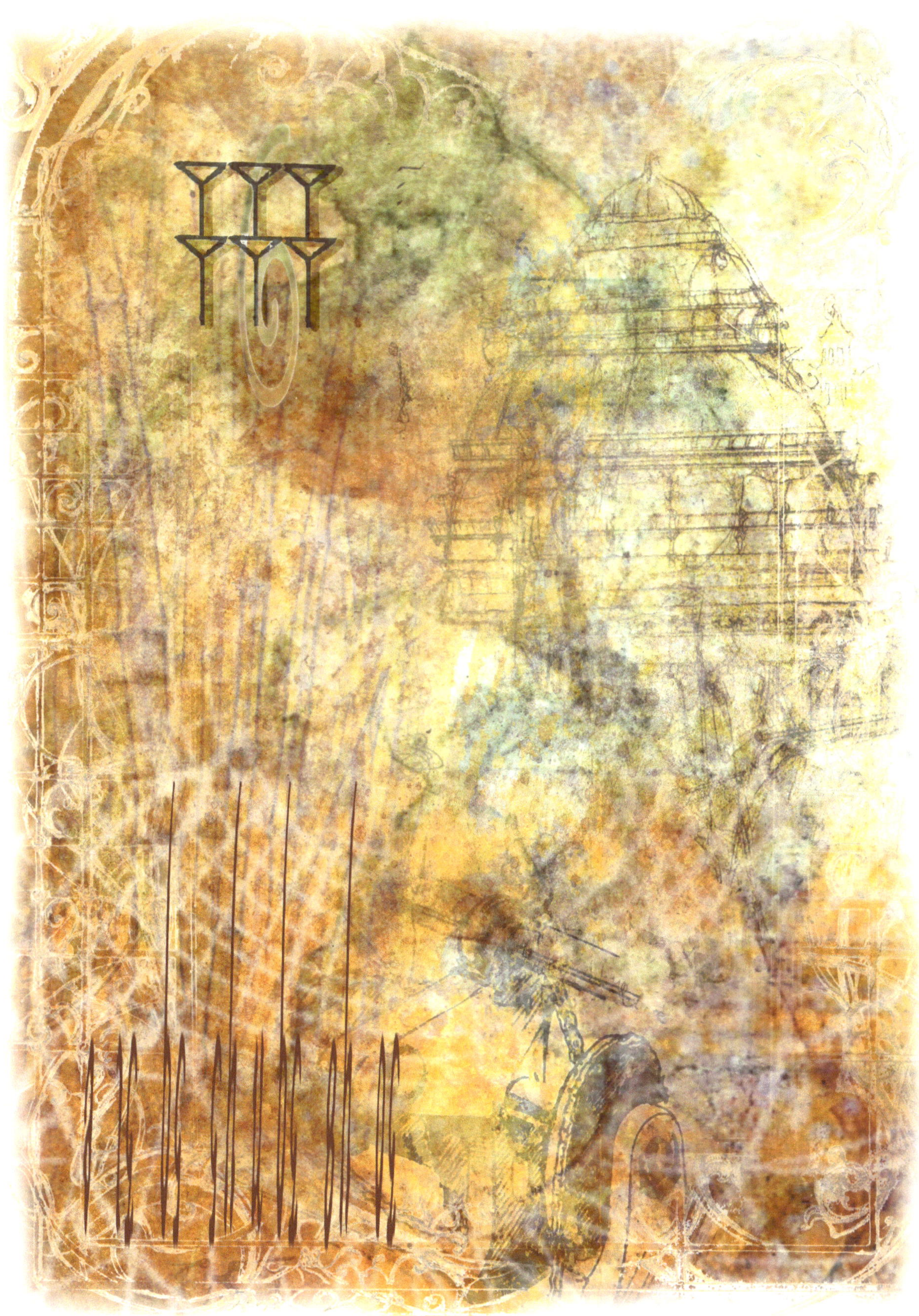

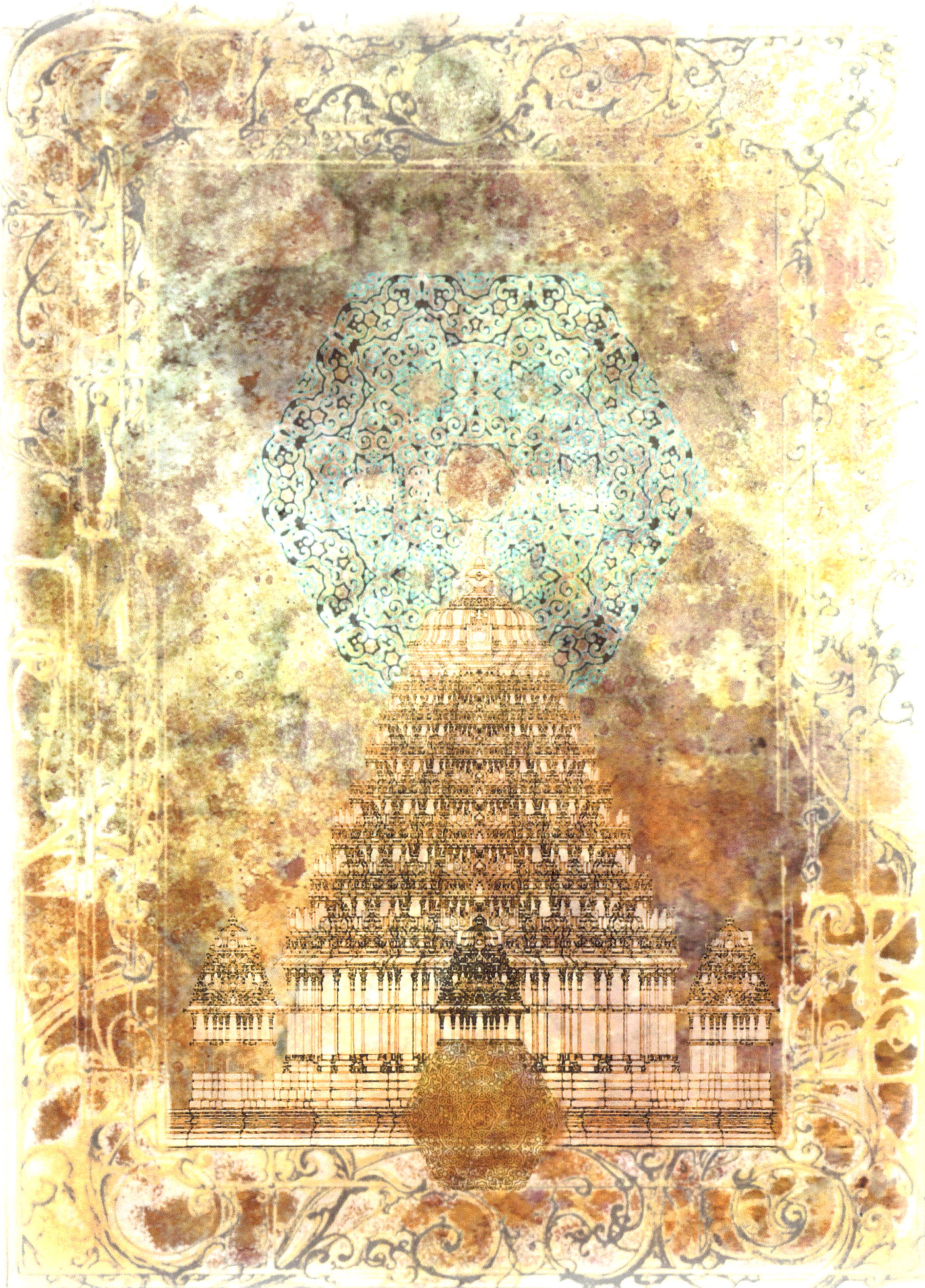

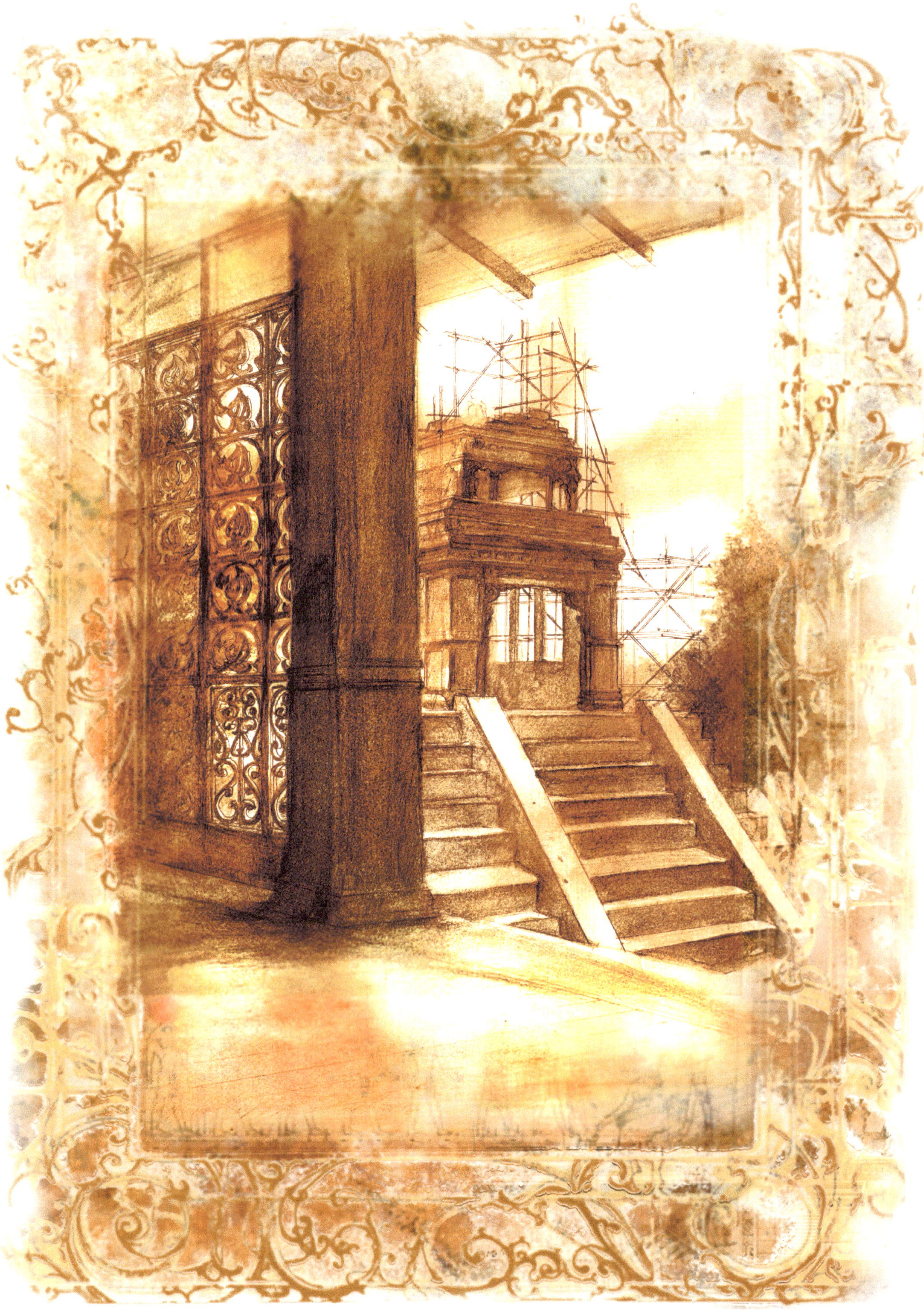

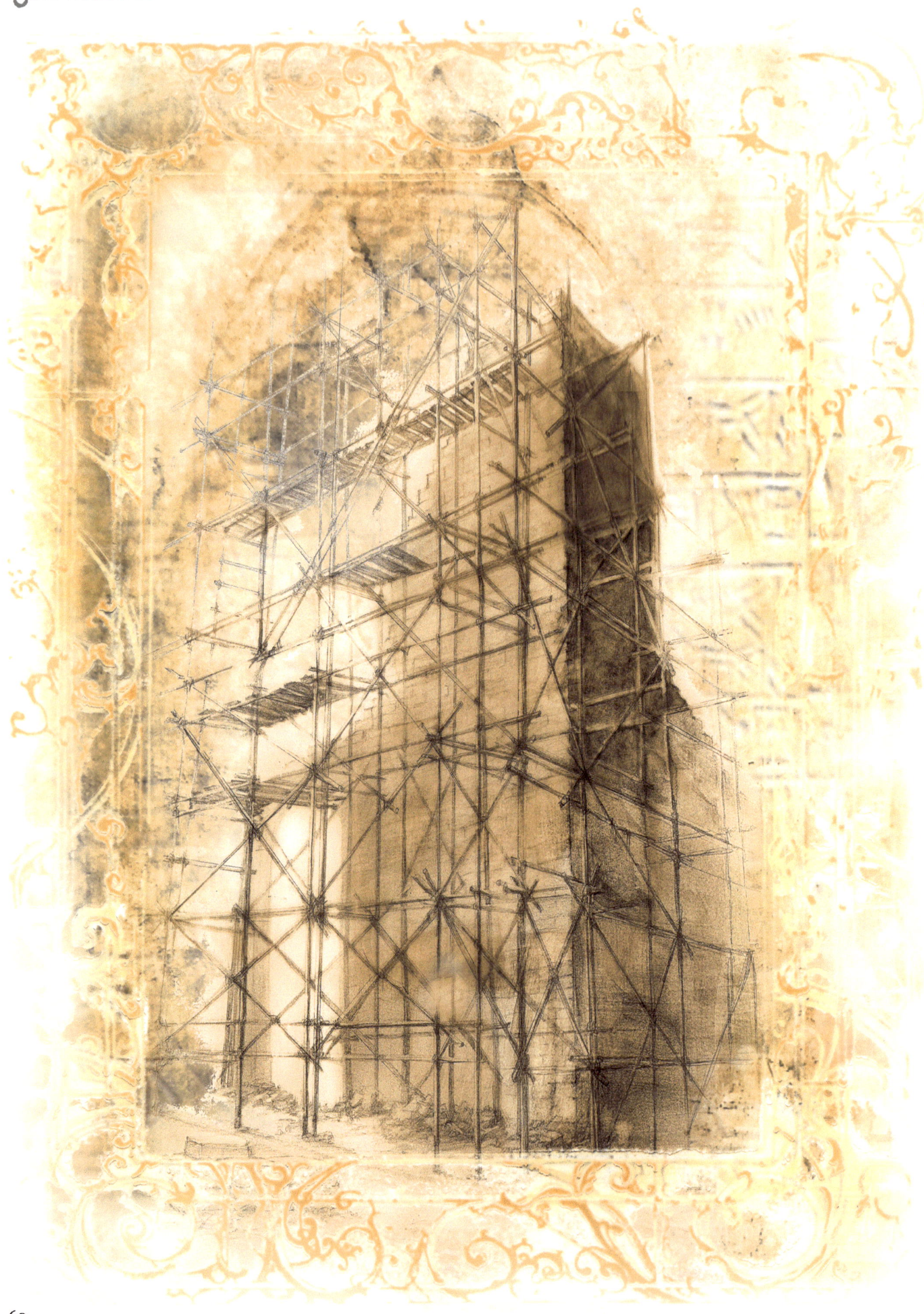

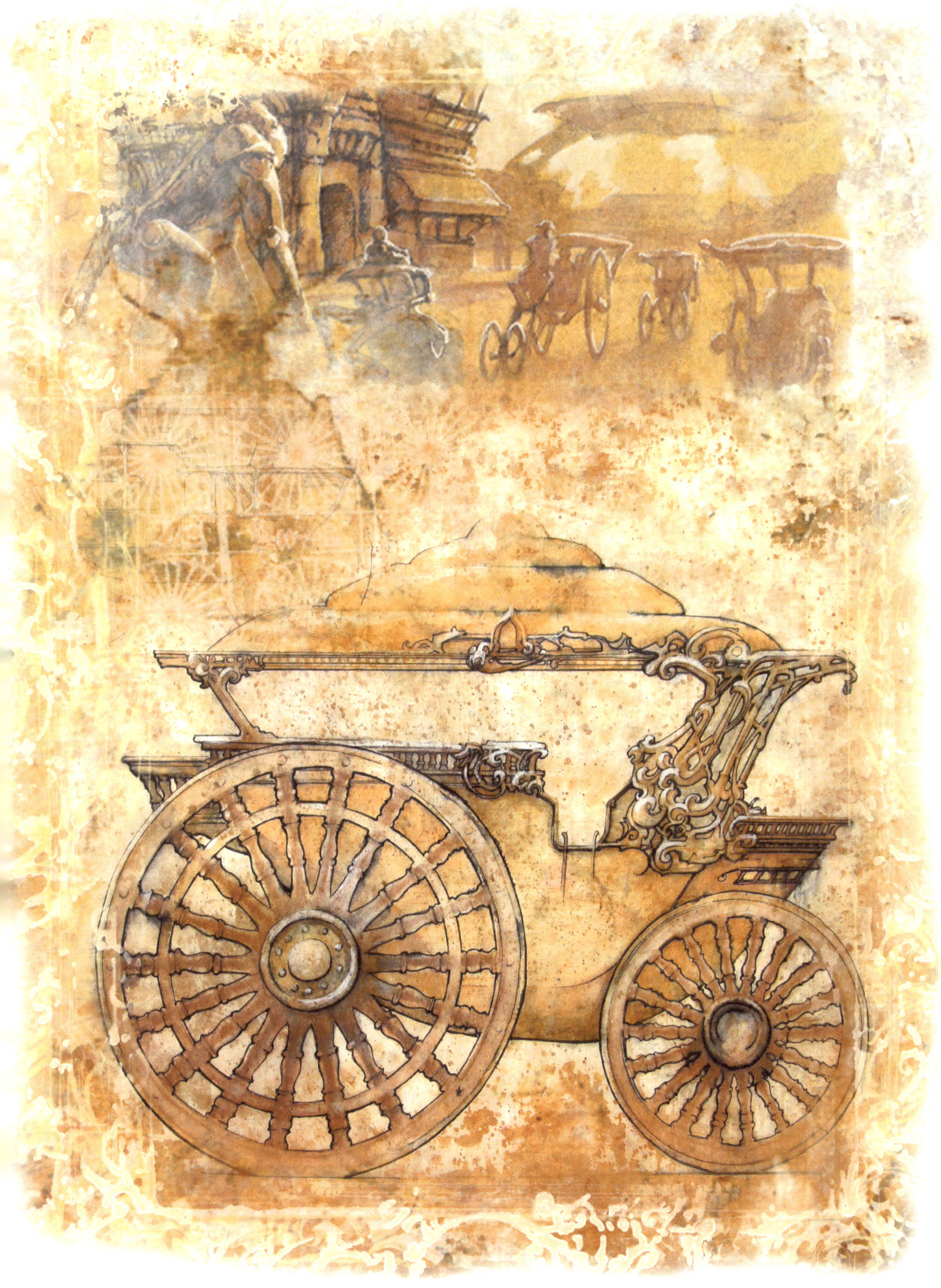

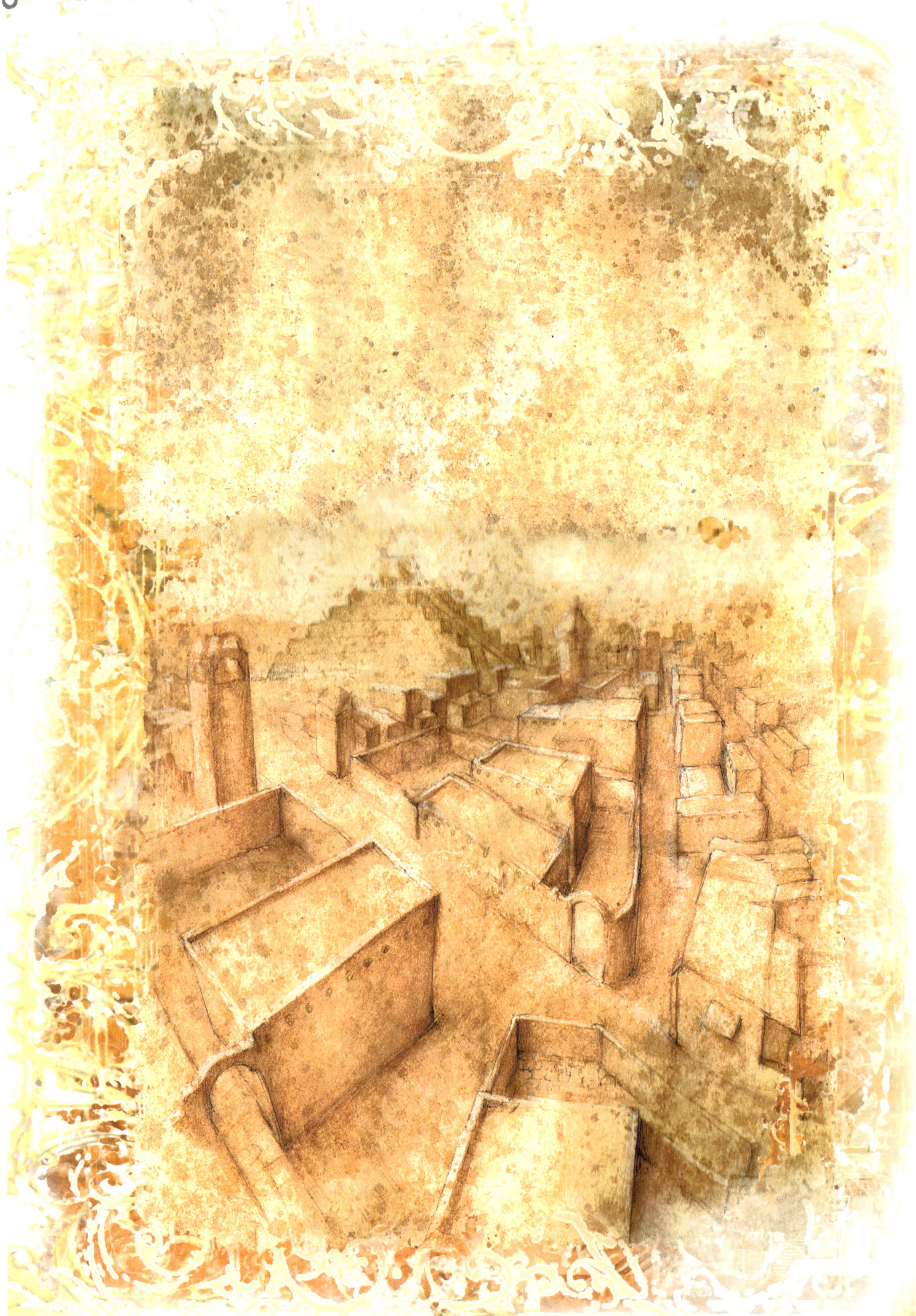

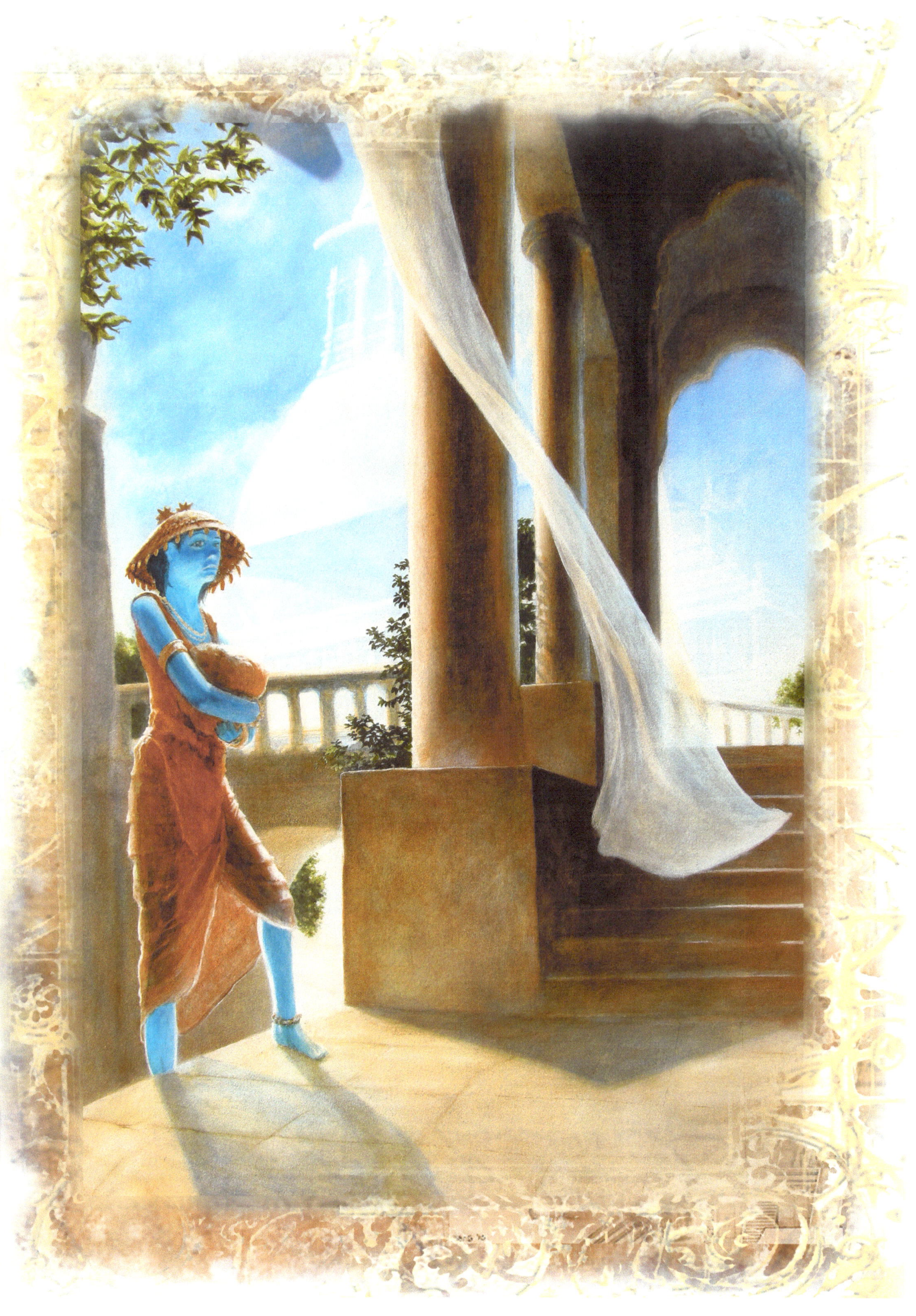

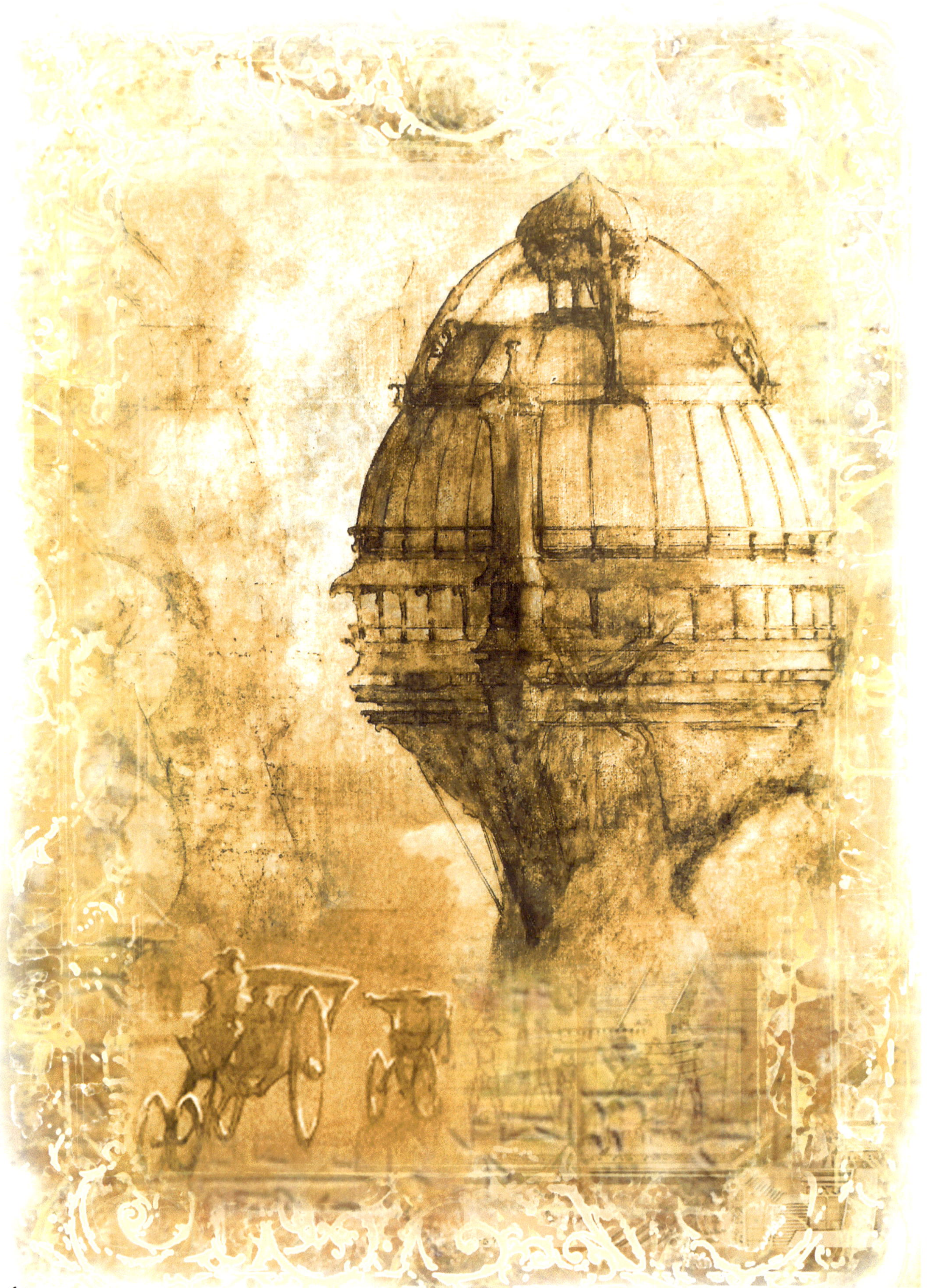

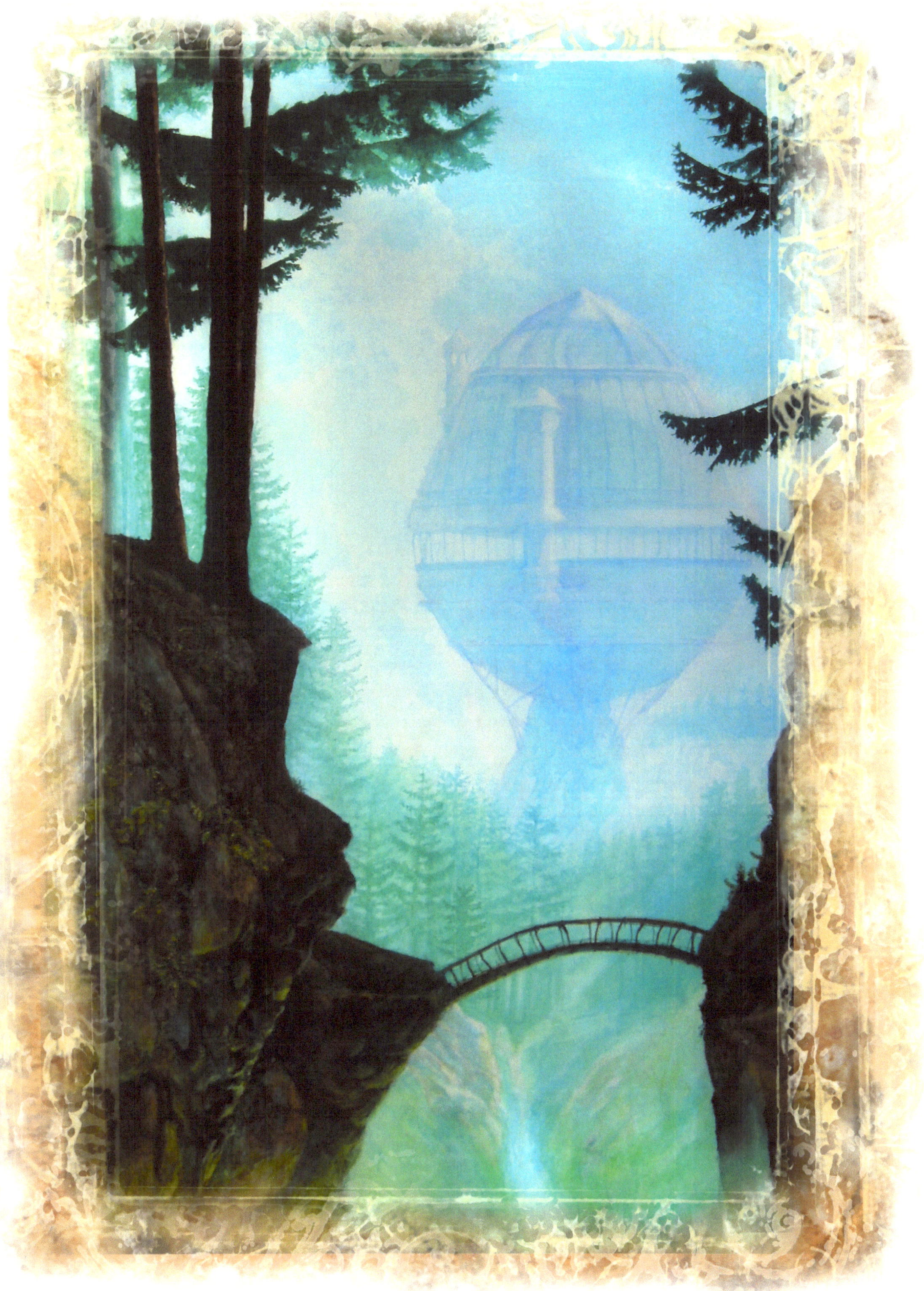

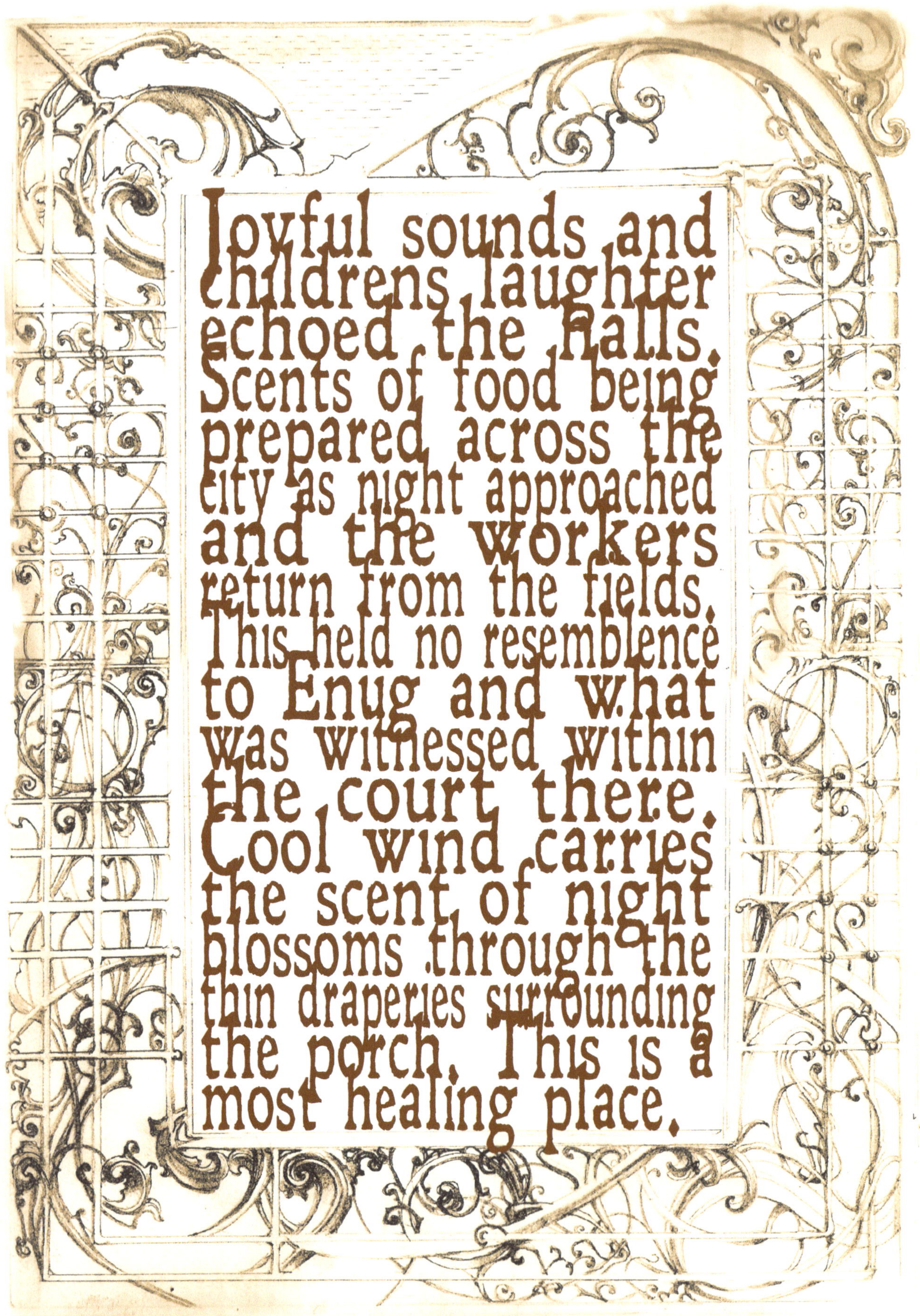
Joyful sounds and
childrens laughter
echoed the halls.
Scents of food being
prepared across the
city as night approached
and the workers
return from the fields.
This held no resemblence
to Enug and what
was witnessed within
the court there.
Cool wind carries
the scent of night
blossoms through the
thin draperies surrounding
the porch. This is a
most healing place.

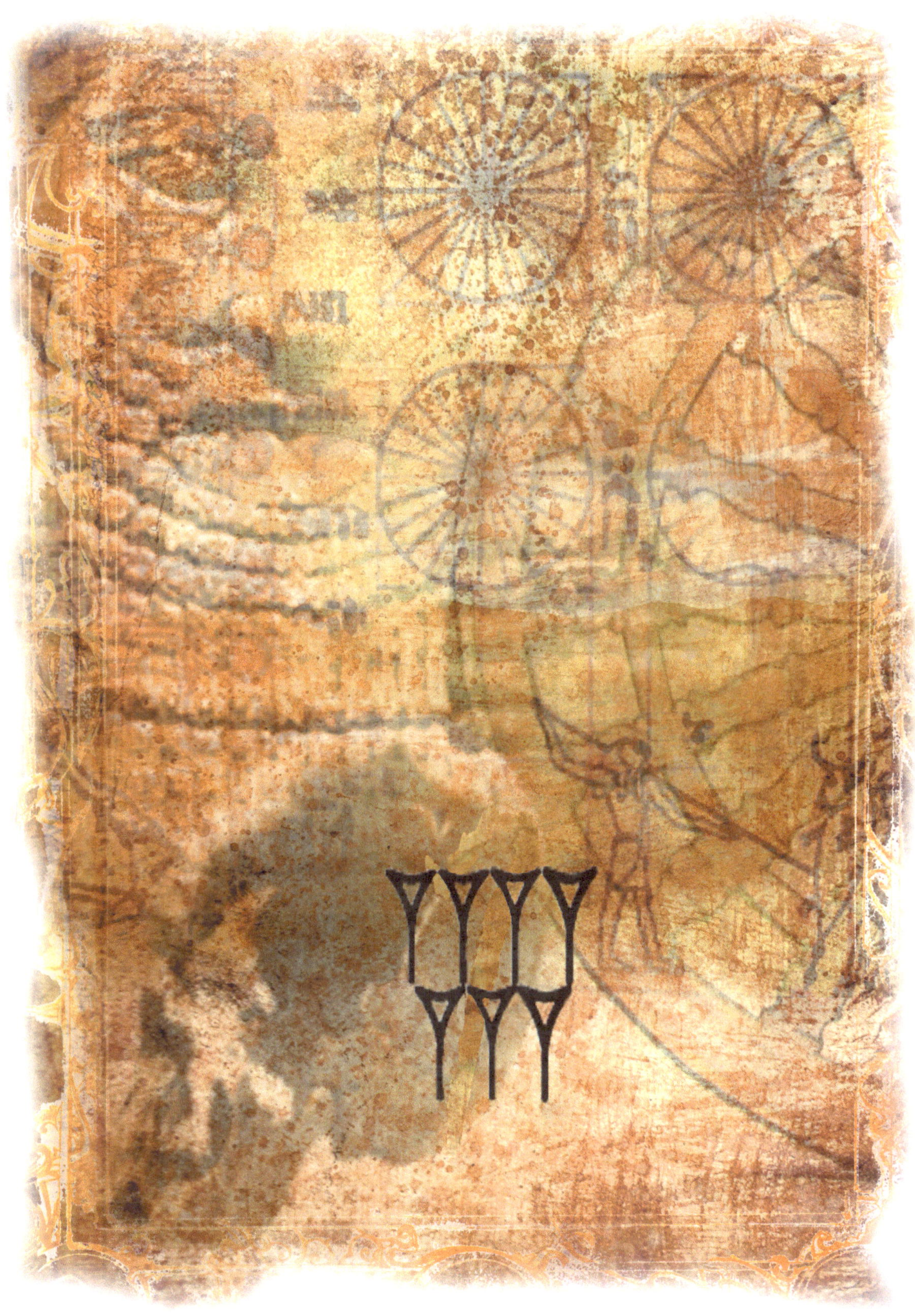

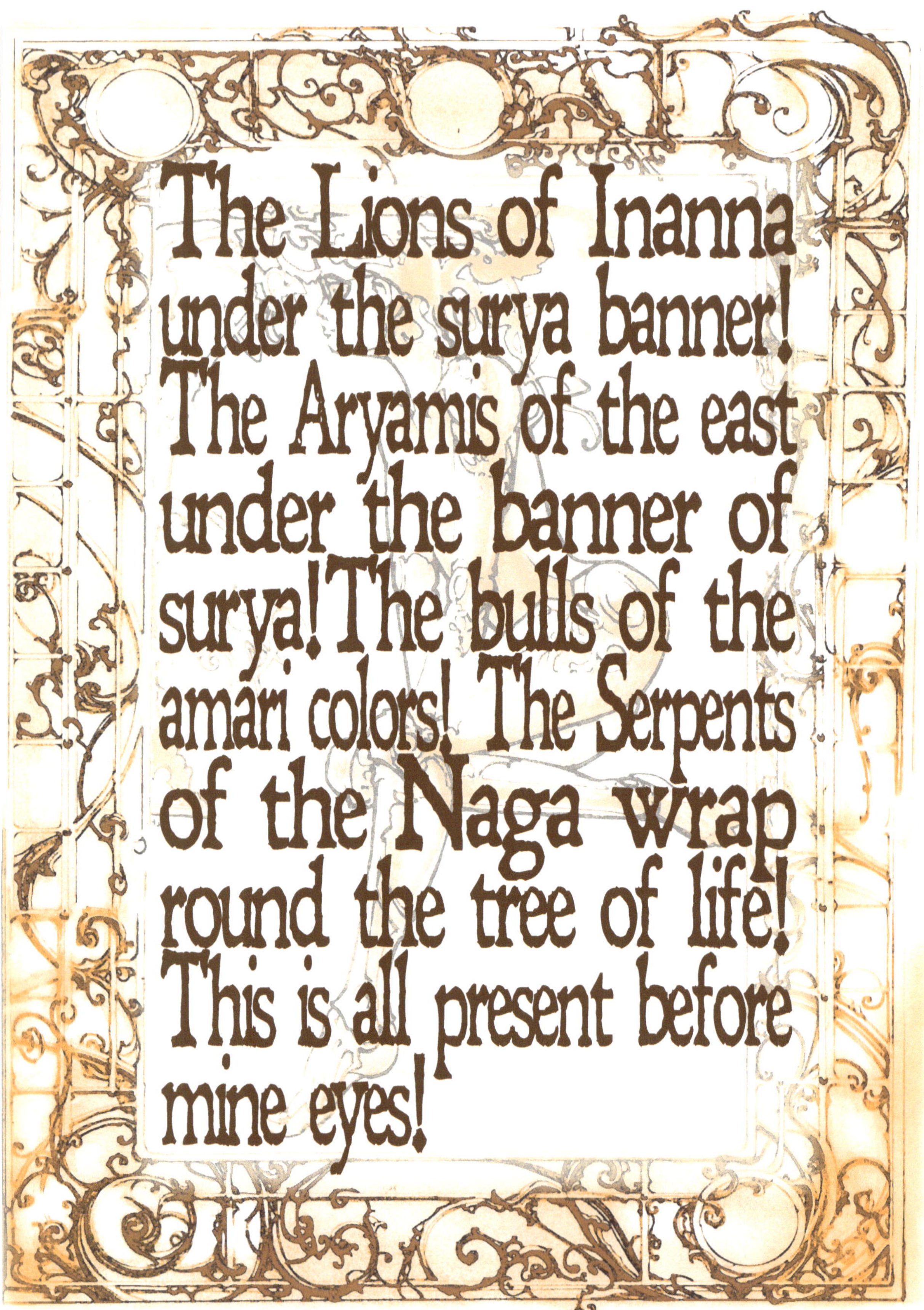
The Lions of Inanna
under the surya banner!
The Aryamis of the east
under the banner of
surya! The bulls of the
amari colors! The Serpents
of the Naga wrap
round the tree of life!
This is all present before
mine eyes!

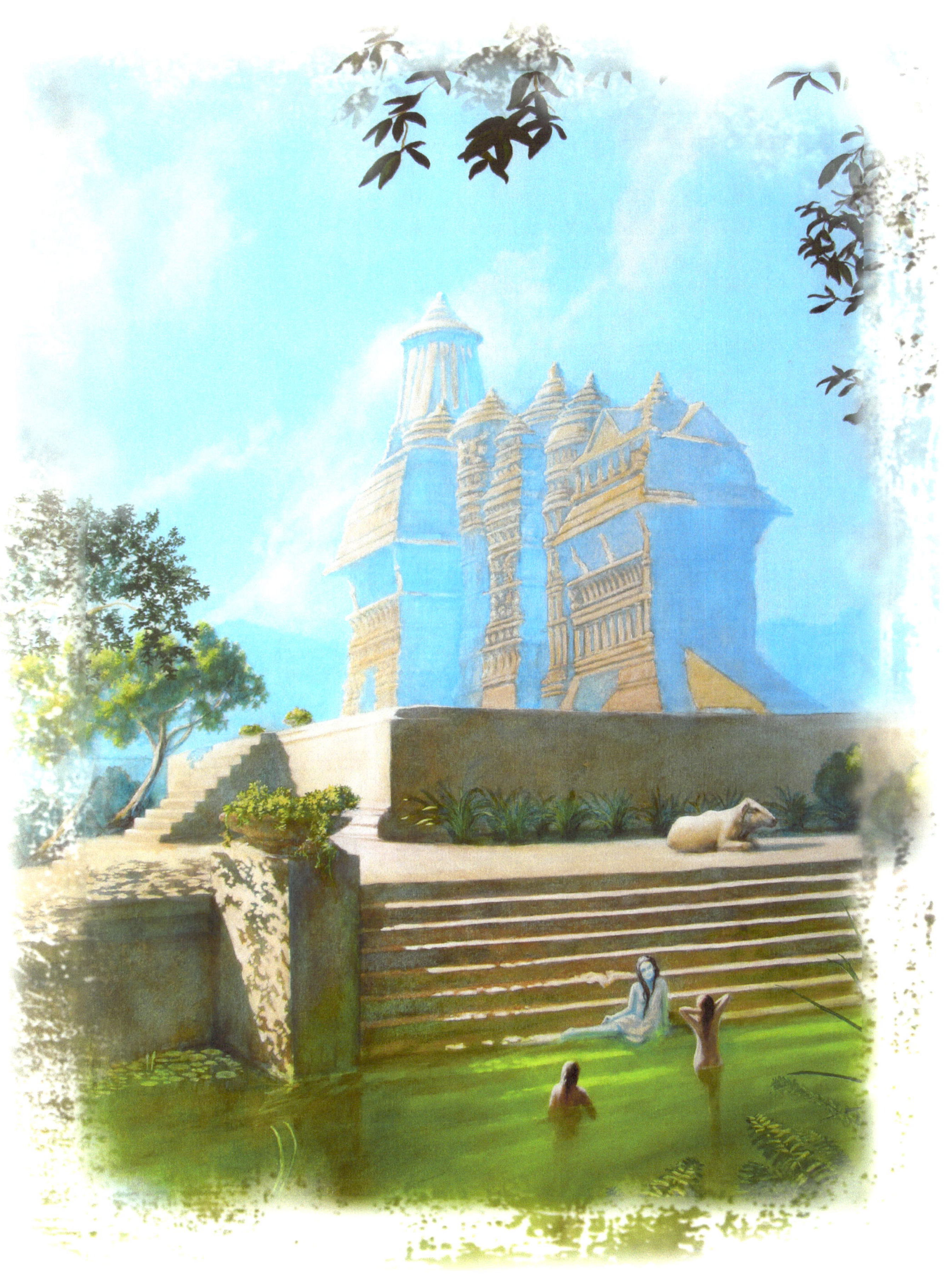

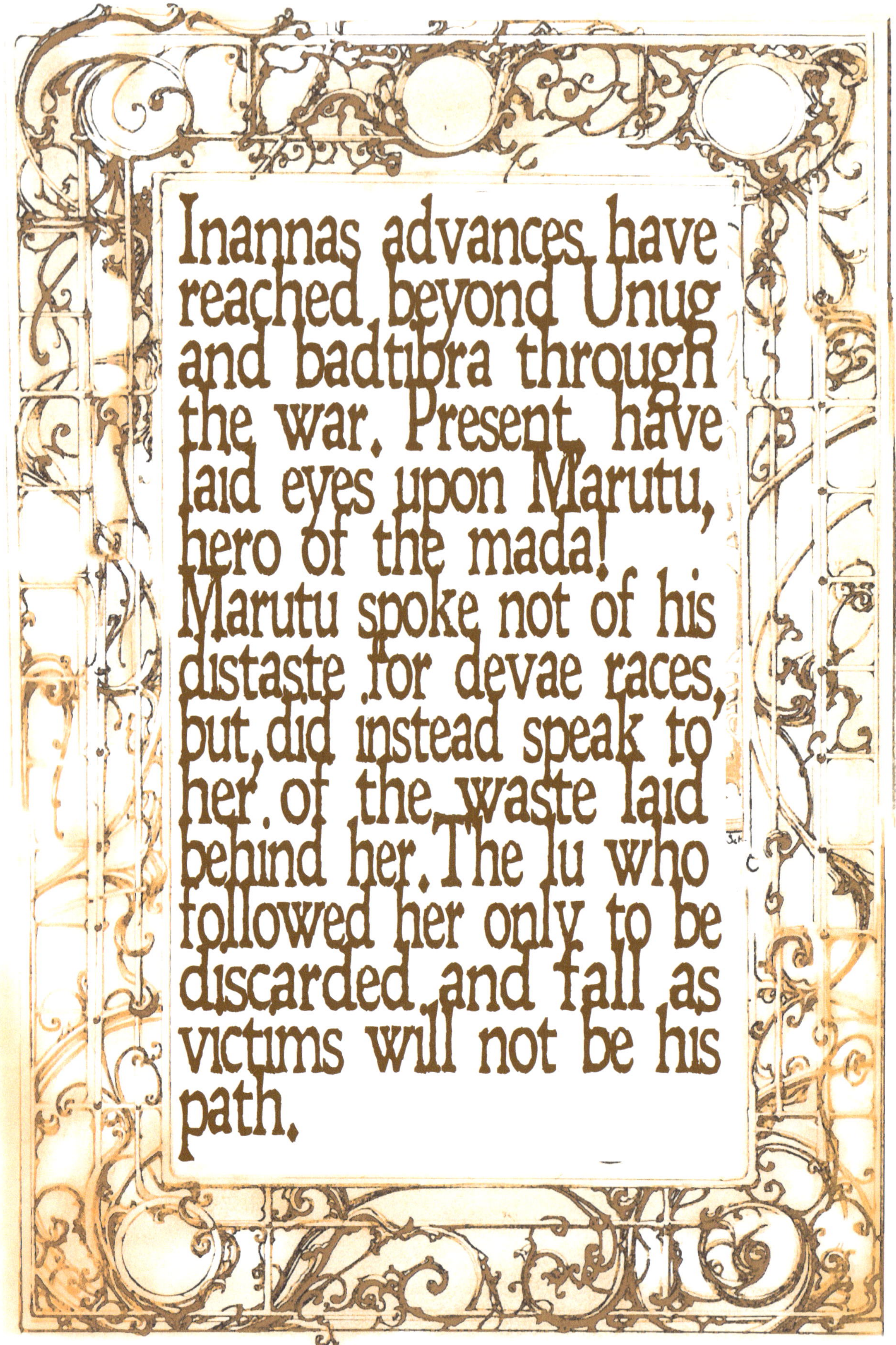
Inannas advances have reached beyond Unug and badtibra through the war. Present, have laid eyes upon Marutu, hero of the mada!
Marutu spoke not of his distaste for devae races, but did instead speak to her of the waste laid behind her. The lu who followed her only to be discarded and fall as victims will not be his path.

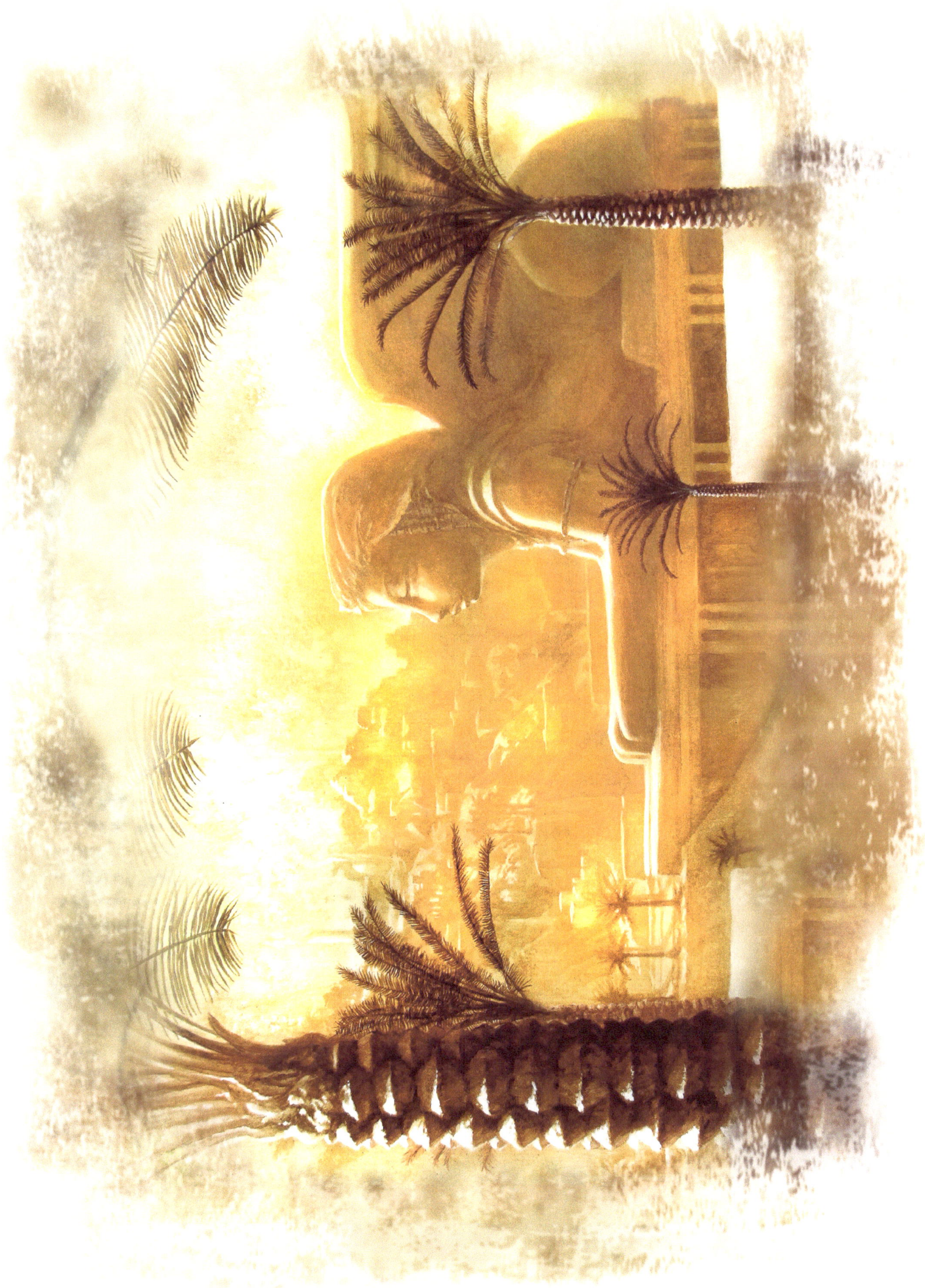

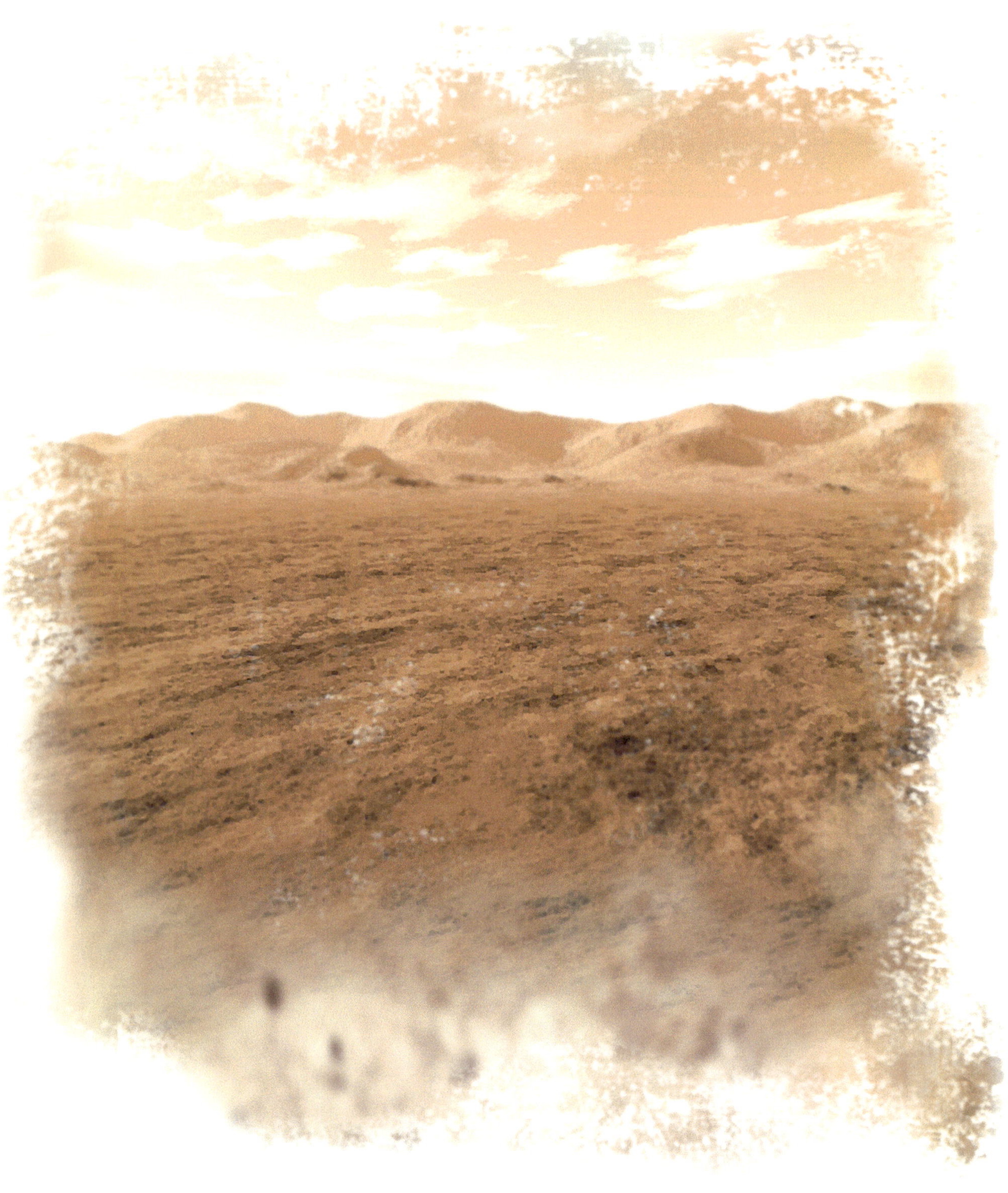

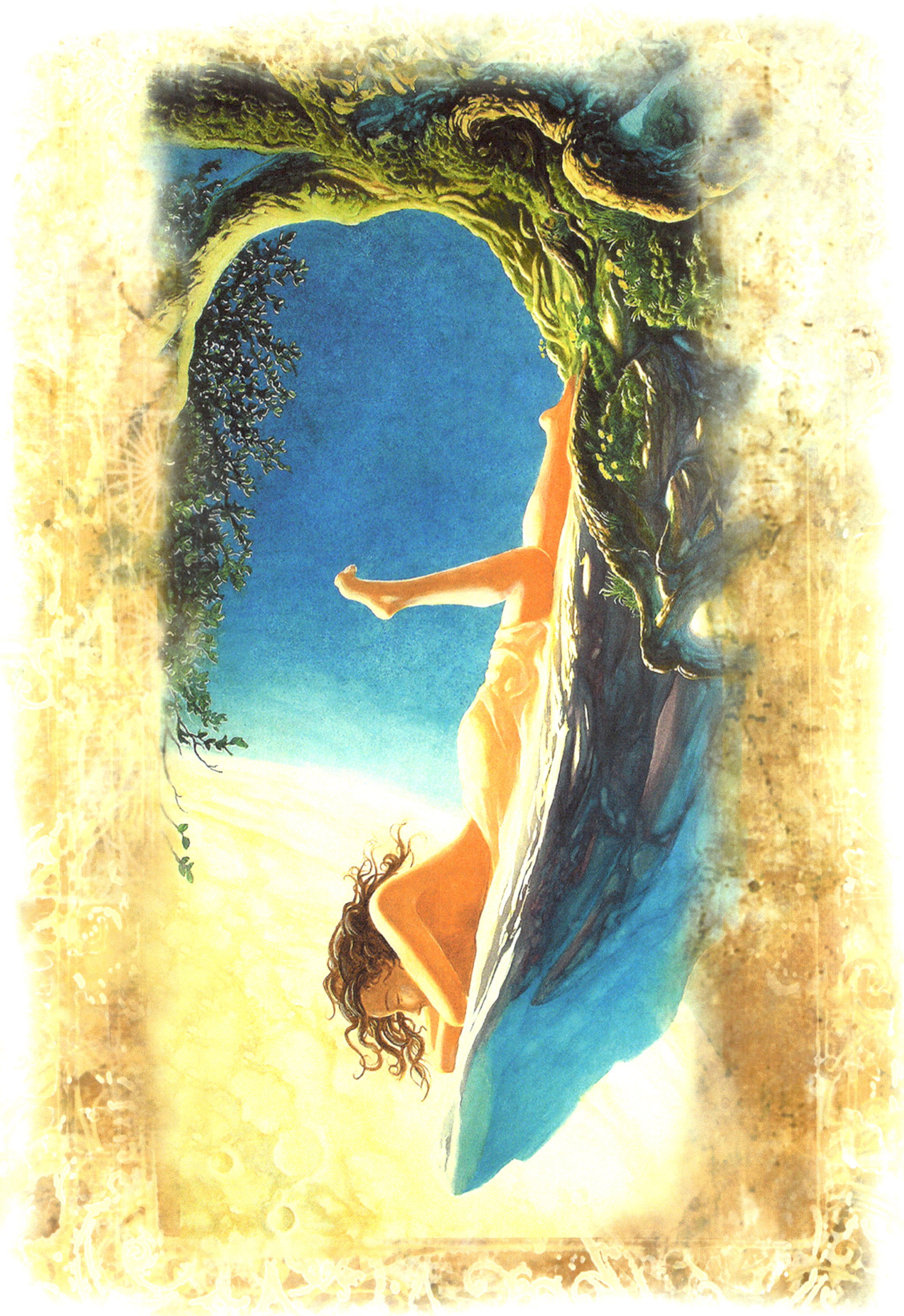

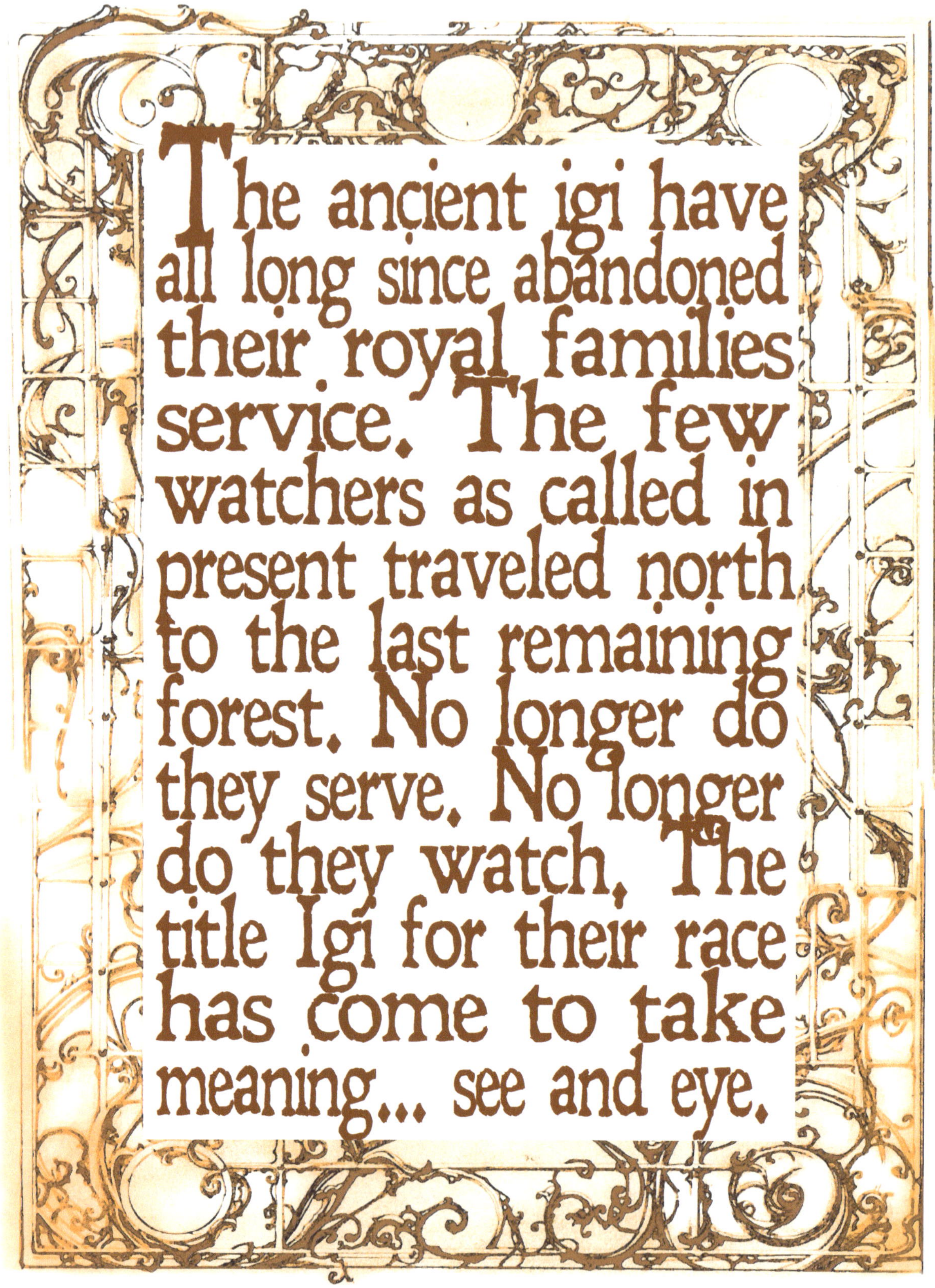

The ancient igi have all long since abandoned their royal families service. The few watchers as called in present traveled north to the last remaining forest. No longer do they serve. No longer do they watch. The title Igi for their race has come to take meaning... see and eye.

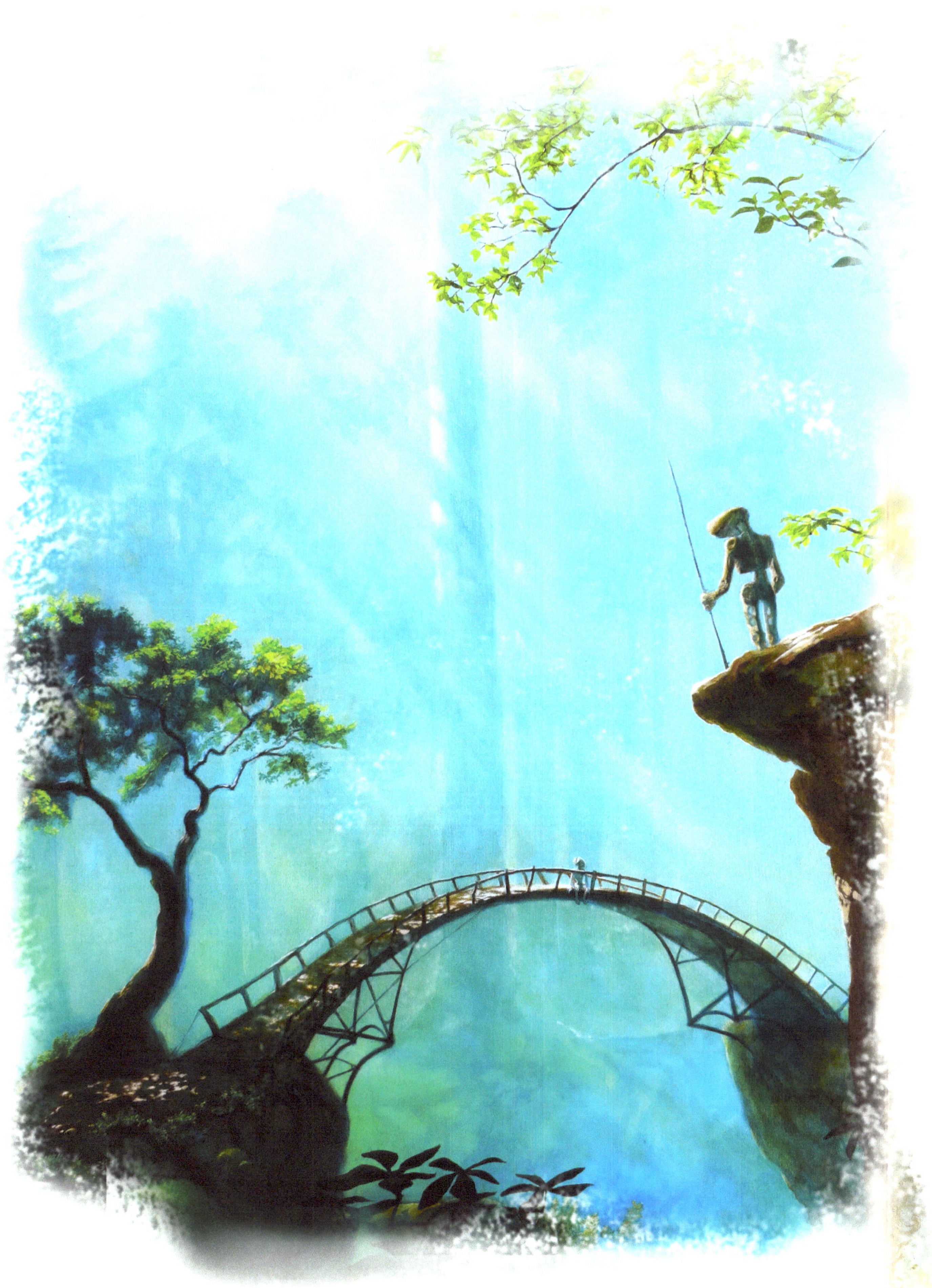

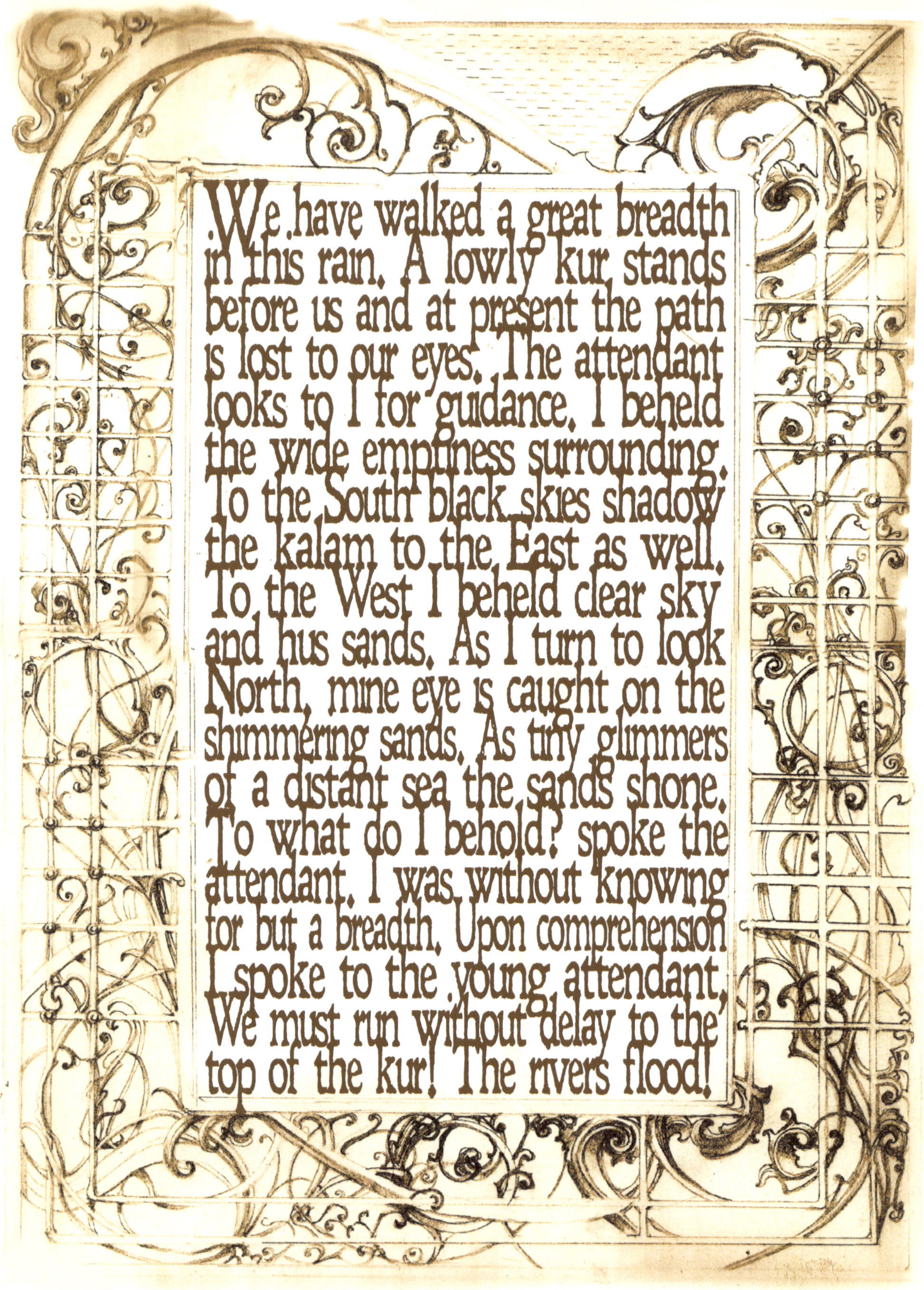
We have walked a great breadth
in this rain. A lowly kur stands
before us and at present the path
is lost to our eyes. The attendant
looks to I for guidance. I beheld
the wide emptiness surrounding.
To the South black skies shadow
the kalam to the East as well.
To the West I beheld clear sky
and hus sands. As I turn to look
North, mine eye is caught on the
shimmering sands. As tiny glimmers
of a distant sea the sands shone.
To what do I behold? spoke the
attendant. I was without knowing
for but a breadth. Upon comprehension
I spoke to the young attendant,
We must run without delay to the
top of the kur! The rivers flood!

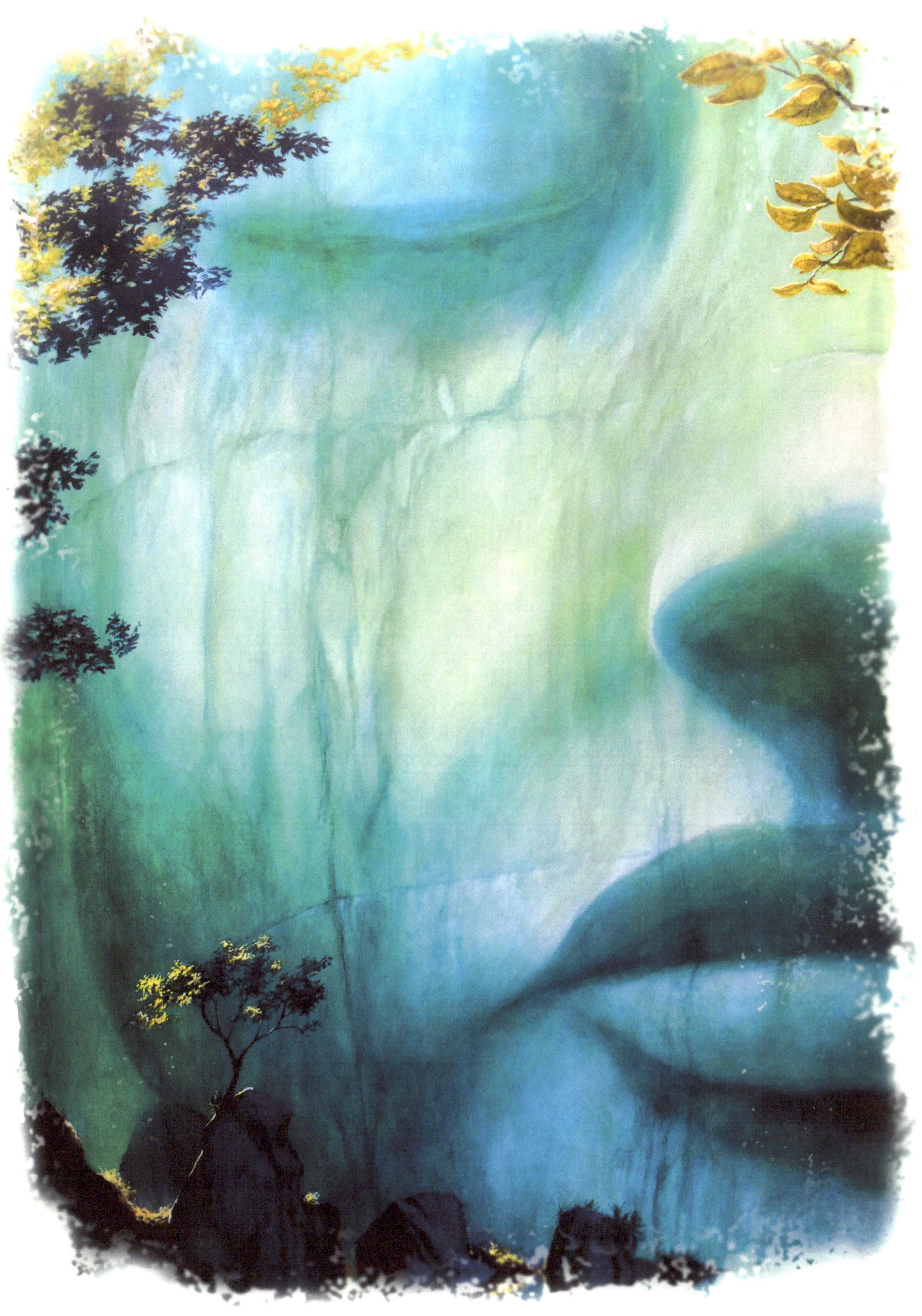

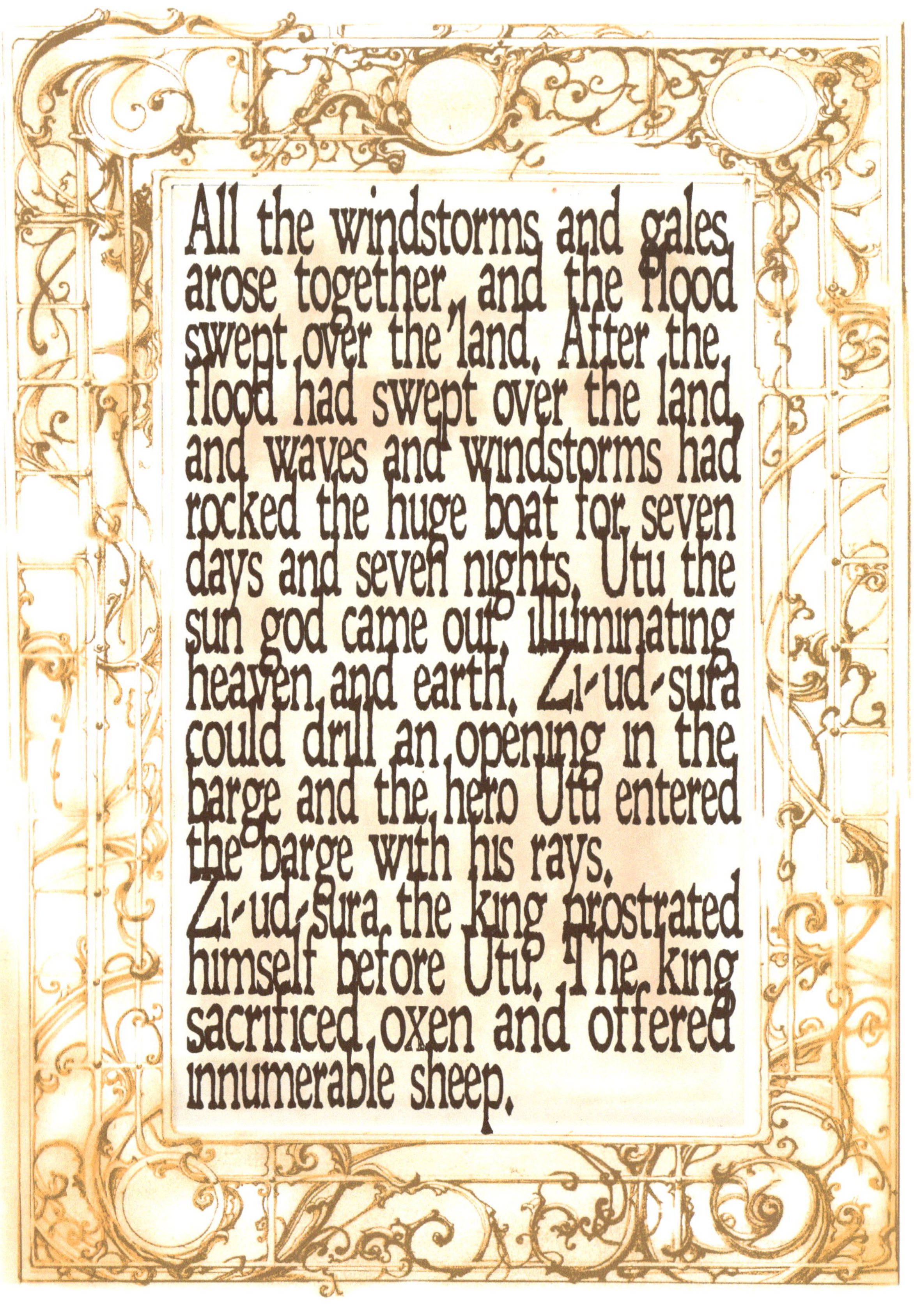

All the windstorms and gales arose together, and the flood swept over the land. After the flood had swept over the land, and waves and windstorms had rocked the huge boat for seven days and seven nights, Utu the sun god came out, illuminating heaven and earth. Zi-ud-sura could drill an opening in the barge and the hero Utu entered the barge with his rays.

Zi-ud-sura the king prostrated himself before Utu. The king sacrificed oxen and offered innumerable sheep.

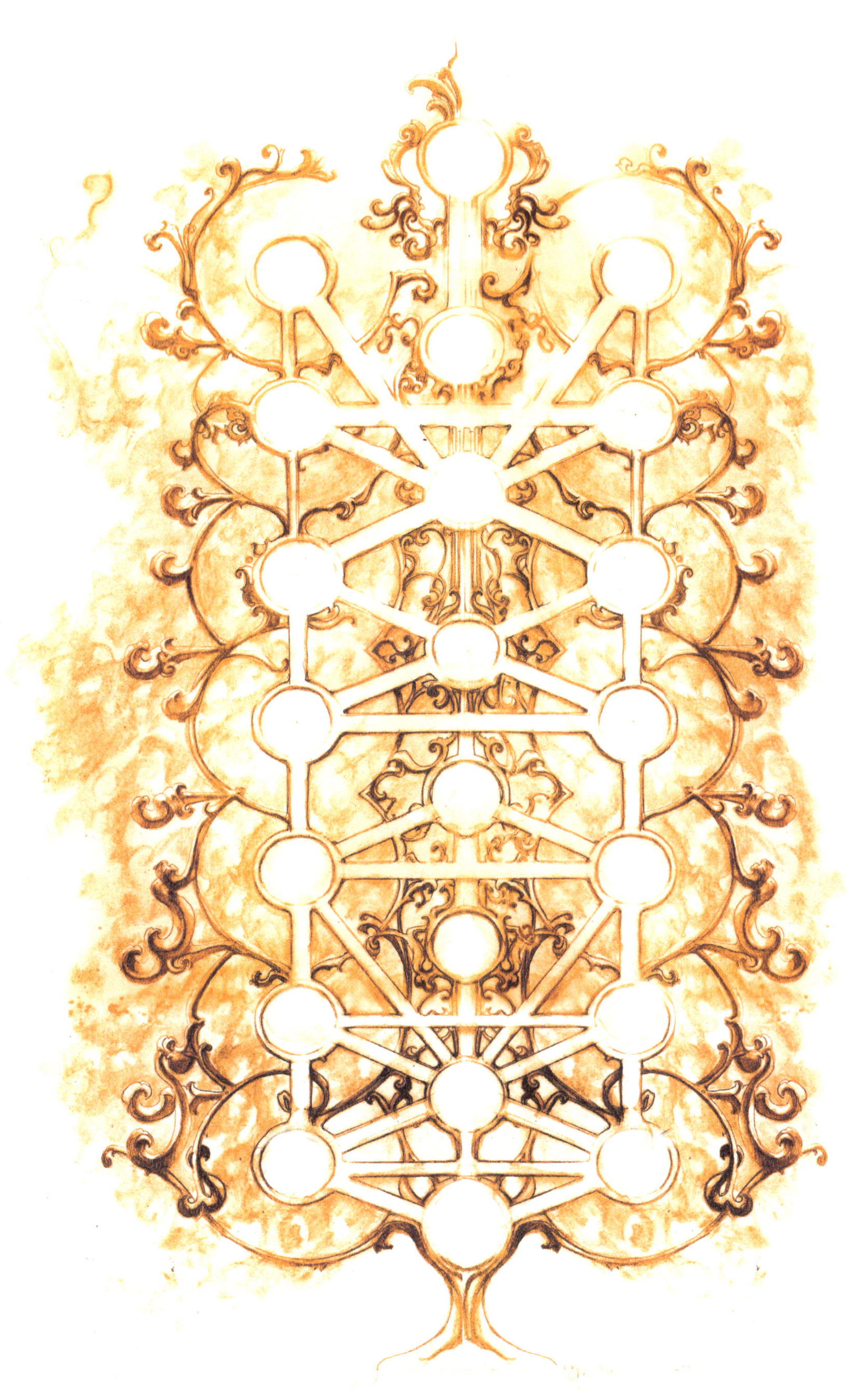

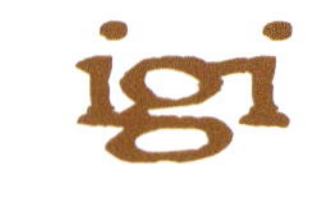

(I' - Gee) - See / Eye

Ancient Sumerian cir 7000 bce.

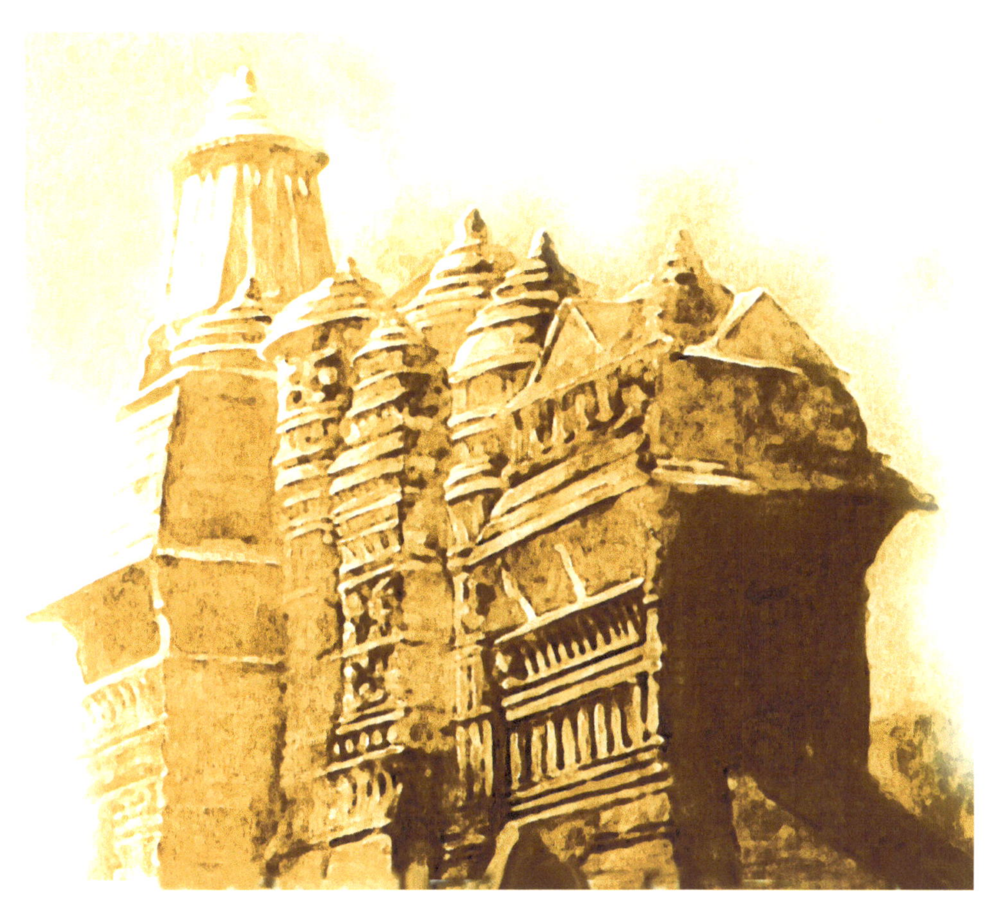

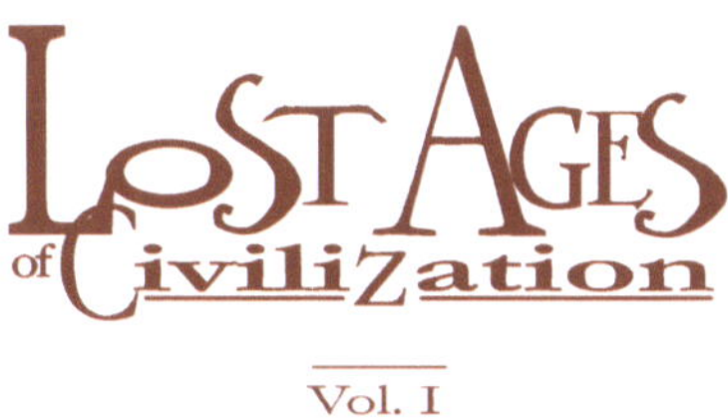

Vol. I

Ink and watercolour works

S K E T C H BOOK

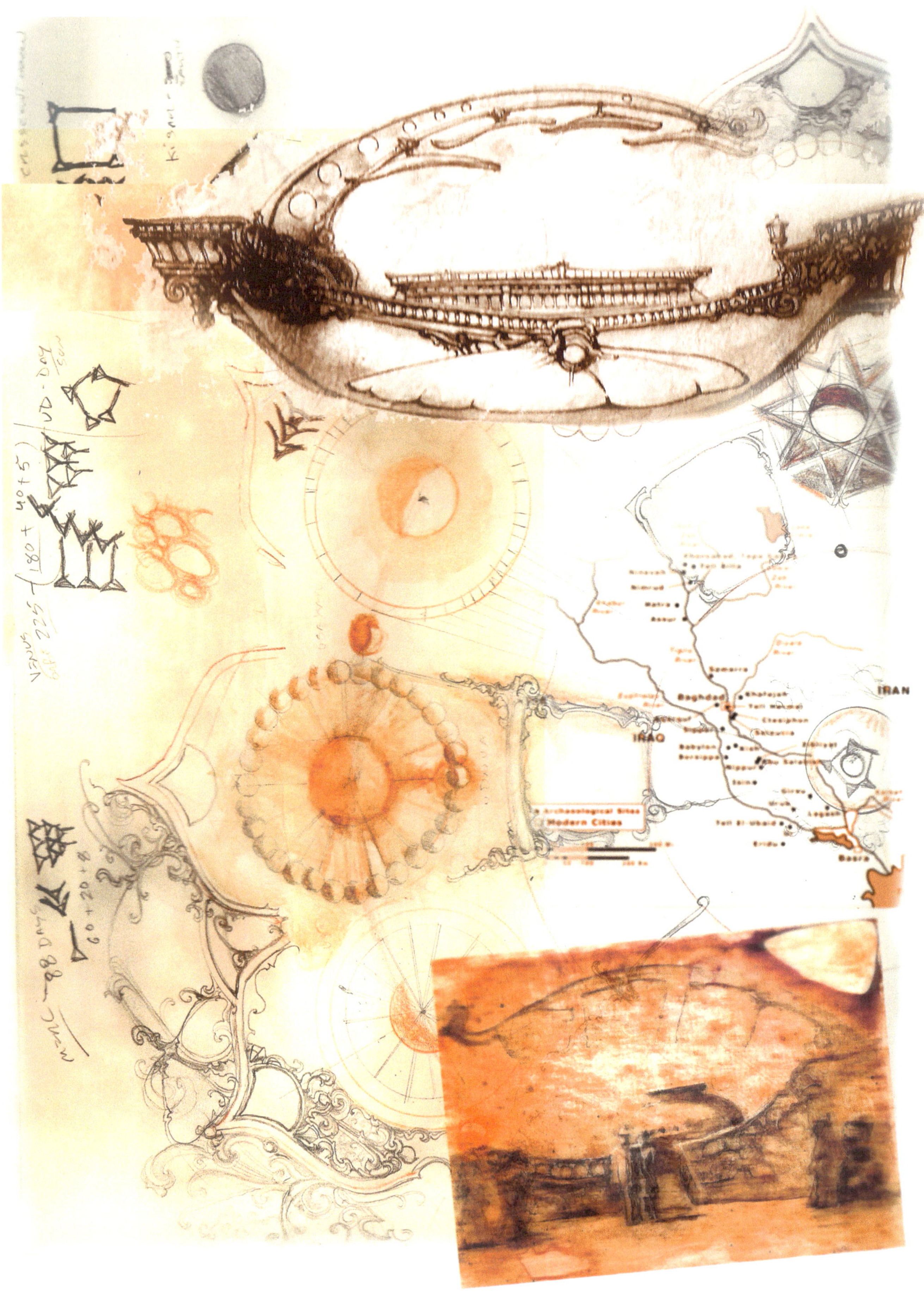
IRAN
IRAQ
Baghdad
Samarra
Ctesiphon
Seleucia
Babylon
Borsippa
Nippur
Isin
Girsu
Uruk
Lagash
Tell El-Ubaid
Eridu
Basra
Nimrud
Hatra
Assur
Modern Cities
VENUS 225
180 + 40 + 5
UD · DAY
88 DAYS
60 + 20 + 8

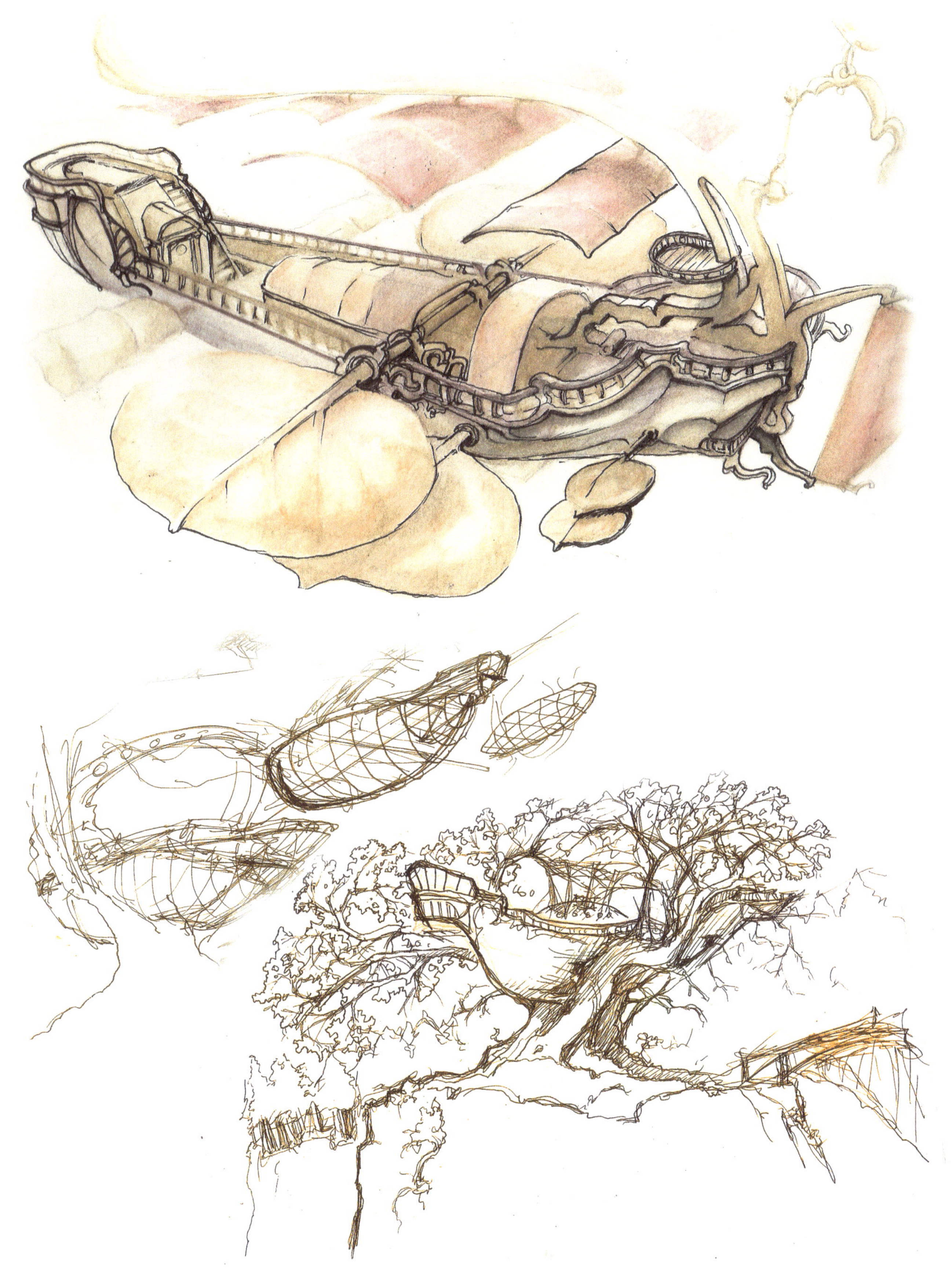

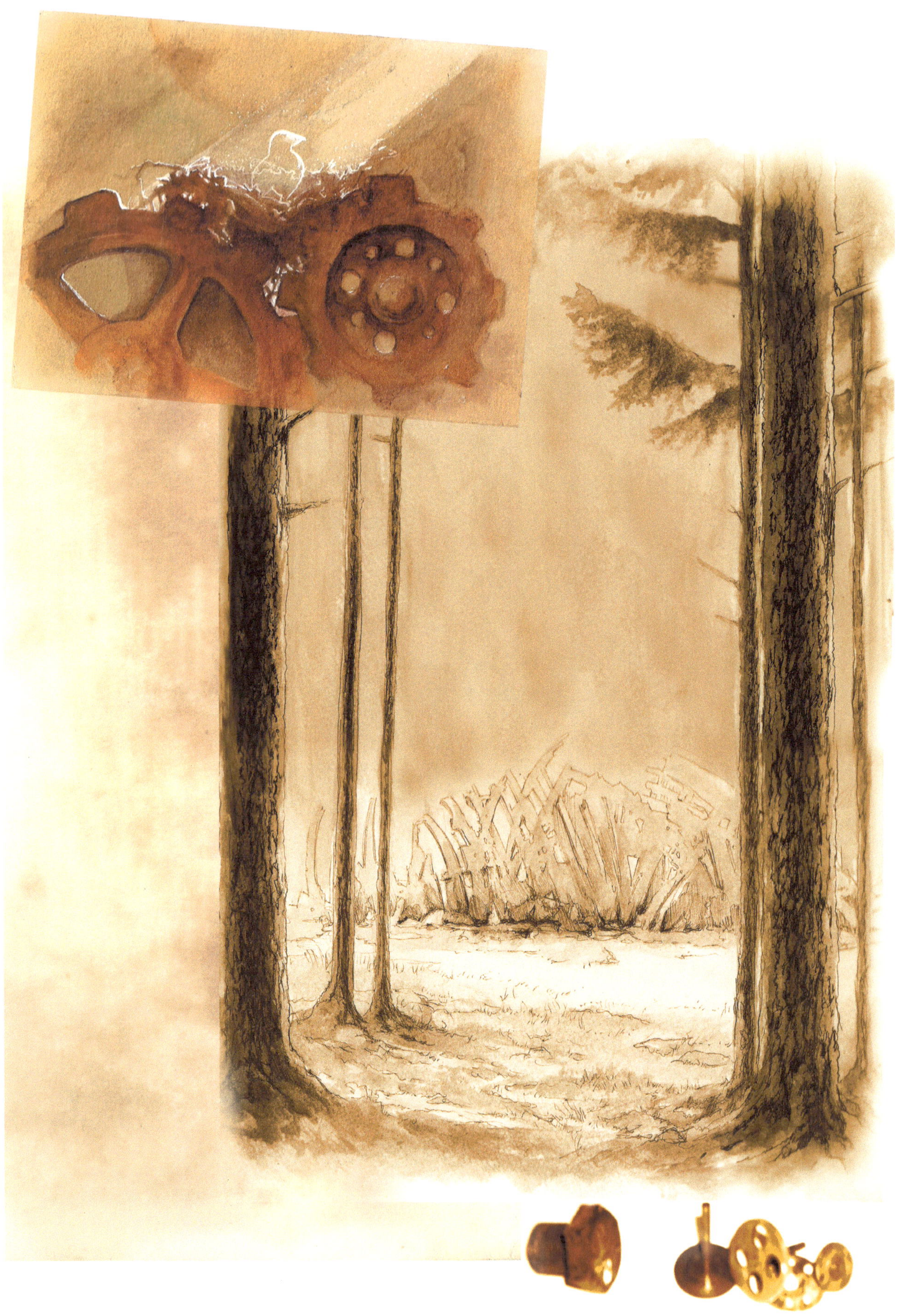

Flying Acorns

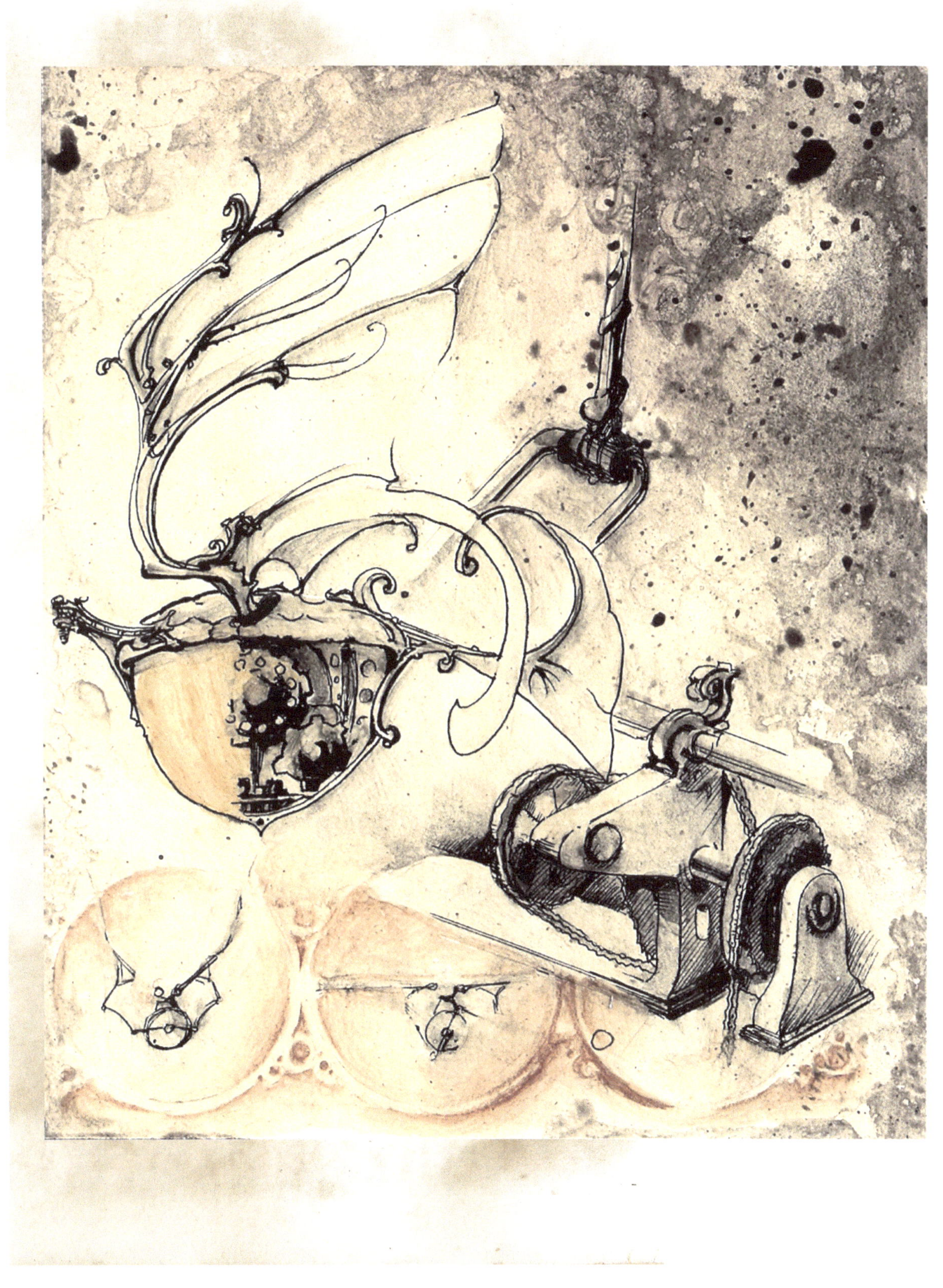

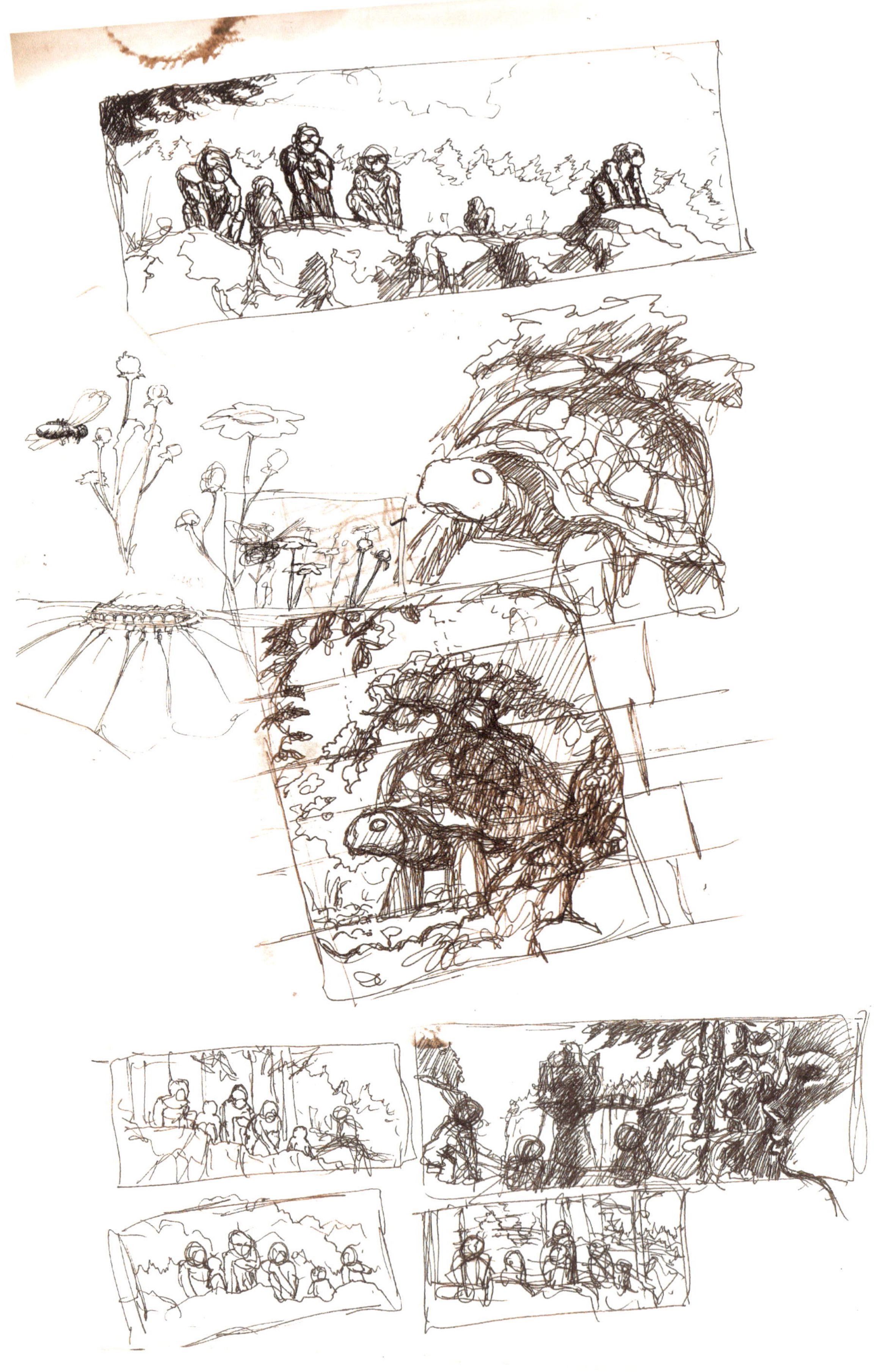

Mechanical to Organic

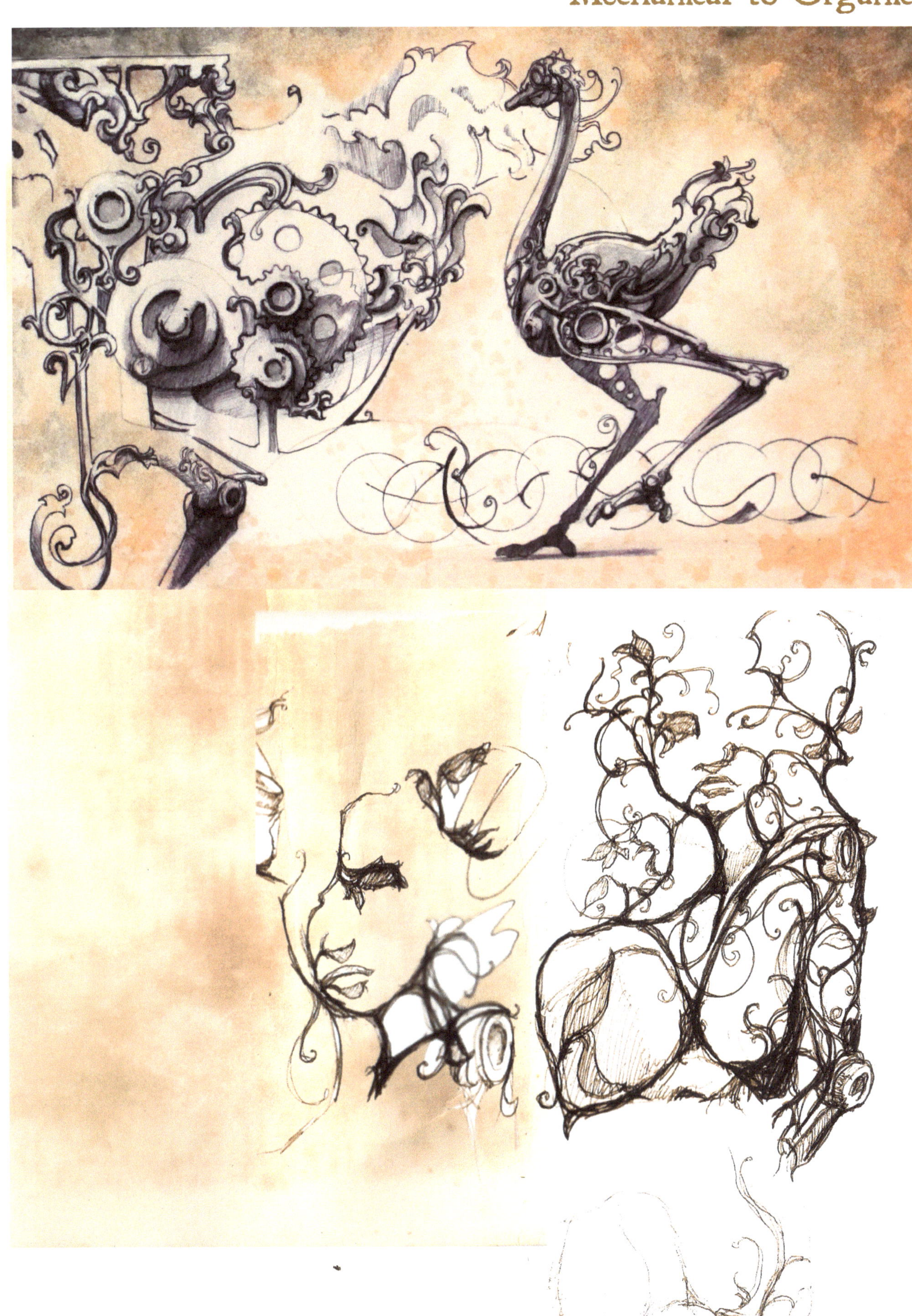

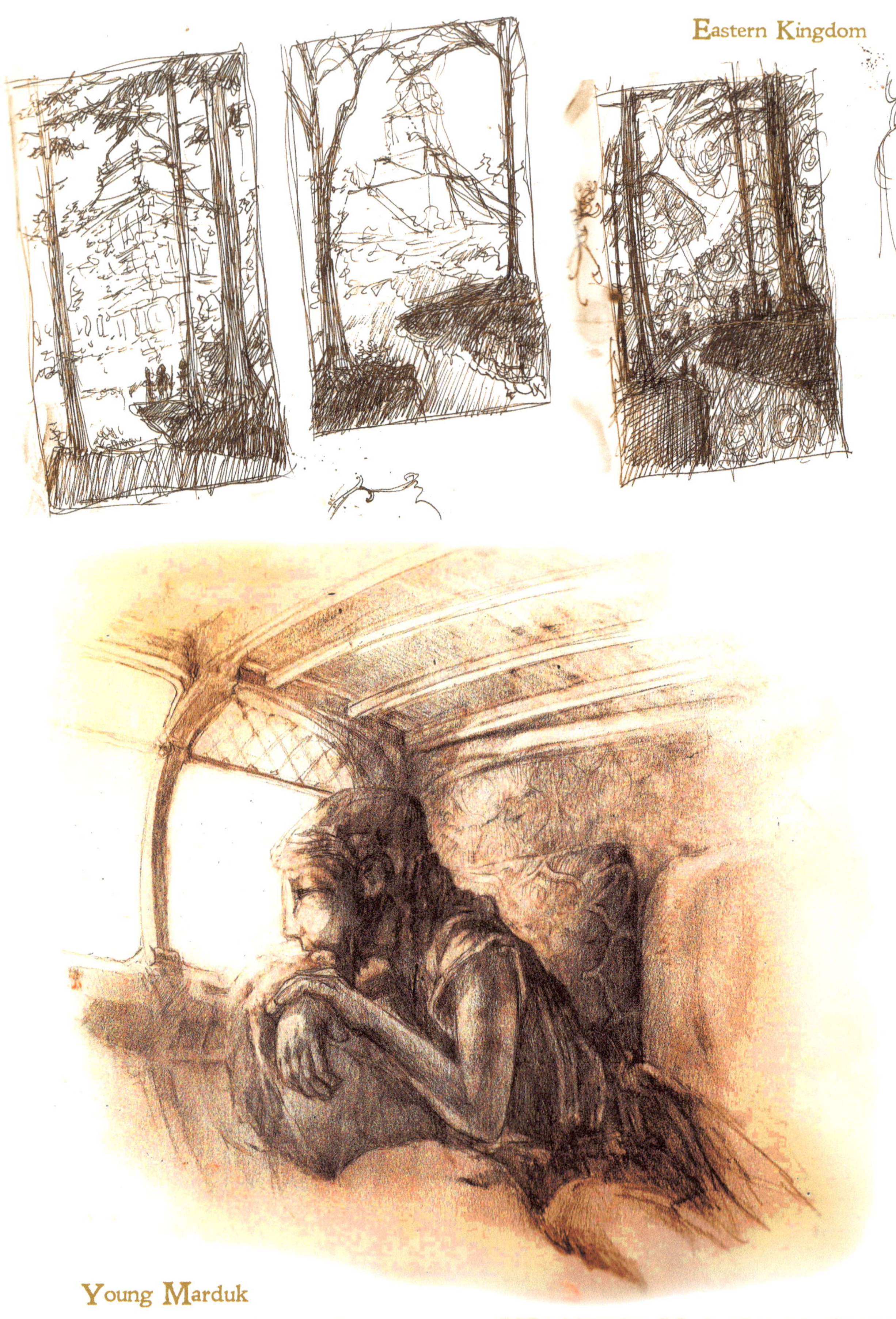

Eastern Kingdom

Young Marduk

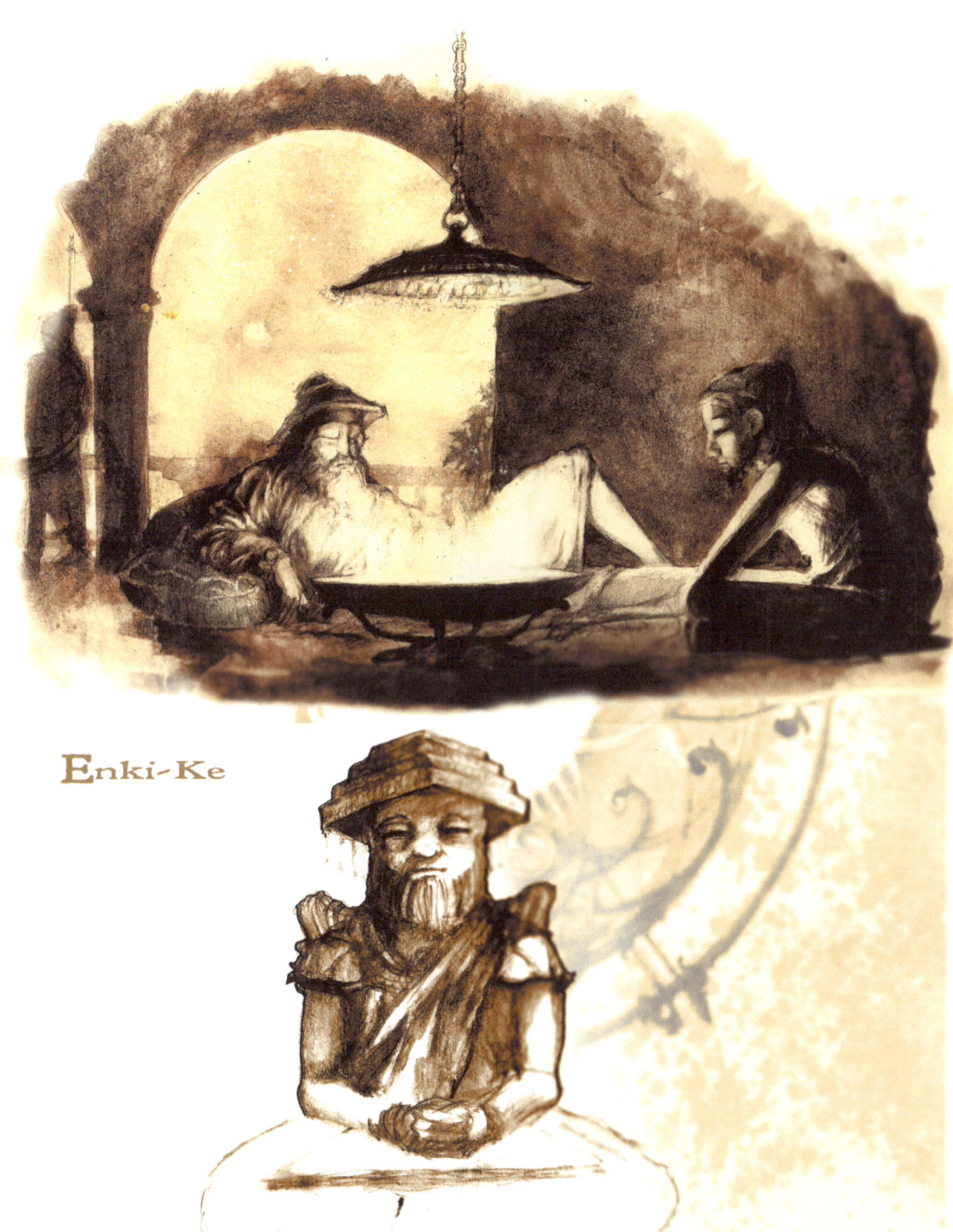
Enki-Ke

the First War of the First Kingdoms

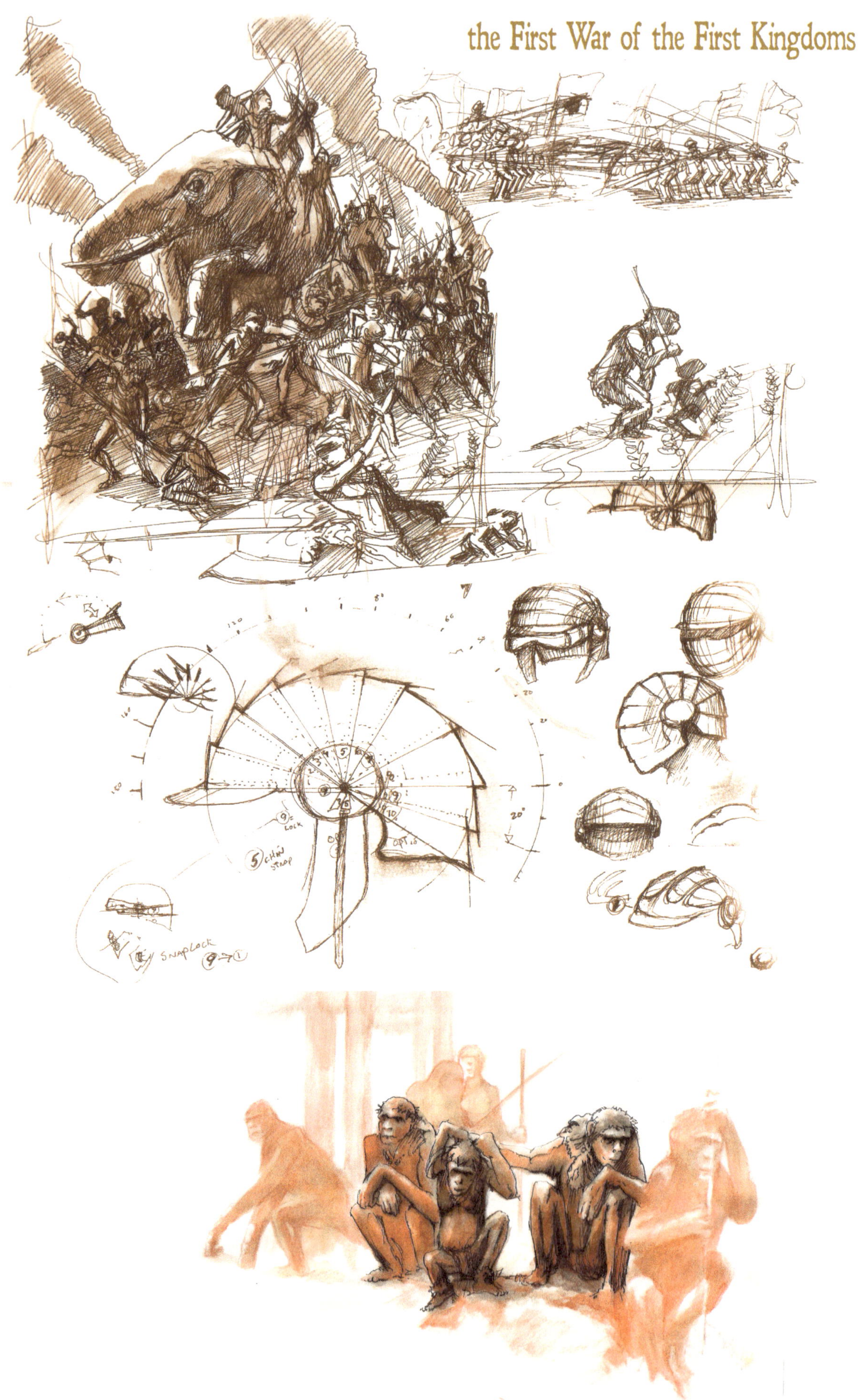

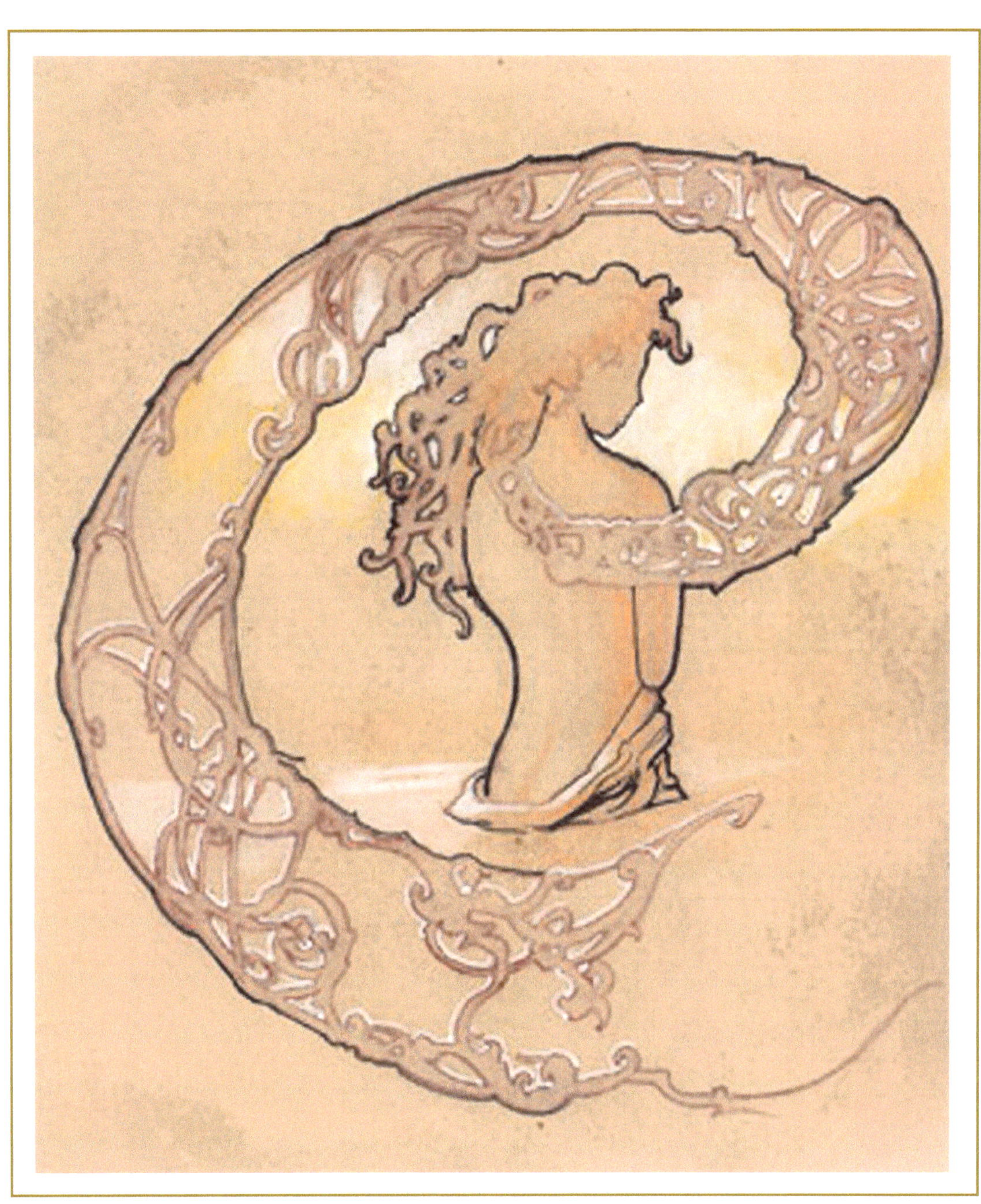

index of images

text references

The ETCSL project, Faculty of Oriental Studies, University of Oxford
http://etcsl.orinst.ox.ac.uk/

t.1.1.3
Enki and the world order
326-334.

1.7.4
The Flood story:

t.4.16.1
A hymn to Nisaba (Nisaba A)
Old Babylonian version

Font - Leander © Copyright 2013
Designer : Michael Tension
www.tensiontype.com
Used with permission of the designer.

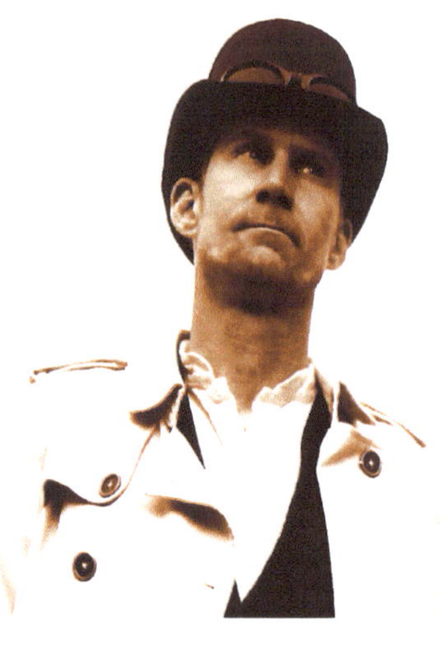

Schel Harris
Artist - Illustrator - Designer

Schel Harris currently lives in Portland, Oregon with his wife Tracie and their 3 dogs. Working as a full-time artist, Schel hopes to produce his multi-volume saga while continuing to show his latest works on his Art-cart.

For more works and monthly updates visit
www.schelharris.com

Bonus material - www.schelharris.com/LostAges

Colour Plates For Removing and Enjoying or Sharing!

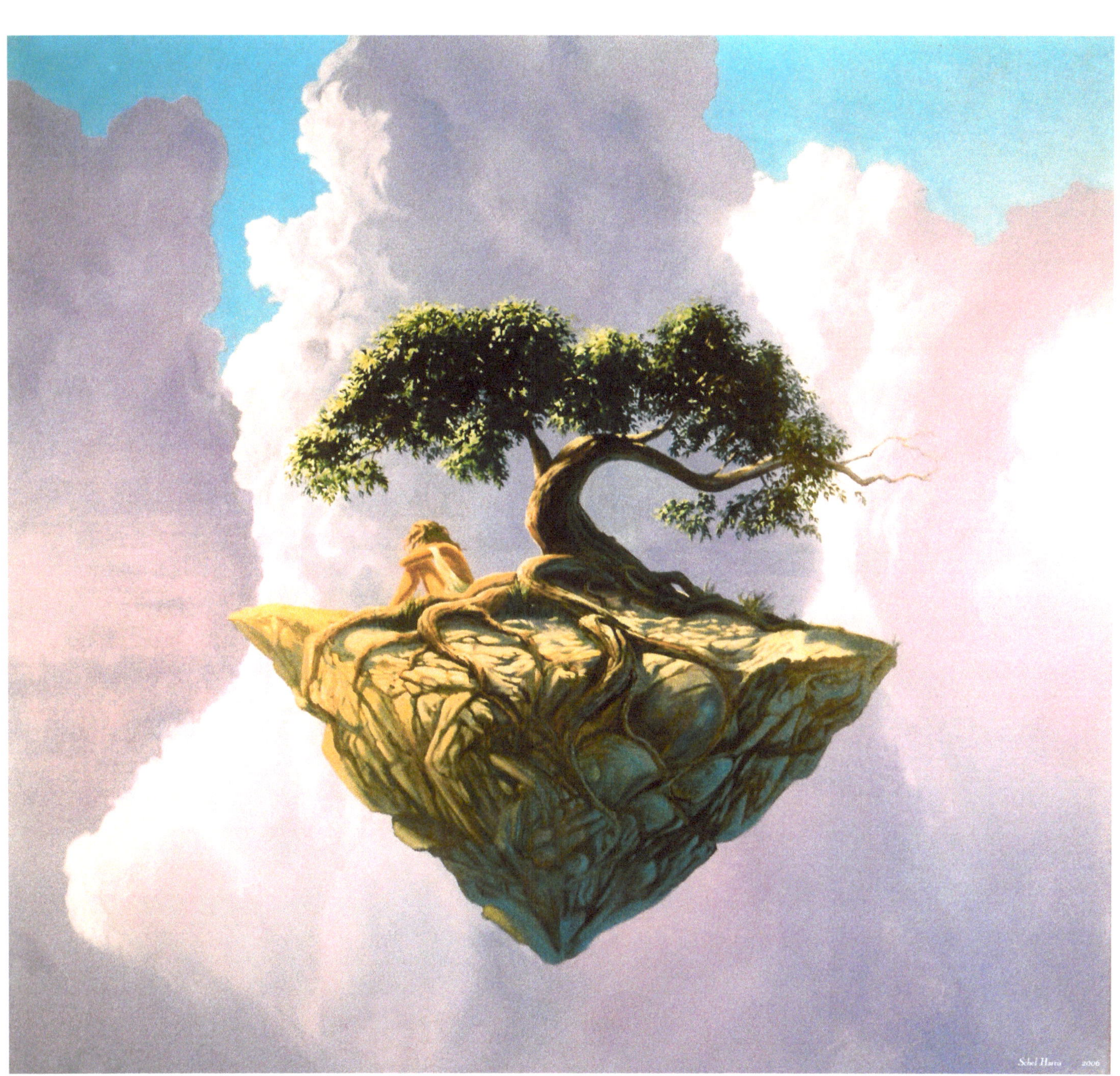
Schel Harris 2006

Solitude

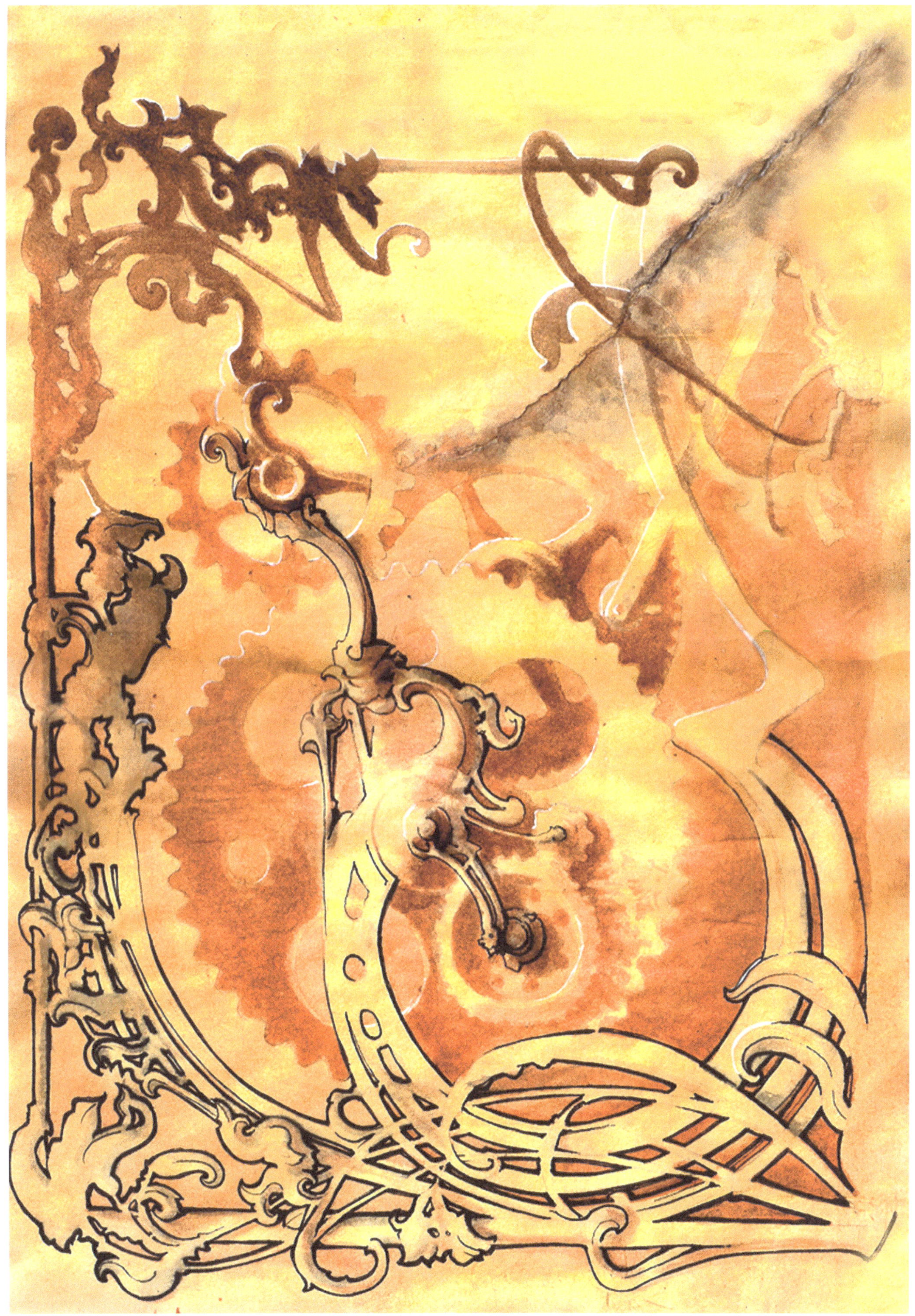

MechPlant Study 5

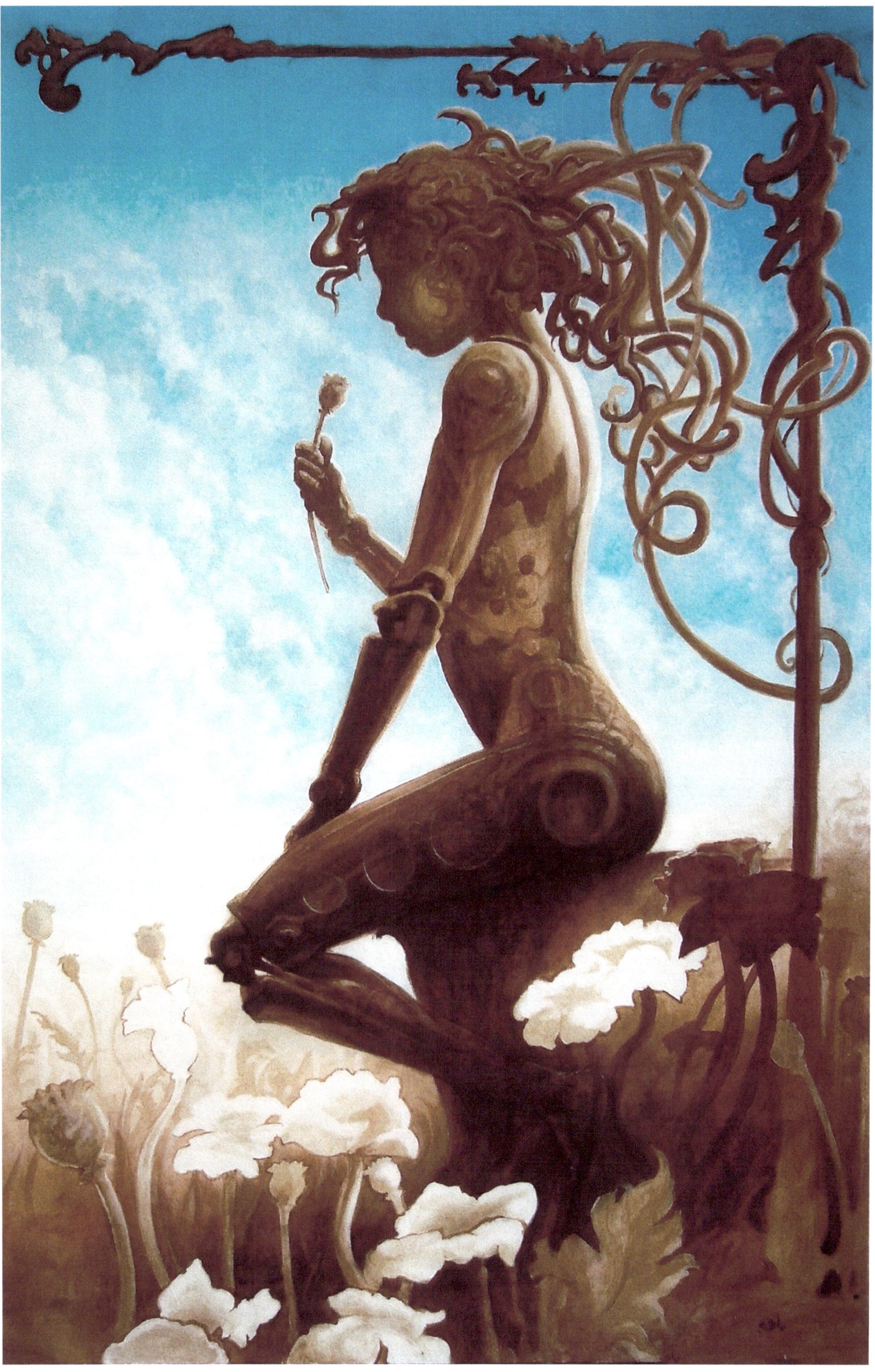

Caitlin Awakes

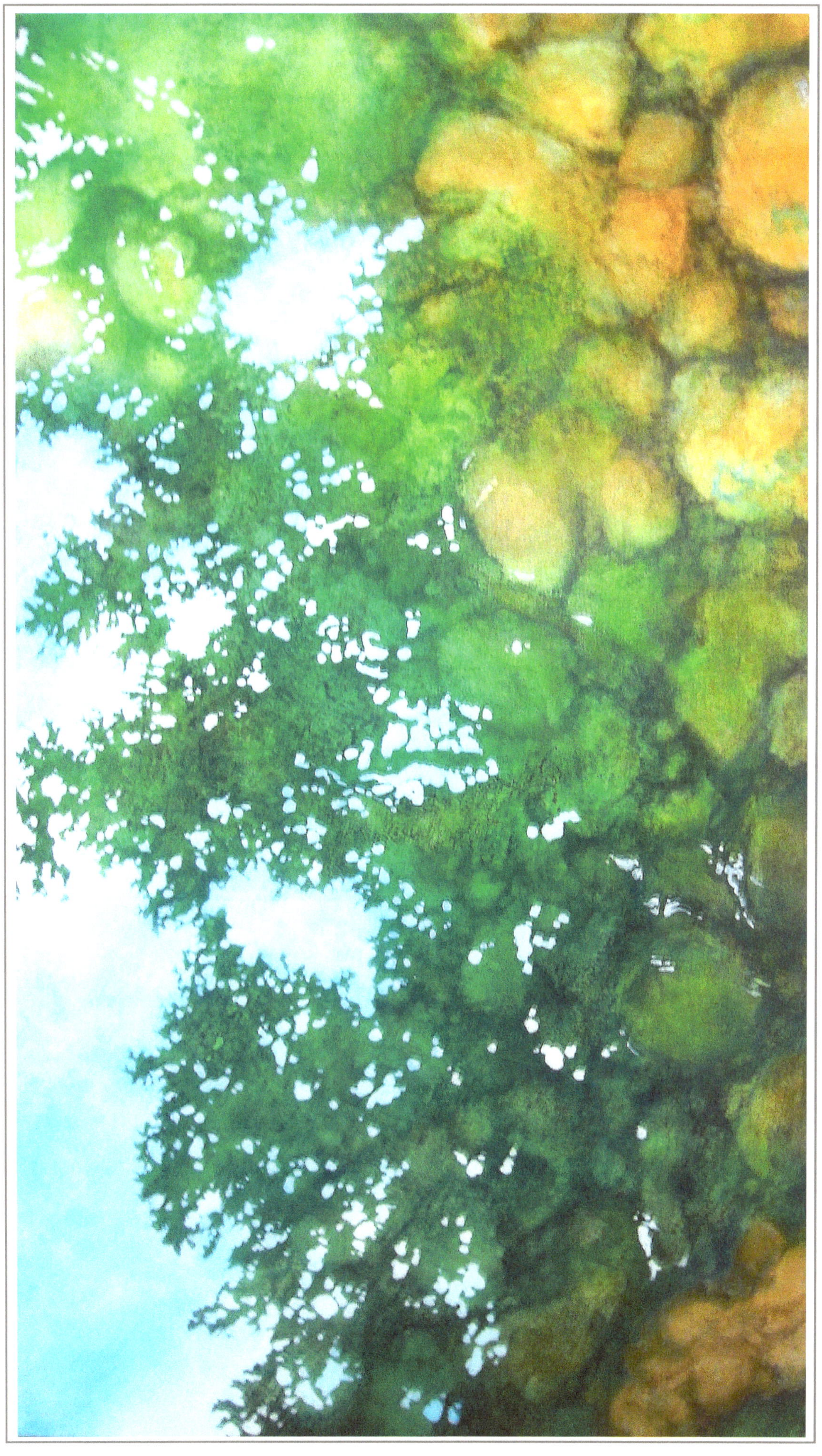

Reflect

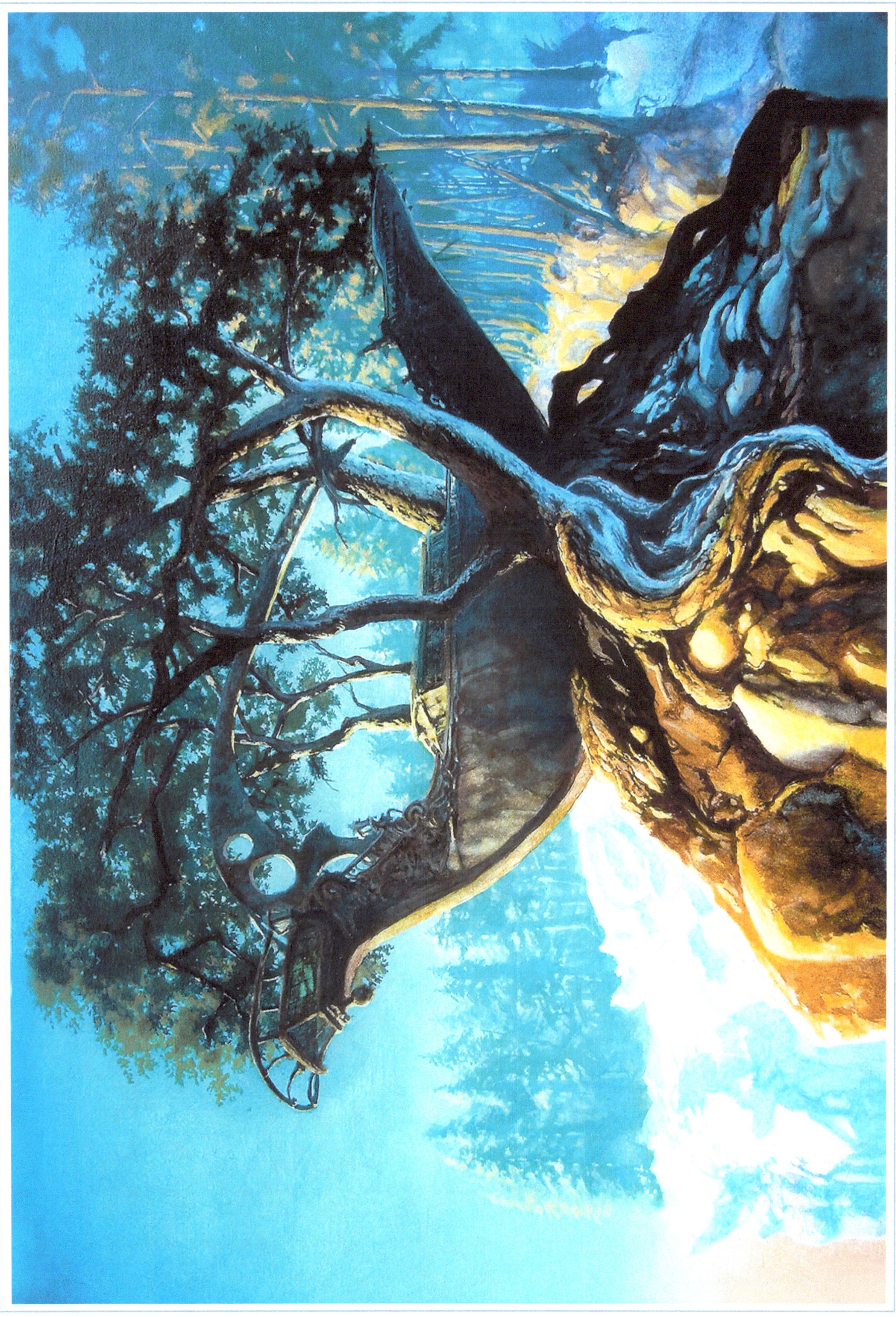

ShipWreck in a Tree

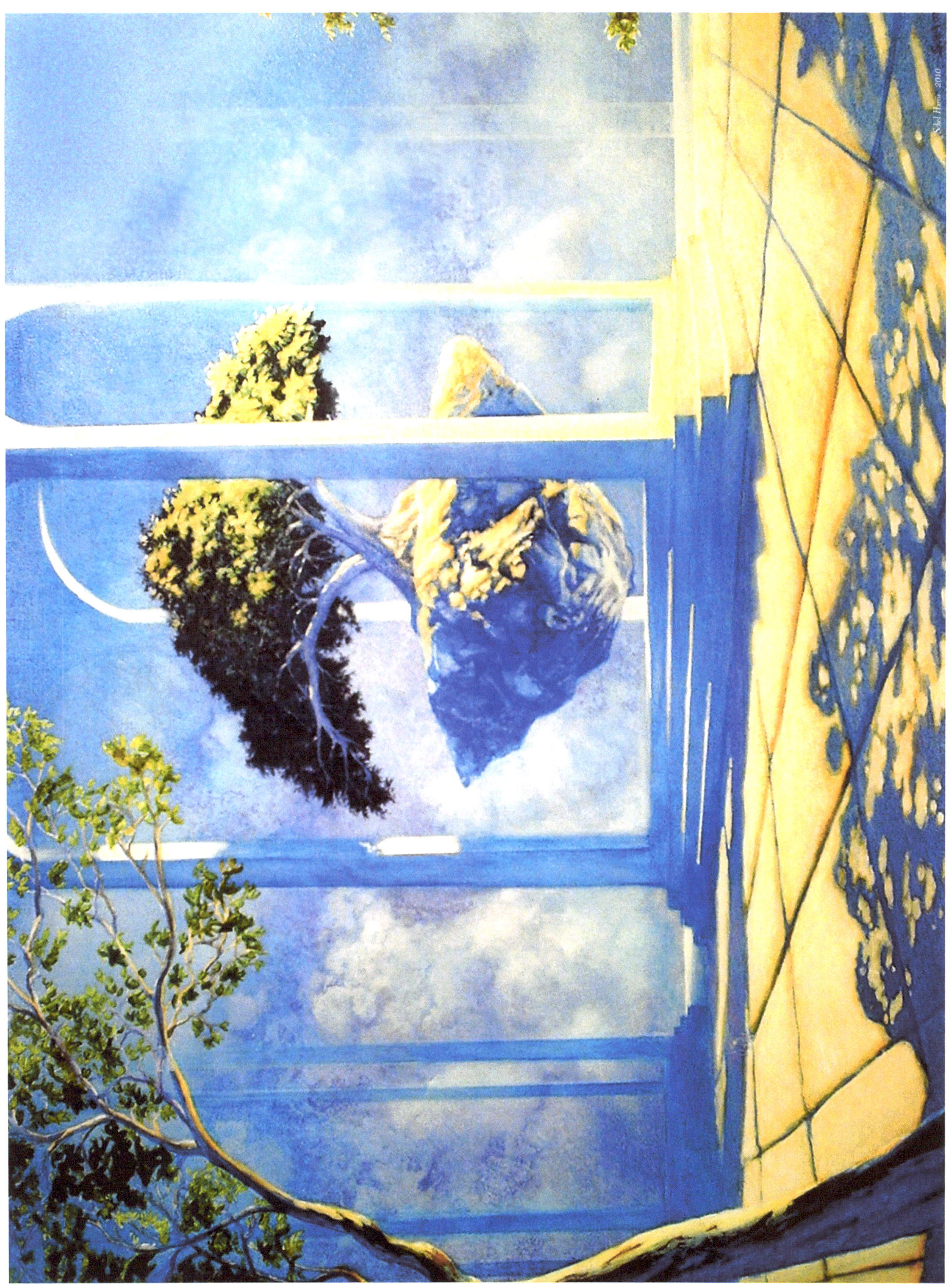

Station II

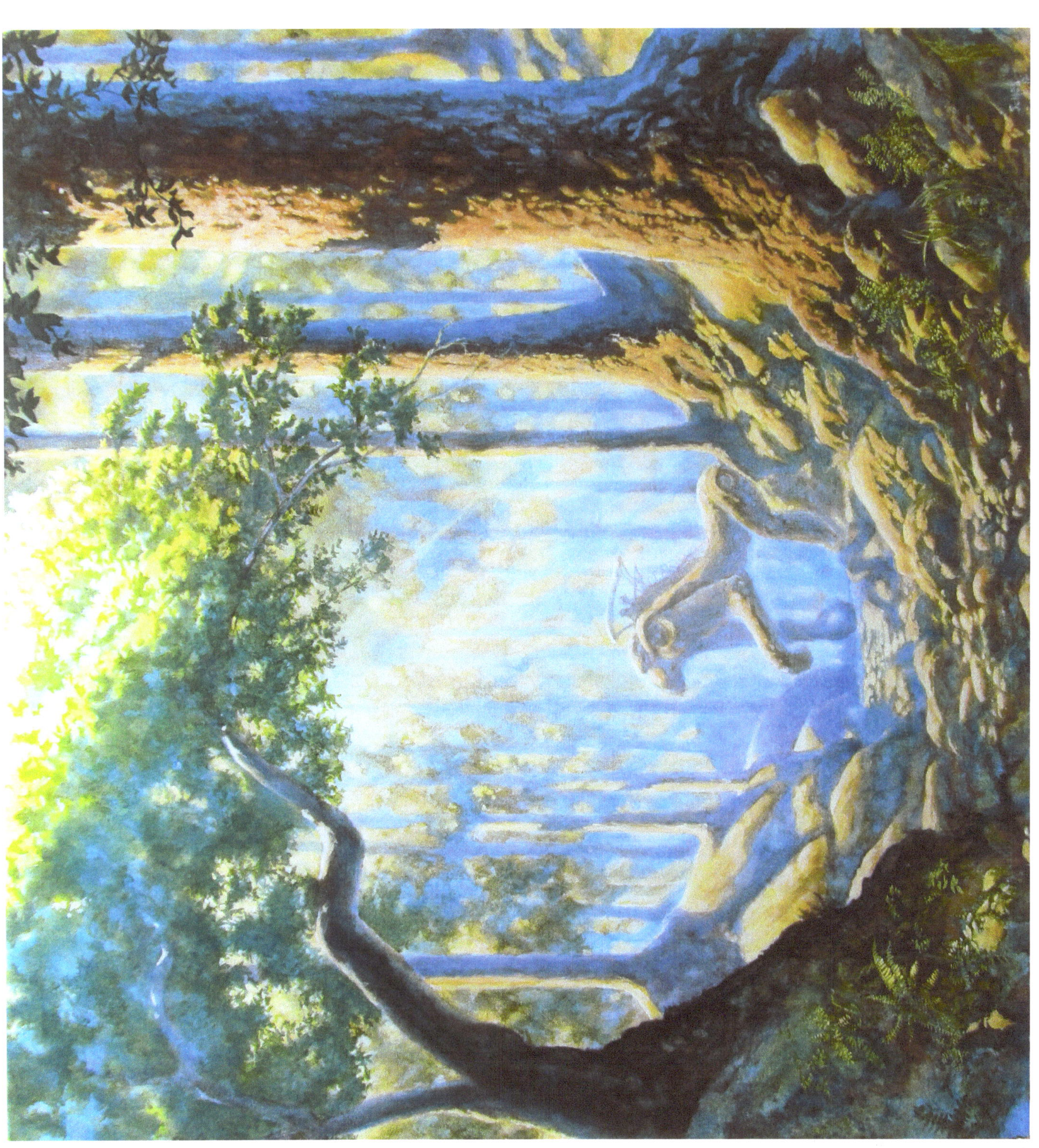

Forest Ape

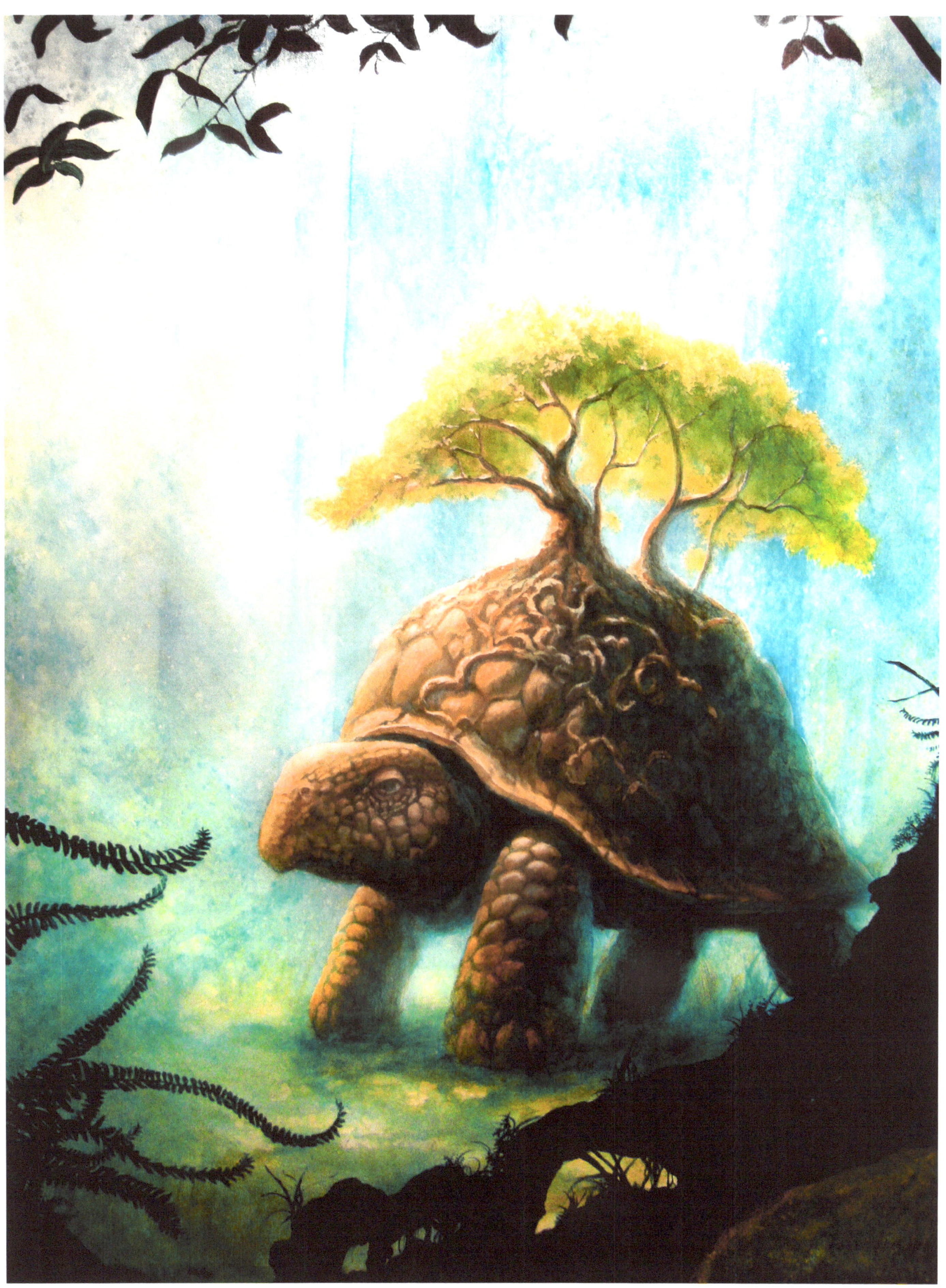

Worldly Turtle

www.ingramcontent.com/pod-product-compliance
Lightning Source LLC
LaVergne TN
LVHW070130110826
845147LV00002B/222

* 9 7 8 0 6 9 2 2 3 6 4 6 8 *